CW00967952

David Shepherd was [...] Lancaster, in 1942. H [...] School in Derbyshi [...] Durham. After University, he was a probation officer in Linlithgow, West Lothian, and a student at the Episcopal Theological College in Edinburgh. From 1968-1979, he was Chaplain of St Paul's Cathedral, Dundee and Anglican Chaplain in the University of Dundee from 1973-1979. Since 1979, he has been Rector of St Mary Magdalene's Church, Dundee.

Since 1992, five of his detective stories have been published – with several more waiting in the wings.

Who killed Sophie Jack? (1992)
Murder Within Tent (1994)
Slaughter at the Polls (1996)
A Christmas Cracker (1998)

Further details can be obtained from our website:
http://www.crime-fiction.com

MEADOWSIDE PUBLICATIONS

A MISHAP IN MAJORCA

DAVID SHEPHERD

A MISHAP IN MAJORCA

A DETECTIVE NOVEL

BY

DAVID SHEPHERD

MEADOWSIDE PUBLICATIONS

DUNDEE
2000

Meadowside Publications
14 Albany Terrace, Dundee DD3 6HR

© *Meadowside Publications, 2000*

Printed by
Burns Harris & Findlay Ltd.
Dundee, Scotland

*The characters portrayed in this
novel are all imaginary and bear
no intended resemblance to any
person alive or dead.*

ISBN 0 9520632 4 7

Meadowside Crime
is a © imprint of
Meadowside Publications,
Dundee.

CONTENTS

The story is set in the holiday resort of Puerto de Pollensa in September 1988.

1: *0 Quanta Qualia!*

"Inspector, you need a holiday!"

Mrs Debbie May was standing resolutely in the middle of her kitchen, wearing a full-length, white satin housecoat, loosely knotted at the waist. Although it was still early morning, her dyed gold hair was immaculately brushed – not a wisp was out of place. Her face was pale – devoid of make-up – and her eyelids too looked a trifle bare; but even without the benefits of mascara, her beautiful brown eyes took in every detail. She looked at Raynes with professional concern.

"When you arrive, you're tired; when you speak, you're crotchety; when you're about to perform, you can't stop yawning. You talk in your sleep. You toss; you turn. Then you wake up and ask what time it is. And in the morning, you creep out of here looking half-dead. A very poor advertisement, I must say! Your mind is about three miles away from your body. You have lost your powers of concentration – not to mention your sense of proportion. In fact, you're completely run-down. No fun. About as romantic as a piece of dead cod!"

It was unusual for Debbie to be quite so scathing to one of her customers; but then, the Inspector was more than a mere client. He was – well – a friend. In fact, it was beginning to trouble her conscience that she still charged him for her favours. However, she reckoned that if he wasn't paying for it retail, he'd probably be paying a great deal more for it wholesale – so, on balance, she was probably doing him a good turn. And for all she knew, he might be charging it to expenses. So who was she to complain?

Raynes looked up from his bacon and eggs with some surprise. Her criticism had caught him completely off-balance. For once, he was speechless.

Whilst he thought about it, he buttered a second piece of toast.

"You're still thinking about that dead scout – instead of concentrating upon a real live woman!"

Raynes nodded.

She was probably right.

"How much longer will it be before you've finished with it?"

"About a fortnight." His voice seemed a little faint so he repeated himself. "About another two weeks. There's a lot of paperwork needed for the Court."

"Well, I think you should make a decision now – this morning – to have a complete break. For a week or ten days; and blow all the cobwebs away. Are you due for any holidays yet?"

Raynes thought he might be due a week and several public holidays. He'd worked fairly non-stop since coming to Grasshallows in June and Debbie was probably right. A holiday would make all the difference.

"What do you suggest? Cyprus, Morocco, Florida, Acapulco?"

"What about Spain?"

Raynes shook his head.

"Dreadful place! Benidorm! I couldn't bear the thought of staying in one of those great concrete blocks. Ten thousand people all trying to sunbathe on one small stretch of sand! No thank you!"

"It's not all like that. There are some nice places. I stayed in a lovely place in Majorca..."

"Germans!" said Raynes. "Overrun with Germans. Send me to a place where at least they speak English; where I can buy a copy of *The Daily Telegraph* and drink a gin and tonic without being mobbed by foreigners!"

Debbie raised her eyebrows.

"Everyone seemed to speak English where I was staying. There were no concrete blocks. And the restaurants were terrific. But I'm not sure whether you could get a place out there at the last minute. You'd need to ask."

"Bit difficult getting single rooms at the last minute."

Debbie turned back to the cooker and turned off the percolator. She smiled to herself.

"Who said anything about going alone? You're not the only one who needs a holiday. I need a holiday too."

Raynes felt a deep glow of excitement tingling within him. All of a sudden, a holiday appeared to be not just a necessity but a prospect of utmost bliss.

"That would certainly make all the difference," he said. "Have you been plotting this for a while – or is this a spur-of-the-moment decision?"

Debbie poured out two cups of coffee, making sure that she left the right amount of space for the hot milk.

"I didn't think of it till last night. But when you staggered in, looking like Richard Burton with a hangover, it set me thinking. I made up my mind at about 2.00am when you fell asleep on me for the second time."

"Did I? I'm sorry."

"Well, if you don't know what you're doing, it proves my point. A fortnight in the sun – with no work, no papers, no crime, no telephone and you'll be almost human again."

Raynes nodded.

"It sounds a very good idea. I'll ring up one of my old chums who's in the travel business. See what he can rustle up. He owes me a favour or two." Raynes smiled. "I'll phone you at lunch-time and let you know what's cooking. Will that be all right?"

Debbie nodded happily.

"That's fine. Except that you've forgotten the most important detail! The essential point!"

Raynes looked puzzled.

"What's that?"

"Where are we going? A girl does like to know whether she is going to eat snails, slurp spaghetti, watch a bullfight or ride on a camel. It does help one to choose the right 'couture'..."

"Well, this place in Majorca sounds OK. If you liked it, I expect I shall find it tolerable. You said it had decent places to eat?"

Debbie nodded.

"Puerto de Pollensa. Don't forget the Puerto!"

Raynes produced his diary and took out his pen.

"There we are. A week on Saturday. A holiday for two in Puerto de Pollensa." He smiled. "I'm looking forward to it already."

2: *Machina Quae Daedalus*

Standing in the departure lounge at Luton Airport, Raynes was beginning to have second thoughts. First of all, he had had to get up at 3.30am after only four hours sleep. Then he had had to drive over to Debbie's flat – only to find she was still fast asleep. She had forgotten to set her alarm! By the time she had done her hair and her make-up, they were decidedly late and he had had to drive down to Luton like a bat out of hell. Although he conceded that beggars could not be choosers, he did rather wish that his friend in the travel trade could have found him a later flight than 7.40am – particularly since their tour operator, Megatravel, insisted on them being there at least two hours in advance.

Having arrived in Luton, they had spent a happy quarter of an hour trying to find the security park for his car. Booking in the Rover had proved frustratingly slow and the courtesy coach had inexplicably got lost on its way back from the airport. After minutes of nail-biting suspense, they had rushed with undignified haste up to the check-in desk, only to be told that their flight was running at least two and a half hours late!

Inspector Raynes had felt like screaming.

Debbie, however, took the matter more calmly.

"Now we'll have time for a proper breakfast," she said.

So they had eaten a typical English breakfast – with marmalade and butter in little plastic packs, nondescript teabags and cold toast, chewy bacon and over-fried eggs. He had read three different newspapers – on a morning when nothing of real interest had happened anywhere in the world. He had been defeated by every crossword puzzle he had tackled. He was surrounded by ugly people with their restless children. In frustration, he had bought an extra cup of coffee from a vending machine and then spilt it all over his shoes. He had read his passport from cover to cover and all the details of his insurance policy down to every last sub-clause – and there was still half-an-hour to go.

As he sat there fuming, he asked himself a question that every seasoned traveller asks himself again and again: 'Why on earth do people bother to go abroad?'

Mrs May remained calm and placid. She was used to impatient people who got flustered and embarrassed. It was no use getting het up oneself. She had anticipated that the flight might be delayed and that Richard might blow a fuse. She felt that her greatest contribution was to be sweet, serene and hopeful. But when he spilt hot coffee all over his new shoes, she had to laugh. He was so deliciously irritable. She hoped that the flight would be a good one and the sunshine heal every wound – and burn.

Fortunately, nothing else went wrong. The customs discovered nothing dangerous in their luggage and she was spared the wandering hands of the police frisker. (Debbie didn't like other women touching her.) The duty-free shop provided her with a litre-size bottle of peach schnapps and they were ushered into the plane without further delay. Their seats were near the emergency exit over the wing, so there was plenty of room to move. Debbie chose the seat beside the window and Raynes immersed himself in the emergency regulations – discovering what he must do when the plane descended from 37,000 feet and hit the surface of the sea at 500mph. Would he remember to pull his floggle-toggle and blow his whistle? On balance, he doubted it.

"Is this 16D?"

Raynes looked up.

A tall woman in a grey tweed suit was bending over the seat peering through gold-rimmed spectacles at the numbers.

"Well, we're 16E and 16F, so it must be."

"Thank you so much."

She seemed like a retired schoolteacher – one of the old school. Raynes was instinctively respectful and sat up straighter in his seat. Debbie offered her one of her magazines which was graciously accepted.

The pilot, it appeared, was anxious to make up for lost time. Almost before the doors were shut, the engines roared into life. The plane bounced and rattled along the taxi-path and out on to the main runway, whilst Captain Mitchell did his best to apologize for the delay.

French air traffic control seemed to be the problem. They had been on strike yet again and once the airline had lost their slot yesterday morning, the delays had become steadily worse. His apologies revealed a strong streak of xenophobia which Raynes appreciated.

Captain Mitchell introduced his cabin crew whom he described as 'la crème de la crème' (which Raynes doubted looking at their rather dumpy faces), and wished the punters a happy flight to Palma where the sun was shining and the noontide temperature was expected to reach 78°.

Loud music filled the aeroplane.

"Dire Straits!" said Debbie.

"How very appropriate!" said Raynes.

But this perhaps was not the moment to complain. With a roar from its three General Electric powerplants, the elderly Boeing 727 pounded down the tarmac, loaded to full capacity. The take-off run was a long one. Buildings flashed past. Raynes reckoned they must have covered well over 10,000 feet before the nose lifted and the wings swept over the hedge at the end of the runway. 'A near thing,' he thought, wiping the sweat from his brow.

Debbie was happy looking down at the fields and houses growing ever smaller on the ground and the elderly teacher was enjoying herself reading the problem page... 'How can I cure my acne?'... and 'Shall I marry him even though he is Irish?' 'I wouldn't,' said Raynes to himself.

Before long, the clouds had blotted out the earth and the cabin crew were serving... breakfast! Raynes groaned. He had been looking forward to a gin and tonic. He looked at his watch. 10.30am. Two plastic breakfasts in one morning!

With bad grace, he ate it – hot croissant, sausage, bacon,

14

one mushroom and something that looked like a deformed omelette. The coffee tasted good and Raynes began to feel more cheerful. He bought Debbie a set of earphones so that she could listen to Billy Connolly, then he settled back and calculated how long it would take them to get to Majorca.

The elderly lady thumbed her way through the magazine before returning to the problem page.

"Does it interest you?" asked Raynes.

"Young people do get into the most terrible mix-ups. They never seem to think about the consequences."

Raynes looked at her left hand to see if she had any rings and noticed a thin band of gold. Was she widowed or divorced? he wondered.

"Do you have any of your own?" he asked.

"Well, they're scarcely children. They're all completely grown-up. Not that they behave like it. That's why I'm going out to Majorca..."

"To keep an eye on them?"

"Just to be near in case they need help."

Raynes had promised Debbie that he would try to keep his nose out of other people's affairs, but he could not help asking: "What seems to be the problem?"

The elderly woman hesitated – as if she disapproved of discussing family affairs with a complete stranger. Raynes could guess the way her mind was working: 'I don't like talking about it... It's not something I would dream of talking about normally... But perhaps it's better to get it out... This man is friendly and kind... I shall never see him again. Therefore, there would be no harm in saying a few words.'

"It's my daughters," she said. "I have two. Sarah and Joanne. They're both in their late thirties now..." She corrected herself: "Actually, Jo's forty-one; Sarah's thirty-seven. Jo was born in that terrible winter of 1947, when everything froze up. Great snowdrifts everywhere. There was no coal. we lived out in the country and I can tell you it was no fun having a baby at that time. We could scarcely get any hot water to bath her.

15

"We used to call Joanne the 'Labour baby' because she was such hard labour." She smiled at what was obviously an old family joke. "Sarah was the 'Tory baby'. She was born in October 1951 when Mr Churchill came back. Those were really happy days. An end to ration books, identity cards and all that. Do you remember sweet rationing?"

"Before my time," said Raynes.

"One forgets. These things were so long ago. So much water has flowed under the bridge since then."

She sighed.

"They both did well at school. Of course, my husband and I were both teachers, so we were able to help them."

Raynes quietly congratulated himself on placing her occupation so accurately.

"Jo went to University. Did frightfully well. Got an Upper Second in English and married a sociology lecturer. Rex was a nice man – apart from his beard. But they seemed very happy together. Had two children. Peter's fifteen; Annabel's thirteen.

"But Sarah was more of a problem. She went off to France to be an *au pair*. She went off for twelve weeks – and there she met this Frenchman. He said he was the *Comte de* something. Anyway, he completely swept her off her feet. She was young and impressionable – and he certainly looked most charming. Always well-dressed. Before we knew what was happening, she was living with him in Paris. No job. Just living it up in night clubs. I think he was some sort of singer."

Her elderly voice was rich in disapproval.

"Of course, it didn't last. He left her for someone else. So she came home. Fortunately she wasn't pregnant! That would have been the last straw! But she found it very difficult to settle down. It took her another year and a half to get into teacher-training college. After that, she managed to get a post in Bexley. We all breathed a sigh of relief.

"But too soon! One of her pupils had a father who was a very rich man. Had his own printing business. Tall, handsome fellow. Very well-spoken. You know the type. And he was

16

married to this journalist – very happily married. They had two children..."

She shook her head.

"Sarah set her cap at him – and in no time at all they were living together. She didn't tell us he was a married man! Well, of course, there was a most bitter divorce and his wife sued him for thousands in alimony. It was a shameful business – and it was all Sarah's fault! Even though I'm her mother, I have to say that she behaved dreadfully.

"The man's wife took the two children away with her. She wouldn't let him see them. I suppose it was quite understandable but it hurt him terribly. In fact, I don't think he ever got over it. He and Sarah eventually got married but I don't know that they were ever really happy. He always worked long hours and then he died in an awful car crash one winter's night. Sarah got his business and all his money. She must be worth at least six million..."

"Really?" said Raynes, thinking of his own meagre pay cheque and wishing he could lay claim to even half a million.

"Of course, most of it's tied up in the business. Still, she seems to spend a great deal. But money can't buy you happiness. It just brings you false friends. Hangers-on. People who hope to scrounge a few thousand off you. But Sarah's no fool. She's kept on the business and it's doing well. When she's not working, she likes to travel. And she loves Majorca. Goes there every year..."

Raynes felt it was time to ask a question.

"Has she remarried?"

"No, that's half the trouble. It's now five years since Charles died. She's had several affairs, but nothing serious. It just seems to be one man after another. At the moment, she's got a publisher in tow. Neville, his name is. Bit of a shark, if you ask me."

"And what about Jo? The other one?"

The elderly woman paused as if uncertain.

"She's changed. She's definitely changed. She used to be so hardworking, so reliable. But I think she's beginning to copy Sarah. She was always rather jealous of her sister's freedom. Felt she was tied down with children whilst Sarah was enjoying herself. Didn't see the path of virtue as being all that rewarding... Her marriage broke up three years ago. She left Rex – and the children. She just moved out. There was no divorce or anything. They still see each other and, to be honest, they still seem perfectly friendly with each other. But she enjoys her independence – and now she's almost as bad as Sarah. She's had a couple of affairs and now she's picked up this greasy lawyer..."

"You don't sound as if you like him?"

The woman shook her head.

"I don't. I don't trust him. He has the sort of eyes that don't smile – even when he laughs. He seems cold to me. Cold and calculating. What Joanne sees in him, I just don't know... Of course, I warned her; but she doesn't listen to me. Neither of them do."

"How long has she known this lawyer?"

"Just a couple of months. Sarah's never met him. That's why Jo's coming out to Majorca. She thought it would be nice if they could all have a holiday together. Sarah's paying, of course. So they're all going to Pollensa for a fortnight."

Raynes wondered if he should say that Debbie and he were also going to Pollensa. But the anxious mother prattled on:

"They're staying in the *Hotel Aphrodite* – all four of them. I do hope they'll all get on together."

"Are you going to join them at the hotel?"

"Me? No. I'm just going to stay nearby in case I'm needed."

"Are you expecting to be needed?"

The woman turned to Raynes full face, her eyes serious behind the gold-rimmed spectacles.

"I don't know. It's just something Jo said to me on the phone last week. She said: 'Mum, I'm not happy about that publisher fellow Sarah's going out with. I don't like him. I think he's after her money. I'm frightened Sarah's going to get hurt. She's done nothing to encourage him but I think he's got his teeth into her.' That's what Jo said. Now she's known Sarah ever since she was born. She's known all about her

18

affairs. She knows how tough Sarah can be. But the fact that Jo's so worried made me think. I imagine that's why she's taking her lawyer friend along with her. Just to stop Sarah doing anything stupid. Jo may be exaggerating but Sarah's still my daughter and I don't like to think of her in danger of any sort."

Raynes asked: "If anything happens to Sarah, who gets all her money?"

"I don't really know. Jo, I suppose."

"There's no likelihood of Sarah getting bumped off?"

The elderly woman looked even more upset.

"Don't put ideas into my head! People will do anything for money. You read about it in the papers. I wouldn't want anything to happen to Sarah. She's my favourite. I know I shouldn't have favourites... but I do. I feel I should just be close in case she needs me. But I'm probably being stupid and over-protective..."

"But quite understandable in the circumstances."

The elderly woman smiled.

"Well, that's my problem. What's yours?"

Raynes smiled.

"I'm on holiday. Totally on holiday! By divine command." He cast an eye at Debbie who seemed to have fallen asleep. "I'm under orders to keep away from all problems, all telephones – and just enjoy myself."

"You're a lucky man! And your wife too. What do you do for a living?"

"I'm a policeman."

The elderly woman looked most surprised. "A policeman?" she said. "And here's me pouring out all my troubles to you. You must be sick to death hearing other people's problems. I'm sorry to have bored you – going on..."

"Not at all," said Raynes. "It was most interesting. I just hope your daughter will be all right and your fears unfounded."

The woman nodded.

"I hope so."

An alien voice interposed.

"Will you please fasten your safety belts. We're coming in to land."

Raynes turned to Debbie.

"Safety belt time! Wake up!"

"I'm not asleep. What were you talking to that woman about?"

"Her daughters. She thinks one of them is going to be murdered."

"Oh, bloody hell!" said Debbie. "Not in Pollensa?"

"I'm afraid so," said Raynes.

3: *Et in Arcadia Ego*

They saw little more of the elderly woman.

Like everyone else, their chief concerns were fighting their way out of the plane and finding their luggage. Raynes, however, contrived to stand beside the woman when she was collecting her suitcase and noted her name. Hickson. It seemed familiar! Thereafter, she was lost in the crowd. She was not on the bus to Pollensa, so she must have been collected or had a car waiting for her.

Debbie and Richard put her out of their minds as the coach moved slowly round the dreary outskirts of Palma and up the dusty road to the interior, squeezing through the narrow villages of Inca and Santa Maria, the driver deftly avoiding the young boys without crash helmets doing dangerous things on motor scooters.

Just to encourage the holiday spirit, they saw another tourist coach lying in a ditch on the other side of the road, with its windscreen shattered and the baggage scattered all over the road. No one seemed to have been hurt. Two fierce members of the Guardia Civil stood on duty and ushered them past.

As the road curled further northwards, the lower hills became greener and more fertile but the upper crags became sharper, greyer and more rugged. The coach sped along the simple tarmac road and down the final valley before being swallowed up in a clutter of concrete walls.

"Is this it?" asked Raynes apprehensively.

"Wait till you get round the corner!" said Debbie.

And sure enough, round the corner, there was a dazzling transformation.

Suddenly there were the deep blue waters of the bay of Pollensa, reaching across to the distant peaks of Alcudia, with the purple and scarlet sails of the windsurfers floating across the gleaming surface. On the left, there were the tree-covered slopes of Cape Formentor and, in the foreground, a forest of masts rising from the marina, flags and pennants fluttering in the gentle breeze. To the right, a vast arc of golden sand and a lengthy promenade seemingly filled with people in brightly-coloured clothes making their way to and from the beach. Even the buildings seemed to be lit up with a sparkling light.

"This is it," said Debbie.

"That's much better," said Raynes. "You had me worried."

The coach proceeded slowly along the promenade, letting people off at different hotels and apartments.

"Glad I'm not staying there!" said Raynes of one; "That looks better!" – of another covered in purple flowers.

Eventually they reached the *Hotel Aphrodite* and it was their turn to get out into the hot sunshine and lug their suitcases up the steps and into reception.

"What name is it, sir?"

"Raynes."

"Room 301."

A swarthy porter picked up their luggage and led them to the lift. He said little – and did not even smile – but doubtless would expect a tip. Unfortunately, all Raynes' money was in 2000 peseta notes, so the porter departed empty-handed.

Room 301 was quite palatial. It was built on the corner of the hotel, with an oblique view of the promenade but overlooking the private gardens and beach where a select few were still sunbathing. The windows were open and the diaphanous curtains floated upwards in the gentle breeze. The afternoon light flowed peaceably into the room, being reflected in the numerous pictures and mirrors which covered the walls.

Debbie put down her handbag and sat on the window seat, looking down at the beach. She watched the coloured sails fluttering backwards and forwards.

"It's lovely, isn't it?"

"Tremendous," said Raynes sincerely.

He had not had a holiday abroad for several years and he was already beginning to unwind. He undid the buttons of his shirt and kicked off his shoes.

"It's a beautiful hotel."

"Aphrodite was the goddess of beauty."

Debbie looked at Richard standing in his grey socks and creased trousers and thought how unglamorous men were.

"A woman, of course!"

She smiled.

"Come and give me a nice kiss."

They kissed slowly and deeply.

"Mm. That was nice."

She looked down at the beach.

"D'you think we've got time?"

Raynes looked at his watch.

"All the time in the world. They won't start serving dinner till about 8.00pm."

Debbie shook her head.

"I meant for a swim, stupid! There'll be time for other things later. Don't be greedy! First things first!"

Richard watched her spring into action.

The cases were all flung open; dresses and trousers hung up. Beachwear and underwear put in the appropriate drawers. Shoes hidden away. Bottles, tubes and hairdryer transported to the en suite bathroom. Books, tapes and tissues neatly stacked on the bedside tables.

"I've brought a gross of rubberwear with me," said Debbie mischievously. "Should be enough to keep us going!"

Raynes' reply was unprintable.

Within less than ten minutes, they were heading downstairs and out through the cool marble reception to the steps which led out into the gardens. Debbie was in a pale lemon bikini.

She had worn it many times before, but Richard was not to know that! Being a light golden brown from her holiday earlier that summer, she already looked part of the scenery. But the Inspector, following her in a pair of bright red silky briefs, felt very white and very self-conscious.

Debbie wended her way through the grounds as if she had been there many times before – as indeed she had – and dabbled her toes in the clear, cool, Mediterranean water.

It was not quite as cold as she had feared.

Perhaps she could take a quick plunge?

Other people were splashing about.

Richard did not look as if he was ready to plunge into anything. He looked a bit lost, carrying the towels and the Factor 25 sun-block.

She said: "I'm going in. Order some sangria!"

She waded deeper and deeper into the water and gradually let her feet float upwards. She swam slowly out into the bay – about one hundred yards – and then slowly turned for home.

There she saw an extraordinary sight.

Richard was standing poised on the diving board about to dive in. It was about twenty feet deep just there. He bounced lightly on his heels, performed a superb arched glide and entered the water with only the slightest 'plop'.

She swam over to him.

"That was brilliant," she said. "I didn't know you were a keen swimmer."

Raynes said: "You don't know everything about me!"

"Obviously not."

"Because if you did, you'd realize that I've lost my trunks."

"When?"

"As I dived in, they just slipped off. I've got to find them or I'm in trouble."

Debbie laughed so much that Raynes pushed her head under the surface. Whilst she was coughing up water and rubbing the salt out of her eyes, he left her to go and look for his red briefs. He found them floating near the beach. He crawled forwards and grabbed them before Debbie could spirit them away. He then returned to deeper water to make himself respectable.

When he returned to the shore, Debbie had already drunk her first glass of sangria.

"You know," she said, "you look much better without clothes! You have quite a nice figure. I can see why I like you!"

"That's not what you said before we came away."

"No, that was when you looked a bloody wreck. Even after an hour in Pollensa, you're a new man. Have a glass of this. It'll warm you up."

Richard swigged back half a glass and felt greatly refreshed. It seemed a far cry from Grasshallows police station. All these semi-naked bodies lying in the sun. Debbie herself looked radiantly happy with little drops of water shining like jewels all over her body. She had been right to drag him away. He had been very jaded and very tired. He had to concede that she seemed to understand him better than he did himself.

He lifted his glass.

"Cheers, Mrs Raynes!" he said.

Debbie flashed back a contemptuous look.

"Don't you dare mention the dreaded 'M' word – or I'll never forgive you. I'm just an expensive money-grubbing whore – and don't you forget it!"

One or two of the nearby sunbathers raised their heads to see who was making this astounding confession.

"I need to make my packet before my assets run out. When I'm old, grey and knackered – and you're approaching your first prostate, then perhaps I'll settle down. But not before."

She winked at a brown-haired girl who was looking rather shocked. She turned to the Inspector.

"Do I make myself clear?"

"Clear and exceedingly public," said Raynes grimly.

"I shouldn't worry about that," said Debbie gaily. "They're mostly Germans or Scandinavians round here. They won't understand a word we're saying."

She picked up the jug of sangria.

"Have another glass!"

Raynes, as always, was bowled over by her outrageous sense of humour.

"To the holiday!" he said, raising his glass.

"That's better," she said. "To the holiday!"

She downed her glass and stood up.

"Let's go and have a bit of nookie before dinner! Last one upstairs wears the plastic mac!"

She sped off back into the hotel, wrapped in a pink towel. Raynes slowly drained his glass.

He looked at the brown-haired girl.

"*Guardian* readers!" he said apologetically. "They're all the same. Once they start to read the Women's Page, they can't control their fantasies – not even on holiday. Let that be a lesson to you, young woman!"

With as much dignity as he could muster in his wet, red briefs, he walked back into the hotel.

The brown-haired girl waited till he was out of sight. Then she turned to her friend. "Did you hear that? He's bonkers. In fact, they're both bonkers!"

And, for once, she was right.

4: *O Noctes Cenaeque Deum*

The dining room of the *Hotel Aphrodite* was designed to take one's breath away. It was broad, spacious and full of light. Situated on the first floor of the hotel with a magnificent view over Pollensa Bay, its tall windows opened on to a wide terrace which ran the length of the hotel. In the morning and at lunch-time, the bright, translucent light poured in through these windows and was reflected many times over by the large mirrors which hung on every wall. But at dinner-time, when a mantle of darkness surrounded the hotel, these mirrors reflected the glory of two massive chandeliers that hung like spaceships, suspended by invisible cords. Over everything was cast their golden glow. The paintwork of the ceiling, the heavily embossed wallpaper, the silken curtains, the deep pile carpet and even the humble menu and napkin, were all enhanced by the one, rich, dominant, golden theme. Surely the most elaborately dressed diner could hardly fail to realize that this was more than a mere dining room? It was a veritable shrine to the goddess Aphrodite herself!

Raynes paused as he crossed the threshold.

"It's lovely, isn't it?" said Debbie.

"Makes a change from the police canteen!" said Raynes, who had been on the point of genuflecting but had quickly recovered his poise.

"Madam?"

An obsequious waiter escorted them to a table on the right-hand side near a party of four. Raynes gave him a knowing smile: "Thank you, Manuel!"

(His 4000 peseta donation to one of Franco's war orphans had not been wasted.)

Debbie was wearing a very pale green silk dress with large floppy sleeves. Her hair, immaculate as always, blended nicely with the general theme.

Raynes sat with his back to the party of four, but he could easily hear most of their conversation.

Debbie looked down the lengthy menu.

"What'll you have?" she asked.

"Steak!" said Raynes. "If in doubt, always choose steak. Do they have mussels?"

"It's all in Spanish," she smiled. "But they do give you a translation on page five. There are plain mussels in a tomato, onion and herb sauce; mussels in a rich white wine sauce and deep fried mussels in a Majorcan salad. Take your pick!"

"Deep fried," said Raynes. "That sounds delicious."

He caught Debbie's eye.

"All right! Plain mussels it shall be. What are you going to have?"

Debbie pondered carefully.

"Crab, I think. Followed by veal."

Behind them, the party of four were beginning to talk.

"Is your room all right, Jo?"

"Splendid, thanks. Lovely view of the hills."

"If you'd booked earlier, you'd probably have got one overlooking the sea."

"Perhaps when you've been here a day or two, you could get the hotel to do a swap?"

A practical suggestion from Neville.

"Beggars can't be choosers! But the sunset over the hills was quite dramatic."

Another male voice. Presumably the lawyer?

Raynes listened carefully.

It emerged that Jo and her friend had not arrived till after 6.00pm and had only had time to unpack and change before coming down to dinner. Introductions therefore were still being made. Sarah was trying to show interest in Jo's new friend.

"Where did you two first meet?"

Jo giggled.

"In a supermarket, wasn't it?"

"Not frightfully romantic, I'm afraid."

"But we got on jolly well at the meat counter, didn't we?"

"Malcolm was trying to decide what sort of beef he could stir-fry. I told him, didn't I, dear?"

"You did."

"And it just blossomed from there?"

"He invited me to sample some of his cooking. And I just couldn't resist!"

How corny, thought Raynes.

"And is he a good cook?"

"That's just one of his talents!"

Malcolm was clearly embarrassed. He turned to Neville: "And how did you two meet?"

Sarah and Neville exchanged glances.

"Something equally unromantic..."

"...I went down to Sarah's place..."

"...A little printing job, you said!"

"Well, I had to have some excuse. I couldn't say straight out: 'How about me taking you over?' That would have been a little too blunt."

"Even for you?"

"So you were hoping to make Sarah an offer? That would have been quite pricey?"

"A merger was more what I had in mind."

"Which you got!"

Neville smiled broadly.

"But not quite in the direction I was expecting."

Malcolm sounded curious.

"I thought you were a publisher?"

"Publishers need to have a reliable firm to print their books and I thought Sarah's firm would be ideal. Quality printing, good artwork, but not too large to be impersonal. It would have been just right."

"But Sarah wouldn't sell?"

"I wasn't asking her to sell. I was proposing a nice little merger. But she said: 'No'."

"Very wise of her," said Malcolm. "One shouldn't take a step like that without proper legal advice."

"And what advice would that be?" Neville sounded a trifle peeved.

"Finding out the value of the fellow who was making the bid. Discovering if his firm was all it was cut out to be. Finding out if he was solvent. Making enquiries to see who owned all the shares... all those sort of things."

"I'm sure Sarah's quite capable of doing all that. She wouldn't need to employ a legal shark!"

There was no doubt about it. Neville was becoming very irritated by Malcolm's comments.

Jo was defensive.

"Malcolm's not a shark. He's a very sensible, practical person. He wouldn't let people rush into things without examining them properly, would you, dear?"

Sarah intervened diplomatically.

"The situation didn't arise. Once Neville and I set eyes upon each other, we knew we were made for each other."

"There's more than one way to skin a rabbit!" said Malcolm coldly.

Fortunately, at that moment, the first course arrived and the conversation turned to less combustible items such as the taste of the prawns and the quality of the wine being served.

Raynes had the impression that Malcolm had scored heavily against Neville. Would the publisher retaliate? Would Sarah defend him? He looked forward with interest to Round Two.

Debbie had realized almost immediately that the choice of their table was by no means accidental. These were obviously the two daughters of the woman Richard had been speaking to on the plane; and he was listening to their conversation whilst making a great pretence of reading the menu from cover to cover.

Not that it was all that difficult to hear what the foursome were saying. In the quiet hum of the dining room, she too could hear their words quite clearly. To Debbie, it seemed to have the makings of a very unpleasant holiday for all concerned.

She hoped Richard would not get too involved. He had promised to put his work behind him and relax completely. If he was proposing to make this a working holiday, then so would she! A fat, middle-aged businessman had been eyeing her up ever since she came into the room. She gave him a friendly smile.

By the time the waiter had delivered their order, the party at the next table had reached the hiatus before the fish course. Whilst Raynes tucked into a small mountain of juicy mussels, he heard Malcolm say:

"What do you publish anyway?"

"Children's books," said Neville.

"They're under the Tortoise label," said Sarah helpfully.

"I imagine they would need to be!"

Malcolm burst into laughter.

"I'm sorry to be so offensive, old chap; but I didn't like the idea of you cosying up to this lovely lady just to get your hands on her company."

Raynes could imagine Neville wincing with

embarrassment but to his surprise, the victim delivered a cool backhander:

"I fancy I know a bit more about the real world than you do," he said. "At least I offer my authors a square deal. I don't charge them £20 for every letter I write and £5 for every minute I spend in their company."

The last words were spat out with icy contempt.

But Malcolm was undeterred.

"No one ever does anything for nothing in this world. I know what you publishers are like. You give your authors ten per cent. The other ninety ends up in your pocket!"

"We do have overheads," said Neville defensively. "Everyone does. There's printing, advertising, delivery charges, a sizeable mark-up for the local bookseller and a contingency account for loss-leaders..."

"Of which, I am told, you have quite a few?"

Neville raised his eyebrows.

"I wasn't aware I was under investigation!"

"Oh, don't be silly!" said Jo. "Malcolm knows people. He knows about all sorts of things, don't you, dear?"

Malcolm managed to sound faintly apologetic.

"Well, knowing I was going to meet you and Sarah, I naturally took the precaution of finding out a little bit about you. And I must say, what I heard left me very worried. Very worried indeed. I don't like the idea of Jo's sister being ripped off."

Neville controlled his feelings very well.

"No one's being ripped off," he said coldly. "Sarah isn't being taken over. She doesn't want a merger. Her firm belongs to her. Mine stays with me. If she decides to do my printing at cost price, that would obviously be an enormous help to me. And if she offers, I shall be delighted to accept. But, up to now, I've asked no favours, have I, darling?"

Sarah shook her head.

"Our relationship's one hundred per cent personal."

Having made his point, Neville managed to stage a further small rally at his opponent's expense.

"Anyway," he said. "I'm not the only one skating on thin

ice. Some of you lawyers sail pretty close to the wind. I heard about some lawyer in Dartford who charged such high expenses on a property deal that the people involved came out with virtually nothing."

Joanne unfortunately did not get the point.

"Malcolm works in Dartford," she said.

"Some people called Latimer," said Neville.

His shot obviously went home.

There was an unpleasant silence.

Raynes longed to turn round and look at them.

Sarah came to the rescue.

"Have you been to Majorca before, Malcolm?"

"Just once. It was a long time ago... I didn't see much."

"Well, now you've got a whole fortnight to see it properly. Jo knows how much I love the place. We must make sure you see as much of it as possible. It's the ideal place for young lovers – and we're all still young at heart."

Raynes was quite impressed by Sarah's handling of an awkward situation. Clearly there were things about her lover's business life that she knew nothing about. But she had defended him. Malcolm had obviously done his homework and had come primed for battle. His object was to expose and undermine Neville. But Neville had not done too badly. He, for his part, had made certain enquiries about the lawyer from Dartford and these enquiries had also revealed highly fissile material. At this moment, Raynes reckoned, the two contenders seemed to be fairly even on points. Sarah had come out strongly; but Joanne was hopelessly out of her depth.

When their main course arrived, Raynes devoted most of his attention to Debbie. He realized that he had been boorish and unsociable. Besides, he could still hear the conversation behind him. They were now all being terribly polite and discussing the various tourist sights that Malcolm ought to see in Majorca.

"The hotel will fix it for us," said Sarah. "They do it in

conjunction with the other travel companies. One day to Palma, another day to the Valldemosa. That's where Gustav Doré did his illustrations for Dante's *Inferno*. It's quite wild round there. And you must see the monastery where Frederic Chopin had his famous affair with George Sand. The coaches are air-conditioned so it's very comfortable. Much better then being stuffed into some wretched Spanish hire-car when you never know if the steering's safe or whether the wheels are going to fall off. One hears such dreadful stories... Besides, when you see what some of the mountain roads are like, you wouldn't dream of driving. One false move and you'd be right over the edge."

Raynes made a mental note that if he was to keep an eye on Sarah and her friends, he would have to find out which day they were going where and he and Debbie would have to synchronize their travel plans with theirs. He hoped Debbie would not mind.

She said she didn't.

She had been drawing her own conclusions about the foursome at the next table. Jo, she thought, was jealous of Sarah – the more attractive, the more successful, younger sister. Sarah had taken up with Neville because he was smooth and good-looking – but a bit of a con-man. But Sarah had her wits about her. She was only giving him her body – not her business. That was sensible.

But she wondered about Jo and her lawyer. What did he see in her? Jo was a good-looking woman for her age with a fine figure. But the lawyer looked younger. Why should he have latched on to her? Quite clearly, he had come to Majorca to attack Neville and break up the relationship between him and Sarah. He was well-spoken and had nice teeth. Even though he might be a shark, he was quite a pleasant one.

Debbie and Richard exchanged their opinions after the quartet had gone into the lounge for coffee. They agreed that nothing would be lost in their own holiday arrangements by following the others and watching their antics. It would simply to the fun. Raynes said that he did not think Sarah was in much danger, but he could easily see the two men coming to blows. He fancied that Joanne was most likely to be the loser. For if Sarah and Neville did break up, Sarah would blame her sister for bringing Malcolm to Majorca. But, on the other hand, if Neville managed to worst Malcolm, then he could see the lawyer washing his hands of the whole business and going home. Either way, Joanne would lose.

Before going through for coffee, Raynes said that he would have to make a short phone call. He wanted to speak to Detective-Constable Carlisle in Grasshallows and tell him to dig out some information on Neville and Malcolm. But he decided that if he told Debbie what he was doing, she might claim he was 'working' – something that was strictly forbidden.

Debbie, however, instantly put two and two together. She would have done precisely the same. Whilst she was waiting, she stood in the main hallway of the hotel, reading all the lavish details about para-gliding, wind-surfing and all the rest. Having been to Pollensa several times before, she knew all the attractions and all the prices.

She was approached by the under-manager.

He looked a little nervous. "Were you the lady at table No 11?"

Debbie was surprised.

"Yes, I suppose I was."

"There's a message for you."

He handed her a white envelope.

"Thank you," she said.

She looked at Richard in the phone booth speaking vigorously to his colleague. She opened the envelope to see what it contained.

The message was brief and to the point.

'Room 216.'

She crunched up the message and the envelope and put them into the nearest waste-bin. A few minutes later, she made her way over to the receptionist and with a sweet smile on her face, she asked:

"How many pesetas are there to the pound?"

"198, Madam."

Debbie looked over at the telephone booth – and sighed.

5: *Omnia Vincit Amor*

Upstairs, in Room 309, Sarah was sitting in front of her dressing table, brushing her hair. She had taken off her blouse and skirt and was sitting in her white lacy slip. In the background, Neville was lying flat out on the bed, still wearing his dinner jacket and his dark-red bow tie. His eyes were shut and his face looked flushed. Sarah had noticed that he had drunk quite a lot that evening – almost double what he normally drank. Now he was suffering the consequences – a sore head, an upset stomach and an overpowering desire to sleep. If she didn't rouse him, he would be lying there fully-dressed all night.

She could understand why he had drunk more than usual. It was Dutch courage; keeping up his image as a man of the world. She didn't blame Malcolm – even though he had been deliberately provocative. Neville should not have risen to the bait. He should have drunk less and kept a clear head – just as she had done. With a little careful steering, the conversation had avoided the more dangerous pitfalls and the evening had ended quite pleasantly. But it didn't take much imagination to see how easily Malcolm and Neville might fall out – or even come to blows. It was all so stupid. It could only spoil the holiday for everyone, especially for Jo who was obviously proud of her catch.

There was no doubt Malcolm was an astute lawyer. He had a sharp mind, a good memory and a very eloquent tongue. He could charm and entertain – but he could also bite. Just as he had bitten poor Neville during dinner.

Malcolm couldn't tell Sarah anything about Neville that she didn't already know. She was aware of all his problems and difficulties. His efforts to carry on the family firm that was losing money year after year; the accumulating debt that

34

was being bridged by ever larger loans. Neville's attempts to keep up with the bigger publishers, launching new lines and cutting profit margins to the bone to boost sales. The constant hope of major foreign orders which never seemed to materialize because the pound was too strong and his sales force too weak. The whole thing was a recipe for disaster.

Sarah reckoned that the best thing Neville could do was to cut his losses and sell out as quickly as possible. He possessed valuable property at the heart of London. If he could get rid of that, he might salvage something from the wreck. But as for take-overs or mergers, that was quite out of the question. The whole thing was laughable. Neville was certainly no businessman. In Sarah's eyes, he was only good at one thing – and that was not publishing!

But tonight, even that seemed unlikely. Neville was dead to the world and incapable of responding satisfactorily to even the most wanton caress. Normally, the sight of Sarah in her slip with her legs and shoulders bare, would drive him to great feats of passion – but tonight, she had had it.

She threw down the brush on to the table and went over to the useless body lying on the bed. She took off his shoes and socks and pulled off his trousers. She unclipped his bow tie and threw it away. She unbuttoned his shirt and ran her hands over his broad chest, stroking his nipples with her soft fingers. All to no effect. She rolled him over to the left and right to get his arms out of his shirt and jacket. Finally, she tore off his briefs, hoping for some sign of ardour – but everything was dead. She shook her head in disgust and lay down beside him, hoping that he would not be sick – or snore. Perhaps in the morning he would rise to better things.

Across the corridor, Jo was faring much better. Malcolm had just spent the last half-hour licking, kissing, tickling and stroking every erogenous nerve in her body. He had ridden her with consummate skill and she was feeling quite limp and breathless – but deeply satisfied, with her lover's head cradled on her warm, cushion-like belly and her fingers running through his soft, dark hair.

He was all a man should be. Rough and demanding beforehand. Quiet and experienced doing it. Gentle and appreciative afterwards. Malcolm had always known what to do, right from the moment they had first met. She still felt a little ashamed that he had seduced her so easily. Taken her back to his house that first night to enjoy his stir-fry beef and then taken it from there.

Years before, when she was married to Rex and had been surrounded by the children, the dog and the cat, the heap of clothes needing to be ironed, the dirty plates waiting to be washed up, and wearing a thick woolly jumper and brown slacks, she would have thought it incredible to be the woman she was today. Rex had been all right – apart from his beard. But no one could say he was exciting. He spent most of his time reading large books and writing lengthy papers which were published in obscure magazines. For all his expertise in sociology, his understanding of human relationships seemed to desert him once he had shut the bedroom door. He was a selfish man and if Jo ever had an orgasm, she counted herself lucky. More often than not, sex was a final duty to be performed at the end of a long day when she was already tired.

Now she had begun to feel that she was a bird of paradise, a *femme fatale*, an ugly duckling that had blossomed into a swan. She had always looked after her figure and she was thankful that she had. Her skin was still fresh and pink, her breasts not too 'hangy', her legs long and elegant as they had always been. All that she had needed was some professional advice about make-up, a change of style and colour for her hair and a wardrobe of decent clothes. Now she felt loose, free and totally irresponsible. No one would guess that she was the mother of two teenage children. She had recovered her self-confidence and with several lovers in the bag, she felt that she had now caught up with Sarah who had always taken such things for granted.

Malcolm was the latest of her conquests. How long he would last, she did not know – but she liked his home, his car and his dry sense of humour. He had already had two wives –

one he had picked up and put down whilst still at University; the other he was a little vague about... but whose hand was still visible in the furnishing and decoration of Malcolm's home. There were no pictures of her even though Jo had looked for them. Malcolm denied having any children, but she wondered whether he was really telling the truth. She had seen a letter which started: 'Dear Dad...' and she had found a piece of blue Lego in the glove compartment of the Jag.

Very quickly, she had discovered that Malcolm liked to keep his life in several separate compartments. Work was work – and seldom mentioned. The past was past – and rarely referred to. With her, Malcolm relaxed. She was picked up when he needed her; put down when he didn't. It suited her fine. But this was the first fortnight they had spent together. It was the first time they had been abroad. Naturally she had been a little anxious – especially about Neville, but judging by the opening cadenza, it was all going to be a great success.

Malcolm stirred himself – and rolled over on to his back.

"Did we drink all that champagne?"

"No. There's still one-third of the bottle left."

"Marvellous!"

Joanne filled the two tumblers with the golden liquid.

"Just the thing to round off the day!"

"Bet your sister's not having such a good time!"

"Why not?"

"I didn't think Neville was in very good shape. Looked quite plastered, I thought. Didn't look as if he'd be much use to anyone." Malcolm chuckled.

"You don't like Neville?"

"Do you?"

"Well, he's very good-looking. Sarah seems to like him. He's got a good sense of humour. Very much a gentleman."

Malcolm shook his head.

"He's a waster. He inherited a good, solid, family business and he's just frittered it away. Spent money on stupid things like horses. They just eat your money – never give you anything back except smelly stuff in buckets. It appeals to one's vanity, of course. I believe it was his wife who liked riding; so he bought a set of stables out in the country – and a few horses to go with them. Then he had to employ a groom, a couple of stable lads and buy a few acres for a good gallop. Not to mention a couple of horse-boxes and a number of large cars capable of towing them. After that, he took to gambling. Lost quite a lot, I believe."

"Where did you learn all that?"

"Phoned up one of his old school chums. He gave me the low-down. It's not a pretty story. He gambled away about a million before he stopped. By that time, his wife had thrown him out. There was a divorce. She married the groom – and kept the horses. Neville returned to his family firm to find things going from bad to worse. He's got one of the worst sales teams you could ever imagine. Absolutely hopeless lot! Plenty of good ideas but if you can't sell the bloody stuff, what's the point? His firm's been going down the plug-hole for the last five years. It's a wonder it's still there! It doesn't deserve to be."

"Well, if it's as bad as that, he couldn't possibly make a take-over for Sarah's firm. She's doing very well."

"So I hear. But Neville's old school chum said that was what Neville had told him. He said that Neville and your sister were getting on so well that it was only a matter of time before she would sell out and he'd take over. Vertical integration, it's called. Getting everything – publishing, printing – under one roof. It makes sense – but not with Neville's firm. It would be like being married to a corpse. I wouldn't like to see Sarah making a mistake like that."

Joanne took a deep swig of champagne.

"I don't think she'd do anything stupid. She's got her head screwed on very firmly."

"But he's wormed his way into her affections. They've been living together... how long?"

"Six months – perhaps seven. February, I think it was. He gave her a bunch of red roses on St Valentine's Day. I think that was when it all began..."

Malcolm shrugged his shoulders.

"Well, anything could happen. She might marry him – and then he'd be next in line to own the firm. If anything happened to Sarah, it'd be his for the taking. You haven't any shares in it, have you?"

Joanne shook her head.

"None. Sarah owns it all. It belonged to her husband, Charles. But he died in a car crash about five years ago."

"Well, as I say, if anything happened to Sarah – say another car crash – then Neville would be a very rich man."

"I don't think Sarah would like that."

"I bet she wouldn't. But if she marries him, there's another danger. Suppose his firm packs up and his huge debts have to be repaid, Sarah might have to help him out."

"I'm sure she must have considered that."

"I hope she has." Malcolm drank the last of his champagne. "But that's why Neville riles me. It's bad enough hearing about it – but seeing him cosying up to her makes me sick. I'm sure he has some redeeming points – but commercially, he's a walking disaster. I think he's hoping Sarah will take pity on him – and bail him out. But if she's thinking of marrying him, she's marrying trouble – you mark my words!"

Back in Room 309, things had not changed. Neville was still fast asleep – not sick, not snoring. He was now curled up beside Sarah, his arm around her waist. At 2.30am, his throat was so dry that he got up and went for a glass of water. He drank two tumblerfuls and then rubbed some cold water over his face. Sarah switched on the bedside light.

"Sorry to wake you up. I just had to have a drink."

He looked at his clothes – now neatly folded.

"I don't remember taking off my things."

"You didn't. I stripped you."

Neville raised his eyebrows.

"Was I out cold?"

"Just about. You drank too much."

"I know." Neville climbed back into bed and cuddled close to Sarah. "It was that foul creature that Jo produced."

"He seemed quite nice to me."

"Well, of course he was nice to you. You're paying for his holiday. But he'd obviously been making inquiries into my business affairs. He was trying to humiliate me in front of you."

"He didn't succeed. I thought you stood up to him remarkably well."

It wasn't true but it made Neville feel better. She could feel him holding her with a stronger and more confident grip.

Sarah smiled to herself.

"But he wasn't the only one doing a spot of detective work. Who are these Latimer people?"

Neville laughed coldly.

"It's quite unbelievable. The Latimers own a bungalow in Dartford – quite an attractive property – or at least it was. Mr and Mrs Latimer work abroad so they had rented it out for a number of years, intending to use it as their retirement home when the time came. However, the last lot of tenants defaulted on their rent and then refused to leave. The Latimers employed dear Malcolm to take legal action to recover the unpaid rent and to get the tenants evicted. The battle went on for about eighteen months. Letters and writs flew backwards and forwards. There were several court appearances. Eventually, the people got turfed out but not a penny of the outstanding rent was paid. I think it amounted to about £15,000.

"Well, the bungalow had been left looking like a pig-sty. The central heating had been torn out and all the wash-basins and lavatories chipped and cracked. The fitted kitchen will have to be refitted and the whole place will have to be rewired and redecorated. They just couldn't sell it – or rent it – in the state it was. No one would touch it.

"That was bad enough! But to top it all, in came dear Malcolm's legal bill for services rendered. £30,000! I'm surprised Mr Latimer didn't have a heart attack. It was quite outrageous! He'd got the tenants out but he hadn't recovered a penny of the outstanding rent. The Latimers naturally refused to pay. So our dear Malcolm took them to court – and won his case! So now they've had to pay two legal bills – with all the extra costs involved. Malcolm hired an expensive barrister to defend him so the Latimers have lost sixty or seventy thousand pounds and they still have their wretched bungalow needing thousands spent on it. At their time of life, it's quite heartbreaking. That's the sort of man Jo's got in tow! He's a rat – and I don't mind telling him to his face what I think of him!"

"Are you quite sure about this?"

"I don't think there are likely to be two lawyers called Malcolm Clark practising in Dartford! If there are, I should be most surprised. Anyway, you saw his reaction at table. He shut up immediately."

"I don't think Jo knows anything about it."

"I'm sure she doesn't. Malcolm's not the sort of man to mix business with pleasure. The Latimers were business; Jo's strictly for pleasure."

Sarah smiled.

"Well, he's being very nice to her. I've never seen her looking so happy."

Neville was about to say: 'fool's paradise' but thought it might upset Sarah. Instead he said maliciously: "I hope he doesn't send her a bill for services rendered! It might be quite hefty!"

Sarah laughed.

"It's strange to think of Jo being someone's mistress. For years, she was so bloody respectable. A real drone! Talking about nothing except her children, all their ailments and the cost of buying them new clothes. She was a real drag! Now she's almost a different person. I used to think she looked down on me as a loose woman. She used to say: 'Of course, it's easy for you. You've no responsibilities! You can do what you like!' She was always so bloody self-righteous. Now she's gone from one extreme to the other. But I still can't imagine her doing naughty things with Malcolm."

"I think women get a new lease of life when they get to forty."

Sarah sniffed.

"What a load of rubbish! Women are at their peak in their thirties. At least, this one is!"

Neville was reminded that he was very close to a warm, sensuous woman who was pressing herself against him. He ran his hand down her leg and back up under her lacy slip.

"You're still wearing your pants!" he said with some surprise.

"Well, get them off!"

It had taken Neville long enough to recover from his alcoholic excesses but, with a bit of luck, the night might still have a happy ending. Sarah rolled on her back and felt the tingling sensation of her defences being peeled away.

She shut her eyes and opened her arms.

"Slowly, darling," she said. "Slowly."

6: *Cui Bono?*

It was Sunday morning in the main lounge of the *Hotel Aphrodite*.

"Hello, everyone! I'm Angie. We're here to welcome you to Puerto de Pollensa and to wish you a really happy holiday! And this is Mandy! Say 'hello', Mandy!"

"Hello, everyone! I'm Mandy. I'm the excursions organizer for Megatravel. We want you to have a simply splendid time in Pollensa and see all there is to see! It's a fabulous island – no other word for it. Fabulous. We've been working here for four months so we should know! So we've laid on an absolutely superb programme to make sure every one of you has a holiday to remember..."

If the breadth of her smile and the brightness of her eyes could have made people's dreams come true, everyone's holiday in Pollensa would have been a rollicking success. Mandy positively drooled over the treats in store.

"...On Monday, we drive through the mountains to Soller. It's an absolutely fantastic ride – on an incredible road! Sometimes, the front of the bus is right over the edge of the precipice! But you don't have to worry – Pedro is a really great driver! You'll love Pedro! The road was built by the Americans to get them up to a radar station, but now it's *the* perfect way to see the Valldemosa! No one should go home without seeing the Valldemosa and smelling the sweet smell of the lemon groves. Soller is famous for its orange and lemon groves – and it's also got something else! A little electric railway that takes you all the way down to Palma. Just the place for a little shopping, ladies! Four hours in Palma and then Pedro will be ready to bring us all home! A fantastic day!"

Raynes listened with a smile upon his face. How did they keep it up week after week? Were they brainwashed? Who taught them to speak in constant superlatives? He could not believe that anyone could get so hyped-up on Spanish mountains or electric railways. Were they paid on commission? Or did they sleep with Pedro?

And who was Pedro anyway? Probably some dumb bunny who had failed to make it as a Spanish astronaut, who now drove tourists round tortuous bends with a permanent chip on his shoulder, longing to drive them over the edge and incinerate the whole coach-load in a sweet-smelling orange grove! Treasured memories in the Valldemosa!

"Now on Tuesday night, we've got another smash hit! We've got a massive barbecue laid on at a really old Spanish farmhouse right out in the hills. You can eat as much as you want and the food's terrific! The booze is free! Some of you probably know sangria's the local hooch. Well, there's sangria and sangria. Ours is fantastic! All the couriers will be dressing up! You'll have a real laugh! And we'll have a few party games to break the ice. After the meal, we've got a gorgeous disco laid on – with even more gorgeous Marc – wait till you see him, ladies! He'll make your hearts throb. Marc will see us through to the wee small hours. You can't miss this one!"

'Oh yes, I can,' thought Raynes, who had been reading the promotional literature and had discovered that Megatravel planned to sting him for 4500 pesetas if he went to the Barbecue La Calobra. About £45 for two people! Quite a

43

chunk out of the holiday purse! No wonder they could afford to offer free booze. With supermarket sangria at about a pound a litre, someone was going to be making an absolute killing.

"And here is Giles! Come in Giles!"

A rather sad-looking figure with a beard and a pair of dirty white shorts stepped forward, holding a pair of goggles and flippers.

"I'm Giles," he said apologetically. "I'm the scuba instructor here. We have a fabulous sea shore – lots of lovely fish and beautiful rocks..." (He did not sound convincing.) "Until you've been down there and seen it, you have no idea how fascinating the underwater world can be." He waved the pair of goggles in one hand and the flippers in the other. "I suppose you've all seen these before," he chuckled. "But this is your chance to use them!"

Raynes looked at the sprinkling of middle-aged matrons with their white hair and their aged husbands – rheumatic, arthritic, smoking, coughing, doubtless riddled with incurable cancer – looking as if they were permanently wedded to an iron lung. Yes, this was their chance to claim on the insurance money. It could be quite a good racket!

Giles had slightly spoiled the atmosphere. He had gone on for too long. He hadn't smiled much. He had spoken modestly and he lacked sex-appeal. Hardly anyone looked as if they were interested in scuba diving. Even Debbie was drinking up her free champagne and looking round for seconds.

It was time to bring on Brendan!

Brendan was indeed A.1. An Irishman, absolutely lit up, even though it was still only 10.30 on a Sunday morning! He was tall with tousled gold hair, a most wicked smile, wild blue eyes, golden brown legs and immaculately white sailing shorts.

"Hello, folks!"

From the very first syllable, you felt Brendan was going to score.

He had a ship. A fantastic, wonderful ship. He had dug it up from some scrapyard in Barcelona. He had rebuilt it and installed the biggest and best bar in the Mediterranean. He could offer *ten* different sorts of Irish whiskey...

44

(Gasps all round.)

The boat had big white sails, a deep crimson hull and she flew the skull and crossbones at her masthead. Sixty people a day travelled on his boat to the blue grotto – the real blue grotto – on the north-eastern side of Cape Formentor. There you could see the incredible blue light reflecting on the fish, on the pebbles, on the white sand... Brendan made it sound like magic.

At night, his ship took on a different role. Then he would roam along the coast pointing out the villas of the famous. 'The good, the bad and the sex-starved' as he put it. With the aid of a megaphone, Brendan would give an impromptu running commentary on all the sinners who lived there, who they were sleeping with and what they were worth. Even what their hang-ups were reported to be. This was the real McCoy! Not the stuff you would read in *Hello!*

Brendan had it all taped. Six times he had been prosecuted for slander; eighteen times for being a public nuisance – but he regarded these fines as natural running costs in a high-risk business. He was not joking! He had heard it rumoured that the Spanish movie star, Daina Donja, had planned to hire a mini-submarine to blow his boat out of the sea!

So there was a sense of danger! A whiff of gunpowder! The prospect of walking the plank and dropping into the blue grotto blindfold as Mr and Mrs Pirate. Yes – it was a fantastic experience – by day or by night. Brendan and his *Jolly Rioja* were a star turn. 6000 pesetas was a mere snip, with a trip to Devil's Island and sardines and sangria thrown in. Only a real misery would turn down the chance of sailing with Brendan!

So – back to Mandy.

("Thank you, Brendan!"

"Thank you, darling, see you at the pub!")

What could Mandy offer that was not an anti-climax? She had on white shorts and a bright red T shirt with 'Mega' written in large letters front and back. She had golden legs and chubby knees. And she had that electric smile.

Now she was offering an afternoon in the Caves of Drach. An all-star concert in the largest subterranean cave in the world. Not a mere recording of Leonard Bernstein but the entire City of Palma Symphony Orchestra blasting out 'Viva Espana' every half hour. Stalagmites and stalactites. The mites go up when the tights go down! (A rather risky joke for a predominantly elderly audience with a high percentage of 'mites' – but everyone laughed ecstatically.)

And then there was a trip to a real pearl factory. Well, it was a real factory but the pearls were artificial. A bit of a come-down that! But they were the best artificial pearls in the world! Hundreds of Majorcan peasant women spent their entire lives stringing these wonderful pearls together. It was impossible to tell them from the real thing! Surely it was the ideal present to take home for a daughter – or for a loved one? A string for any sucker you could think of.

On Thursday, there was a trip to a monastery. (You thought Megatravel was only interested in money? But you were wrong! Megatravel catered for the spiritual as well as the profane. And anyway, by Thursday, most people were feeling the pinch!) But to resume:

On the way to the monastery, the tour would stop at the old city of Pollensa (from which the Puerto got its name) – the old Roman capital of Majorca, with its narrow streets and its fantastic Calvary. 365 steps from top to bottom. One for every day of the year. Megatravel gave you precisely twenty-five minutes to cover this Via Dolorosa.

From there to Lluc – home of sparkling waters and an exhibition of Mallorquin folk dancing. Then up to the monastery. Time for a quick prayer. A photo of some smiling old codger in a black cassock. Then a chance to dabble one's weary feet in the beautiful torrent of Pareis... and so on to a lingering coach ride home with dear Pedro who was probably by now completely smashed.

Mandy made it all sound like a walk in a paradise garden. But Angie was quick to bring the punters back to earth. Don't drink the water! Watch out for man-eating sharks! Make sure you keep an eye on your handbags when you're lying on the beach! Be careful which car-hire firm you choose! Don't stay in the sun for too long unless you're used to it. Remember to keep your hands off the Spanish waiters and/or maids. And if anything should go wrong – perish the thought – remember! The Megatravel couriers were waiting in their office to arrange immediate hospital treatment or a coffin home. Nothing was outside Angie's remit. You could trust Angie to see that you travelled home fleeced or rigid – preferably both!

But in case you took her too seriously, the couriers would now circulate – to ask which tours and expeditions you would like to sign up for. Book now – pay later, was Megatravel's soft sell. To help you make up your mind, a second round of champagne made its appearance. Raynes thought the word 'champagne' was a bit of a misnomer, but it was just the thing to rekindle the holiday spirit and Megtravel's lucky victims succumbed immediately to Mandy's electric charm. How could one refuse her?

Raynes turned to Debbie and said: "What do you feel like doing?"

She looked at him with half-closed eyes.

"Right now," she said, "I feel like a good ****!"

7: *Quaerebam quid Amarem*

"I thought you were very hard on Neville last night."

Sarah and Malcolm were sitting in the hotel garden on a hot Sunday afternoon. Sarah was wearing a white silk blouse with a long, white, pleated skirt. She looked cool, calm and very collected. Malcolm was also feeling exceedingly laid-back, enjoying his first beer of the day. Sarah was cradling an ice-cold gin and tonic. She had decided it was better to clear the air right away.

"Just thought I ought to warn you."

"I don't need any warnings. I know all about Neville. I have done from the beginning. You only have to look at him to see what sort of person he is."

"He's certainly not cut out to be a businessman."

"No. But he obviously felt he had a duty to carry on the family business – especially after his elder brother died."

"He'd have been better selling up."

"Probably."

Malcolm took a sip of his beer.

He was determined to make it last.

"You know he's heavily in debt?"

"I do."

"Doesn't it worry you?"

"Yes."

"What have you advised him to do?"

"Precisely what any other sensible person would do. Sell it off as a going concern and hope that the property his firm owns would make the package more attractive than it is."

Malcolm smiled.

"Bit of a cheek, suggesting that he should take you over?"

Sarah bristled.

"He didn't suggest that at all. What he said was that we might like to print some of his books and, in return, we might buy a stake in his company."

"A large stake?"

Sarah wasn't going to tell Malcolm that Neville had suggested a 40% stake in Warrenders. It would only make Neville look more silly in Malcolm's eyes.

"The whole thing was a non-starter," she said. "I just treated it as a joke."

"An expensive joke!" said Malcolm. "I heard that Neville had proposed 50%?"

"You heard wrong. I'm very particular about my business. I don't rush into speculative ventures with anyone. We just keep doing what we've always been doing – quality printing and we don't take any risks."

"How long have you been running the firm?"

"Five years. Since Charles died."

"Jo was telling me. A car crash, wasn't it?"

Sarah nodded.

It seemed so long ago. Charles was almost like a figure in a dream. Unless she put her mind to it, she could hardly remember what he had looked like.

"Did Charles build the firm up himself?"

"He and a friend. But his friend got itching feet. He wanted to go abroad. So Charles bought him out and then it was all his."

"And now it's all yours. Quite an achievement..."

"... for a woman! Don't be a bloody chauvinist!"

"Sorry, I didn't mean to sound patronizing. But it is quite an achievement. Did you know anything about printing beforehand?"

"I know quite a lot about managing human beings. Get that right and everything else falls into place."

She sounded hard. But deep down, that was the way she was.

"Didn't Charles have any relations?"

Sarah looked at Malcolm sourly.

"He had a wife. His first wife. But she didn't play any part in the firm. She was a journalist."

"She didn't have any shares in the company?"

"None. Anyway, Charles divorced her. She was well provided for." Sarah's voice sounded bitter. "She got the house and about half a million. I don't think she could complain. She screwed Charles for every penny she could get but she didn't get her hands on the business. She'd probably have liked to – just out of spite."

"Did Charles have any family?"

"A boy and a girl."

"You never see them?"

"No."

Malcolm looked thoughtful and took another sip of beer.

"So what happens to the company if anything happens to you? Who gets it then?"

Sarah looked at Malcolm coldly.

"Surely, as a lawyer, you don't have to ask me a question like that! It's perfectly obvious. It would go to my sister. She's my next of kin. And if you married Jo – and anything happened to Jo – it would pass to you. I'm sure you'd worked all that out long ago." She smiled. "We women are not as green as we're cabbage-looking! We can read you men like a book! Jo's a splendid person, but if anything happened to her sister, she'd be worth a small fortune. Makes a chap think, doesn't it?"

Malcolm laughed.

"Unless you happen to marry Neville?"

Sarah smiled.

"Ah? The 64,000 dollar question! The unthinkable possibility! If Neville married me and got his hands on all my millions! What a wailing and gnashing of teeth there would be – especially in Dartford!"

She was being cruel.

Malcolm managed not to appear irritated.

"But you've already agreed that he's in no way equipped to run a business..."

Sarah laughed.

"... But he's very well-equipped to be a husband! And I should know!"

Malcolm grinned.

"Good for him! But his first wife didn't think so."

"Did you know her?"

"No. But one or two of his friends have told me what their marriage was like."

"She liked horses."

"She liked horses more than she liked Neville. And once Neville was gone, she married the groom. She knew what she wanted."

"Are you suggesting that I don't?"

Malcolm smiled broadly.

"I was just going to say that there are other people around who are both skilled in business and who also know how to make a woman happy."

"Is that a proposal?"

Sarah was amused.

"No, just a compliment. You are a very attractive woman and I would hate to see you make a foolish mistake."

Malcolm was at his most charming.

"Surely," said Sarah, "it would be an even greater mistake for me to even contemplate falling in love with someone whom I only met twenty-four hours ago – who happens to be in love with my sister?" She corrected herself. "Whom I thought was in love with my sister? But could it be that he is only using her as a stepping stone to greater things?"

Malcolm took her criticism in his stride.

"Jo is a splendid person – and we have great fun together. There's no doubt we are very happy together. But I've given up saying I love anyone..."

"You love yourself!"

"Don't we all? Jo and I have never tried to pretend we had any sentimental attachments. We just enjoy everything we have..."

"Until you find something better...richer...younger?"

Malcolm shook his head.

"That's very unfair. I've got no thought of leaving Jo. We're very happy – and, in time, it is just possible that we might get married. It depends on how she feels about me. But we haven't got to that point yet. If I did meet someone younger...richer...and more attractive, would it be a crime to change horses? You wouldn't want me to make another foolish mistake?"

"Have you made one?"

"Several."

"Perhaps coming on this holiday was a mistake?"

Malcolm shook his head again.

"Not at all. In fact, I think it's one of the best things I've done in my whole professional life. If I can save a rich and beautiful woman from marrying a fool – and a rogue – then this holiday will have been more than worthwhile. Added to that, the joys of sex, sun and sangria – what more could a fellow want?"

Sarah could not let him get away with that.

"Malcolm," she said, "you are a very dangerous man! You play with people. I suppose – being a lawyer – you do it every day. People's lives lie in the palm of your hand. Some, you advance – others, you destroy. My sister has put a lot of trust in her relationship with you. I wouldn't like to see it destroyed – especially not by me!" She swigged down the rest of her gin and tonic and put her glass down firmly on the small white table. She looked Malcolm calmly in the eye. "I won't say that I don't find you attractive. You have a way with women. I can feel it. You may say that you like my body – or my bright blue eyes – but, flattering as it is, you know – and I know – that you are interested in only one thing. Money! And I have no intention of letting you – or anyone – dominate my private life or my business. So there!"

She smiled.

"Bravo!" said Malcolm. "A brave speech."

"But you got my message?"

"Loud and clear. But I also hope you got mine?"

He looked at her glass.

"Time for another round, I think."

8: *Audi partem alteram*

Whilst this conversation was taking place in the hotel garden, a second – more serious – conversation had been taking place in the *Aphrodite*'s cocktail bar. Neville had met Joanne on the main staircase and taken her aside.

"I just wanted to have a quiet word with you."

"Couldn't we have a drink whilst we are doing it?"

"Oh, sorry! What would you like?"

"A Cinzano would be nice. Bianco with ice."

Neville called the barman over.

"A Cinzano Bianco with ice and a large San Miguel, please."

He returned to Jo.

"I'm sorry to have to say these things to you, but I'm very worried about your friend, Malcolm."

Jo smiled.

"I thought *he* was worried about you and Sarah?"

"It's all very complicated. Really it is. He thinks I'm a scheming capitalist trying to lay my hands on Sarah's company."

"Aren't you?"

"Of course not! Sarah wouldn't do anything stupid. I

52

thought at one time she might be able to help me, but things have gone a bit too far for that. My firm's going rapidly downhill; we're heavily in debt – and it's proving the devil of a headache trying to decide what to do."

"Sell it!"

"But to whom?"

"To Sarah! Let her buy it from you – and then she can sort out the mess. If there's anything that can be salvaged, I'm sure she'd do it..."

Neville looked doubtful.

"... unless you're completely bankrupt, in which case you ought to be applying for a receiver."

"It's not as bad as that."

"Well, sell it to Sarah for one pound. Prove that you love her. That you trust her. That you're not interested in her only for her money."

"She knows I'm not."

"That's not what Malcolm was told. He was told that you'd been boasting to people that you were going to take her over. It was only a matter of time before you became the boss."

Neville looked apologetic.

"I suppose I did say that – but they were only words. Words covering up a very humiliating reality. I did ask her to buy a stake in my firm, but she just laughed. I don't think she has any illusions about what's happening."

"None whatsoever. It's *your* company. She doesn't want to get involved. But she can see what it's doing to you. I'm sure she'd be only too glad to see you get the burden off your back. The longer you let things drift, the more damage it'll do to the two of you." Jo sipped her drink cautiously. "Malcolm wasn't telling her anything she didn't know."

"It's a bit rough, coming from a complete stranger," said Neville. "Especially from one who's not exactly above criticism himself!"

Jo raised her eyebrows.

"And what's wrong with Malcolm?"

"How much do you really know about him?"

"He's good-looking, he's kind, he's generous, he's a

successful lawyer, he's got a good sense of humour, he's a talented cook – and he's a splendid lover."

Jo felt that there was scarcely any more she could say about Malcolm without going completely over the top.

Neville looked serious.

"But what d'you really know about him? D'you know if he's been married before? D'you know if he's got any children? Is he actually divorced? Has he told you anything important about himself?"

Jo was silent.

She didn't want to admit that there were parts of Malcolm's life that were a closed book. She had no wish to pry. She was sure that Malcolm would tell her in due course. It was better to wait.

Neville understood what she was feeling.

"Well, let me give you a few facts. Malcolm has been married twice..."

"I knew that."

"He was married to a girl called Karen when he was at University – but he divorced her the moment he qualified as a lawyer. His second wife was called Helen and they have three children – Robert, Elaine and... I forget what the last one's called. Helen divorced him three years ago on the grounds of adultery. Adultery – not just with one woman but with a whole string of them. Helen bided her time till she'd got chapter and verse. Photographs. Video film. Tape recordings. She hired a private detective to get all the information. When it came to court, the case was so cut and dried, Malcolm didn't even try to defend himself. That says something, doesn't it? He just conceded that, brilliant lawyer though he thinks he is, Helen had run rings round him – and then proceeded to claim the most generous settlement for herself and the children."

He looked at Jo.

"You didn't know about any of this, did you?"

Jo shook her head.

"I thought not. But ever since that moment, Malcolm has been a killer. I don't mean he strangles people or anything like that. But, in Court, he goes for people. He rips them off for every penny he can. He's absolutely ruthless. Almost as if he's trying to get his revenge."

Jo sat silent and upset.

"Did you hear me mention some people called Latimer last night? Some people from Dartford?"

She nodded.

"Well, let me tell you what happened to them."

Neville proceeded to repeat the story he had told Sarah, but in slightly greater detail.

Jo looked very shocked.

Neville concluded: "That is what Malcolm is really like! One of my salespeople lives in Dartford and he told me. I thought at first he might be making it up, but I checked with a lawyer friend and he said every word was true. People are frightened to face Malcolm in Court. Sometimes, even his own clients wish they had chosen someone else. The sting's in the tail! He wins the case – then he stings them!" Neville paused. "I'm sure that with you, he's been very kind, very generous, very loving – but that's only one side of Malcolm. There's another side to him which is completely inhuman."

There were tears in Jo's eyes.

"Why did you tell me all this?"

"I thought you ought to know the truth. Malcolm's said enough against me. I just thought you ought to have the whole picture."

"Thanks for nothing!"

Jo shook her head.

"Why did you come to Majorca?" Neville asked.

"To meet you and Sarah."

"And whose idea was it?"

Jo thought for a few moments.

"Malcolm said he would like to meet my sister. I'd told him about her and you. He said it would be nice to have a weekend together. I told Sarah and she suggested it would be even better if we could all meet out here in Pollensa. She even paid for it. I'm sure she had no idea you two would fall out."

Neville downed the last of his beer.

"Don't you think there's something suspicious in his desire to meet Sarah?"

"No. Do you?"

"I don't know. I find it strange that Malcolm – normally such a busy, successful lawyer – should show such a touching interest in other human beings. It seems out of character."

"Everyone needs a holiday – even busy lawyers! I think you're making a mountain out of a molehill."

"Perhaps I am. But everything we know about Malcolm suggests that his two interests in life are money and women. Your sister combines both."

Jo laughed.

"You're not suggesting that Malcolm's interested in Sarah? That's ridiculous! They've only just met. Just because he's rattled your cage, you're jealous!"

To Joanne, the matter was quite simple. Malcolm had been teasing Neville – but in doing so, he had touched a raw nerve. In return, Neville was determined to blacken Malcolm's reputation – something which he had done most effectively. In Jo's opinion, Neville was being petty and spiteful.

Neville said nothing.

Joanne picked up her bag.

"Well, if that's all you've got to say to me, I think we'd be better joining the others outside."

She looked at Neville who was still fingering his glass and biting his lip.

"Give Malcolm a chance," she said. "Don't prejudge him. Even if he can be a brute in Court, he's here to enjoy himself. And if you keep attacking him, it'll only spoil the holiday for all of us. Try and be nice to him."

Neville looked up.

"You're probably right. I am being a bit sensitive. I didn't mean to spoil things. But I can't help thinking he's a wolf in sheep's clothing – and I keep wondering why he's interested in all of us. All I can say is: 'Be careful! Be very careful in what you're doing!'"

9: *Latet anguis in herba*

Even though she dismissed Neville's worries as the jealous resentment of the failed businessman towards a successful lawyer, Joanne could not forget what he had told her about Malcolm's background and the shocking iniquities of the Latimer case. Not surprisingly, her attitude towards her lover was somewhat altered by the new perspectives she had been given.

She could now understand Malcolm's reticence in talking about his wife and children. It was a bitter experience – a humiliating experience – which he would obviously want to bury. Bury deeply. It was not something he would have wanted to discuss with her. A new woman... a new chapter in his life. It would be a measure of progress in their relationship together when he felt able to share his bitter memories with her.

As for his activities in Court, she did not entirely agree with Neville's strictures. Malcolm had to spend a lot of time and effort preparing his cases – and the eviction of unwanted tenants was, she imagined, one of the most lengthy and unrewarding cases a lawyer could take up. Of course the tenants would not leave voluntarily; they would avoid payment if they could. The Latimers had wanted them out. Malcolm had got them out. It was not his fault the tenants had wrecked the house. She could understand the Latimers' feelings, but Malcolm was perfectly entitled to charge them for his work; and if the Latimers refused to pay, then they deserved to be sued. It was an unpleasant business, to be sure, but the more she thought about it, the less she blamed Malcolm. If the Latimers had been more careful in their choice of tenants, the situation would never have arisen. Malcolm had really made the best of a bad job.

Jo and Neville came out to join the others in the garden. Sarah immediately noticed that her sister had been crying and looked suspiciously at Neville. What had he been saying to Jo?

Malcolm was in his most expansive mood; he gave his beloved a kiss, found a chair for Neville, arranged for a fresh round of drinks and challenged his rival to beat him out to the end of the breakwater. The loser would pay for the cost of the barbecue at La Calobra on Tuesday night.

Sarah said: "It's already been paid for! What about making the loser pay for all the drinks at the dance tonight?"

"Suits me," said Malcolm. "Are you game?"

Neville took off his shirt and shorts. Underneath, he was wearing a small pair of briefs which accentuated his manhood to great effect. Sarah looked at him admiringly and even Joanne found it difficult not to notice the difference between the two men.

Malcolm and Neville strode purposefully down the steps towards the beach.

Richard and Debbie were lying sunbathing not far away. The Inspector raised himself on one elbow to watch them.

"Going off to drown each other!" he said cynically.

Debbie was rubbing oil into her skin.

"Neville's got a beautiful bum," she said. "Really exciting. Those muscles are quite mouthwatering. I do hope he murders Malcolm!"

She turned on to her stomach and popped on her sunglasses.

Raynes looked at her with merriment.

She was wearing a pink, blue and yellow striped costume with a small straw hat on her head.

For Debbie, men's bodies and their performance were every bit as fascinating as that of a yearling competing in its first race. A trainer had only to look at a horse to know how it would perform. Debbie had uttered her considered judgement – and it was final.

Raynes' eyes followed the two men down to the beach. He watched them slowly entering the shimmering, blue waters.

"My money's on Neville," he said.

"So's mine," said Debbie, not even looking.

The start was as fair as one could wish and both men struck out vigorously for the end of the breakwater which was about three hundred yards off-shore. Long before they had reached the finishing post, it was obvious that Neville was well ahead.

As he reached the slippery stones, Neville turned round and watched Malcolm struggling to catch up.

"Well done!" said Malcolm. "You had the edge on me. Obviously, you're in better shape. I just couldn't keep up with you."

"I've always loved swimming. Don't get as much as I would like to."

Malcolm was tempted to say that once Neville was bankrupt or in jail, he would have all the time in the world. But he checked himself. Neville was not bearing any grudge; neither must he.

"It's lovely out here," he said. "Sheer heaven!"

"You can see why Sarah enjoys it so much."

Malcolm nodded.

Up on the terrace, Sarah looked at Joanne.

"Did Neville upset you?"

Jo nodded.

"It was nothing really. He was just warning me about Malcolm. Filling me in on all the gory details about his past and urging me to beware of the beast!"

"Neville does seem to feel very strongly about Malcolm."

"I think he's jealous of Malcolm's success."

"That's not surprising."

"And I think he's a little frightened that Malcolm might be interested in you."

"In me?"

"You – and your money. He seems to think Malcolm engineered this holiday simply to get closer to you. I told him it was quite ridiculous."

"Quite!"

Sarah sounded more emphatic than she felt. There might well be some truth in what Neville was saying.

"I told him that if he went on, he'd spoil the holiday for all of us."

"Quite right!"

"So I suppose that's why they're both out there on that rock. Proving that they're friends for life!"

Sarah smiled.

"Men are funny creatures. They see the world in such a different way to us. At heart, they're still like prehistoric cavemen, fighting it out with clubs, staking their claim to land or women, enjoying their little moment of victory." She looked out into the bay. "By the way, who won? I didn't notice."

"Neville," said Jo sulkily.

She was thinking how much more manly Neville looked without his clothes. Malcolm was still so white – and inclined to be flabby. Perhaps he'd look better when he'd been a fortnight in Pollensa?

"Well, that'll make one of them happy," said Sarah. "We must remember to congratulate both of them when they get back."

Raynes nudged Debbie.

"They're coming back."

Debbie turned over lazily and sipped slowly at her sangria.

Raynes lay back and shut his eyes. It was more her scene than his.

She sighed.

"Yes," she said, "those briefs are far too small. Massive, he is. Massive. Poor Malcolm doesn't stand a chance."

She continued to sip her drink as the two combatants marched by. But although Neville had received her gold seal of approval, it was Malcolm who looked at her as he passed by.

That was the pretty little blonde he had seen in the dining-room the previous night. Very slim, very brown, very petite. Lovely legs – and no wedding ring! He must make sure he got her on her own one night. Her boyfriend looked a bit of a deadbeat. A middle-aged salesman of some sort. If he could pull her, it might make the holiday even more interesting. He smiled quietly to himself.

Debbie noticed the look. It spoke volumes to one so used to the slightest hint or innuendo. The bait had been nibbled at. She looked back at Richard – still with his eyes closed.

"You're quite safe," she said. "Adonis has passed."

But in her mind, she was doing a few quick calculations.

198 pesetas to the pound?

Well, he could afford it!

Shortly before dinner, Joanne was having a shower when the telephone rang. Malcolm answered it. With the water still pouring down around her, Jo could not hear a word of what was being said.

"Is that Malcolm Clark?"

"Speaking..."

"It's Wendy."

Malcolm froze perceptibly.

He listened to the voice at the other end of the line with one ear – and the sound of the running water with the other.

He managed to make his replies as banal as possible: "I think it is quite unnecessary... The matter is safely in hand... I assure you, you have nothing to worry about... You can trust me to handle the matter to your satisfaction... Well, if you insist...! Please leave any message at reception. Thank you."

He put down the phone and was thankful to hear the water still running in the shower. In a few moments, the water was turned off and there was the distant buzz of a hairdryer. Malcolm was glad to have a few minutes on his own.

Why on earth did people have to be so awkward? Couldn't she just leave him to do things his way? He sighed. And now she was coming out to Majorca 'to be on the spot!' That was the last thing he wanted! One slip and the whole thing would blow up in his face.

"Bugger!" he said to himself. "Bugger!"

He was very angry.

But when Joanne came back into the bedroom, Malcolm was lying calmly on the bed, stark-naked, reading the *News of the World* which had eventually arrived at the hotel at about 4.00pm. He looked up at her.

She was wrapped in a primrose-coloured bath-towel, her face pale without make-up, her hair soft and sweet-smelling.

"Who was that on the phone?" she asked.

"A client! A very inconsiderate client who ought to know better than to disturb me on holiday!"

"I didn't think you'd given anyone our number."

"Just my secretary. She has erred."

Jo thought it unlikely that Malcolm's secretary had done any such thing. They had left England on Saturday afternoon. Surely the secretary would not be back in the office till Monday morning? It sounded a little suspicious.

"It wasn't anything serious?"

"No," said Malcolm. "It was nothing serious."

But even though he dismissed the call so lightly and pulled her down roughly on to the bed, tore away the towel and ravished her body with his tongue, Joanne felt that his love-making was not entirely single-minded. Something was worrying him. She wondered what it was.

After dinner that night – and every Sunday night – there was a dance in the main downstairs lounge of the *Hotel Aphrodite*. A local group, Los Pescadores, were all dressed in sailor suits and naval caps, giving it great licks and clearly enjoying themselves.

Raynes was not a great dancer but he could cope with the basic steps. If it was a waltz, a tango or even a foxtrot, he could manage – but anything more exotic and he was out of his depth. Scottish dances such as the Gay Gordons, the Dashing White Sergeant and Strip the Willow were more his cup of tea – but he could hardly expect such things to be played in darkest Spain! Debbie, being more versed in the ways of the world, was an excellent little dancer. She informed Richard discreetly that her first extra-marital affair had been with a teacher of Latin dancing. He had taught her a wide variety of steps; she had taught him the twist... and a few other things as well!

She was wearing an almost see-through, black chiffon dress, with a gold choker, a gold bracelet and a pair of gold sandals. Looking at her many different outfits, Raynes was able to understand why she had needed such a large suitcase. As always, she was the most eye-catching woman in the room and there were a number of envious looks as they swept round the dance-floor together.

In between times, they retired to the bar, where Debbie ordered fruit juice and wiped the sweat off Richard's brow. Her brown eyes kept teasing him and the unending stream of scurrilous stories kept him laughing. He was so glad she had tempted him away on holiday. Grasshallows now seemed so remote, it might well have been on a different planet. He kept wanting to touch and stroke her – her arms were so smooth and brown.

Across the room, Malcolm was also watching her. Every few minutes, his eyes flickered over to the bar. Jo did not notice, but Sarah did. Eventually, Malcolm's vigilance paid off. After another couple of dances, Debbie went away to the ladies' toilet and her partner returned to the bar to order a fresh round of drinks. Quick as a flash, Malcolm excused himself and, using a circuitous route, he left the room and stationed himself in the passage outside the ladies'.

Debbie was not long in emerging.

She was not entirely surprised to see Malcolm standing there. Her first reaction was that he must be desperate. Her second reaction was that he must be a very cool customer. If his girlfriend were to catch him speaking to her, their holiday romance could take a rapid nosedive.

"I'm sorry to disturb your evening," said Malcolm suavely. "I just couldn't resist your dancing. Not so much your dancing as the body that goes with it..."

Debbie smiled sweetly at the compliment.

"... I was looking at you in the beach garden this afternoon and I thought it would be fun if we could share a little time together."

"No problem!" said Debbie.

"No problem?" Malcolm was delighted.

"Just arrange the time and the place and leave a message at reception. I'll be there. Afternoons are best!"

Malcolm could scarcely believe his good fortune. His eyes sparkled. "That's great!" he said.

"Cost you though!" said Debbie coldly. "Forty thousand pesetas..."

"Forty thousand pesetas!" Malcolm was shocked. "That's £200!"

Debbie nodded.

"Just about."

She was joking, of course.

He smiled. "I wasn't expecting to pay for it."

"People like you never are! They expect everything on a plate. If you want it, you know the price. If you can't afford it, you'll have to do without!"

Malcolm tried to cover up his embarrassment.

"Most people pay me for my services."

"So I believe. But it's different round here." She smiled as she thought of Richard sitting peacefully at the bar. "I'm sorry," she said, "but my boyfriend wouldn't accept anything less. He's a very hard man!"

With that, she sped off back to the main lounge.

Malcolm went into the gents' to think it over. Two hundred pounds! What cheek! He had never thought that she was a tart – or that man with her, her pimp. But probably it made sense. They would be recouping the cost of their holiday by ripping off the more gullible guests. At that price, it wouldn't take them long to break even. Perhaps even make a hefty surplus! He wondered if she took Visa? He laughed at his stupidity in approaching her. Why should he pay £200 when he had got Jo? Still – she did have a delicious body. It was available. He would think it over. He had a whole fortnight to decide.

Malcolm returned to the main lounge and danced first with Sarah – then with Jo. Sarah noticed that he was no longer looking over to the bar with such frequency.

"Good," she thought. "She's turned him down. Given him the cold shoulder."

But as he turned his thoughts away from Debbie, he pressed closer to Sarah and ran his hand softly down her bare back. As they swept into one of the darkest corners near the band, he bent his head and kissed her gently on the lips.

Sarah did not resist.

There was something about Malcolm that captivated even the most level-headed woman. It was power. A sort of animal power. You felt that any moment he might carry you off to his lair and rape you. Nicely, of course! To feel those hands caressing you – made you tingle all over. As she had said that morning, Malcolm was a dangerous man. She could see what Jo felt about him. It would be very easy to let yourself go. Malcolm was obviously completely amoral.

As he swept Sarah around the dance-floor, Malcolm sensed that the barriers were crumbling. She was not holding back – she was not pushing him away. He pressed his groin against her thigh so that she could feel what he was feeling.

Sarah looked up.

"You're a wicked man!" she said. "A very wicked man!"

"But you're not resisting!"

Sarah smiled.

"Not tonight."

'Win some, lose some,' thought Malcolm. At least Sarah would not be charging him £200. She would give herself freely. Like an over-ripe plum, she would fall into his hand. She wouldn't make a big scene. She wouldn't say anything to Jo. It would be a little secret between the two of them.

He returned to his seat and finished off his glass of beer.

"Your turn next!" he said to Jo.

But even as he spoke, he couldn't resist a glance over towards the bar. But she had gone. He felt a little disappointed. He had everything he could want – and more; and yet, in his heart of hearts, he knew he would have to stump up that two hundred pounds.

10: *O tempora, O mores!*

At 9.30 on Monday morning, Raynes found himself standing under a palm tree which looked rather like an overgrown pineapple. Puerto de Pollensa had quite a large number of such palms, planted about every ten yards along the promenade on both sides of the road. But every now and then, the municipal authorities (with a rare sense of humour) had left a gap with no palm tree – just a square hole, with no earth, about three feet deep – providing an unforeseen but possibly tragic hazard for the blind, the starry-eyed or the just-plain-drunk to fall into on their way home.

Raynes was not alone.

About forty other people were waiting for the same bus. He noted that Angie from Megatravel was busy ticking off names on her clipboard to make sure all her charges were present. Raynes urged Debbie to hold back the moment of self-disclosure to keep their shepherdess anxious till the last moment, but Debbie said he was being mean.

Raynes cast his eyes around his fellow passengers to see whom he was fated to travel with – possibly even to die with! They were a motley crowd.

First of all, the inevitable geriatrics, making the most of their retirement. The women, plump and bulging, in flowery dresses and floppy hats, carrying large white leather handbags. And their husbands, tall, thin and grey-haired, exquisitely drilled over the years, all wearing clean shirts and pressed shorts, with ankle socks in various pastel shades and sensible canvas shoes – each one faithfully carrying a small bag with a towel, sun-tan oil, the daily paper and a sleeveless cardigan in case it got cold on the way home (which, of course, it never did). There were six of each specimen, making up a round dozen.

At the other end of the spectrum, there were an equal number of sweet young couples – some on their honeymoon, others anticipatlng their honeymoon and perhaps the odd pair still in the first flush of marital bliss. Their men appeared a little more macho – with strong brown shoulders and dark blue vests; their girls, eyes half-shut, their hair wild and loose – looking as if they had been ridden hard all night (as perhaps they had), entwining themselves around their steeds in low-cut tops and ragged denim shorts.

Raynes looked at Debbie to see how she compared. She was wearing a cerise blouse and a tiny pair of white shorts. She wore white sandals and was carrying a small white leather handbag. Her sunglasses were attached to a black cord around her neck but at this moment, they were tucked into her hair.

There was a small, grubby girl who seemed to be on her own. She had very dark-brown skin and long, dark-brown hair. Raynes wondered if she might be a pickpocket and watched her movements carefully. Her shorts were creased and dirty and her green and white striped T-shirt made her look rather like a football club mascot down on her luck. Raynes decided to christen her 'The Brown Baby'.

More aloof was a student in a bright red and blue tracksuit with a baseball cap in the same brash, distinctive colours. On his back, the tracksuit boldly proclaimed: 'University of Arkansas'. Raynes doubted whether there was any such place. The student was wearing large, dark, reflective sunglasses and was plugged into his Walkman. His mouth was constantly in motion, chewing gum, which he periodically spat out on the pavement. Raynes made a mental note not to sit anywhere near him.

Sarah and Joanne were there with their escorts, who looked as if they would much rather be back at the bar in the *Hotel Aphrodite*, reading yesterday's newspapers. The girls' pleated skirts and silk blouses marked them out as a cut above the rest. They had a look which said: 'Why do we have to mix with all these unpleasant people?'

Finally, as there are in any holiday crowd, there were parents who seemed determined to inflict their offspring upon the world – whether the world wanted them or not. There was Mr and Mrs Average with their perfect poppet who said nothing and rarely smiled. She had carrot-red hair, pouting lips and wore a hideous mauve and green dress. Her parents fussed over her interminably and were rewarded with innumerable compliments: 'What a well-behaved child!' – ignoring the fact that the little soul might have been retarded or brain-damaged.

By contrast, Mr and Mrs Tabloid, fresh from their greasy English breakfast at the Union Jack café, with their two uncontrollable and noisy sons, both in black shorts and white T-shirts, sporting the logo: 'It's in *The Sun*!' Unlike Mr and Mrs Average, the Tabloid parents tried for the most part to ignore their children – except to say: 'Shut up, Brian!' or 'Get off him, Glen!' – hoping against hope that the two of them might batter each other insensible and give them and the other passengers some peace.

Fortunately, the Tabloids elected to sit on the back seats of the bus. The geriatrics bagged the seats at the front and the young couples headed for the nether regions. Richard and Debbie sat halfway down the bus, two rows behind Sarah and Jo, but conveniently close to the Brown Baby, whose lithe, wriggling body held Raynes entranced.

The first part of the journey – to Lluch – was quite straightforward, but the road through the mountains to Soller was a terrifying experience. The bus soared higher and higher between the grey, rugged peaks. It reeled happily round complete blind corners; it bowled confidently along the edge of huge precipices with sheer drops to left and right, One soon learnt not to look sideways out of the bus windows if one dared to look out at all. The hairpin bends had a stomach-turning nightmare quality which was not helped by the screams of Glen and Brian in the back seat: 'Dad, we're going over!' Very often, it seemed impossible to believe that the coach would ever reach its destination. Now and again, it was brought to a sudden halt and obliged to reverse, so that part of the bus was actually hanging over the abyss. Passing cars counted themselves fortunate to squeeze by. And all the time, Pedro cheerfully took one hand off the steering wheel to point out objects of local interest which Angie, who seemed to have nerves of steel, translated for the benefit of the passengers.

Raynes realized that he had greatly underestimated Pedro's talents. It was very much a case of 'your life in his hands'. He was so shaken by the journey that as he left the bus outside the station in Soller, he gave Pedro a 5000 peseta note. In normal circumstances, he would never have thought of giving him anything, but his acute gratitude for still being alive prompted him to make this handsome gesture. Pedro accepted the note with a broad smile and said: "Gracias, señor!" which seemed to sum things up rather well.

By contrast, the journey in the little electric train from Soller to Palma was sheer bliss. Raynes wandered around under the trees and crossed the narrow gauge tracks to look at the highly-polished brown wooden coaches, with their ornamental, cast-iron platforms – rather like the carriages one saw in the old cowboy films from the American mid-west. They were almost sixty years old, having been built in Zaragoza in 1929. The Inspector was secretly a bit of a railway buff. (One of the things which greatly disappointed him about Grasshallows was that the station had been closed down several years before.)

It gave him enormous pleasure to hear the three blasts on the whistle before the train moved off. It reminded him of the older type of police whistle he had been issued with when he first walked the beat. The whistle blew again as the train plunged into the first of eleven tunnels on the line. The walls of the tunnel seemed alarmingly close and the feeble lights in the carriage cast strange shadows upon them. The carriages rattled furiously as the train gathered speed but the ride was quite smooth. On the second part of the journey, the train was going downhill – travelling through the bare and barren tracts on the outskirts of Palma.

After the all-too-brief forty-five minute journey, both Debbie and Richard were feeling very much restored and ready for the main business of the day. A quiet lunch. A glass of Rioja. Perhaps two? A trip to the Cathedral and shopping. Debbie was looking for a blue leather handbag. Raynes had yet to discover how many shops in the Majorcan capital sold leather handbags! It was an expedition he would not forget.

Every tourist to Palma visits the fourteenth century Cathedral – probably because it is the one, recognizable historic object in an otherwise modern city. Floodlit at night, its picture appears in every holiday brochure advertising

Majorca. On a hot summer's day, it is one of the coolest places one can find. So it was no surprise that all the Megatravel party found their way there in the course of the afternoon.

Debbie and Richard arrived there shortly after an over-indulgent lunch. Debbie was feeling deliciously lightheaded and had the impression she was walking on air. Richard tried to stop her giggling and told her that if she was good, she might meet an angel.

"So long as it's a real male angel," she said, "I shan't complain. But don't give me a hermaphrodite. I wouldn't know what to do with it!"

Raynes hurried her past two devout-looking nuns before she could make any further indecent comments.

He noticed that the foursome from the *Hotel Aphrodite* had reached the Cathedral before them. Malcolm was sitting in the choir stalls looking faintly bored. The superb carving by Juan de Salas did nothing for him. Neville was walking up and down with his arms folded, whilst Sarah and Jo were discussing the finer points of the beautiful Gothic altar screen – one of the Cathedral's greatest artistic treasures. Raynes was sorry they had not brought Sarah's mother with them. He felt sure she would have enjoyed it.

When Malcolm saw Debbie, his eyes lit up. In them, there was a mixture of lust, jealousy and contempt. He was not sure which feeling was most in the ascendant. But he could not help looking at her and his eyes followed her round the building. Richard was not aware of Malcolm's malevolent stare but, even in her less than sober state, Debbie was. She didn't like men like that.

The student from Arkansas made a slow pilgrimage round the Cathedral – making full use of the official guide. He explored the building thoroughly – examining every pillar and each window with deep interest. He looked so lonely that Raynes began to feel sorry for him. He wondered if he should go over and say a word. But he knew – to his cost – that when you take people up, it is sometimes very difficult to shake them off.

The elderly couples had seen many a cathedral in their

time. It was something that could be 'done' in double-quick time. Raynes noted the speed with which they advanced up the main aisle. An anxious, whispered conversation at the transept – and on with the sleeveless cardigan, in case the husband caught a chill. Then a camera shot of the altar screen to show the vicar back home. Another of the organ. Fifteen seconds admiring the two Renaissance pulpits and thirty seconds in the Royal Chapel – long enough to appreciate the fine baroque altar – which the guide book said one should appreciate!

Then a look of good Protestant disapproval at the crowds lighting votive candles before a statue of the Virgin. Eyes left as they pass the box asking for donations to maintain the fabric of the Cathedral. Out through the magnificent Almoina doorway and into the sunlight. Ignore the children begging on the steps, but feed the pigeons with a left-over sandwich. Off with the sleeveless cardigan. On with a drop or two of sun-tan protection. And away to a nearby café for a cup of coffee and a cream cake. Culture is such an exhausting business!

Mr and Mrs Average dragged their pathetic child round the Cathedral. She had only been persuaded to enter after being bribed with a large, double-scoop, strawberry ice cream, which she licked without much obvious enthusiasm. Drops and drips on the beautifully clean stone floor marked her *via dolorosa* around the building. Finally, the ice cream slipped from her grasp and landed plum in the middle of the tomb of King Jaime II in the chapel of the Holy Trinity. Vergers, gibbering furiously in Spanish, rushed in with pails and mops to clean up the mess. The child was led out of the church weeping piteously.

Young couples glided sinuously into the shadowy chapel of St Jerome, getting a cheap thrill from the ghostly presence of the Marquis de la Romana. Time for a quiet, lingering kiss. Others, predictably, went much further.

One of the Tabloid boys wrenched open the centre door of a confessional box, revealing the unexpected sight of the Brown Baby passionately embracing a Catholic priest, her shorts around her feet.

"Shut that cupboard immediately!" shouted Mrs Tabloid.

Reluctantly, Brian closed the door.

"What was that?" Glen asked his father.

"Adam and Eve, son."

"Gee, Dad, I didn't know the Bible was so exciting!"

Mr Tabloid gave him a friendly clip round the ear.

Mrs Tabloid decided that the Cathedral was no fit place for a decent British family.

For a further two hours, the British contingent roamed the streets of Palma – mostly window-shopping. They bought a few postcards. Walked along the Paseo Sagrero looking at the millionaires' yachts bobbing in the paintbox-perfect blue waves. Glasses of San Miguel were drunk and a few tips left. Richard faithfully escorted Debbie from shop to shop in the quest for a blue leather handbag – an elusive holy grail. He felt footsore and weary.

"I know just what I'm looking for," said Debbie, now stone-cold sober. But she didn't see it – at least, not in Palma. "There's a very nice one in Pollensa; but it's terribly expensive!"

Raynes did not take the hint.

Instead, he thankfully wended his way back to the coach where Pedro was his grinning, cheerful self. Perhaps he had spent an idyllic afternoon with Angie on some deserted beach. Raynes felt more confidence in Pedro's driving after his experience that morning. He reflected that the main road home was both straight and level. It would be a peaceful end to an exhausting day.

Two by two, the passengers returned to the coach, where Angie ticked them off. She then counted them in their seats just to make sure. Her soft thigh brushed twice against Richard's arm. Everyone was in a mellow, sleepy, forgiving mood. They had seen Palma. They had no desire to see it again. But they took back with them a kaleidoscope of treasured memories – some more treasured than others. And perhaps the Brown Baby most of all.

11: *Iacta Alea est*

On Tuesday afternoon, Raynes and Debbie went for a long walk along the promenade. They had agreed it was just too hot for sunbathing or swimming. Walking would create a nice breeze and if they found a shady corner, they could settle down and enjoy a brief siesta. They had walked far beyond the houses and hotels of Pollensa and found a small grassy patch under a couple of old trees. It had been a very peaceful afternoon.

Now it was about 4.30pm. Almost time for the first gin and tonic of the evening. They were slowly making their way back to the *Hotel Aphrodite* along the shops' side of the road, pausing every few minutes to look at postcards or menus. Debbie had gone into a supermarket to compare the prices of various brandies and Raynes was wandering ahead.

Although he was completely off duty, he never lost the habit of looking at the faces of those who passed by or the people sitting at the tables of the little pavement bars.

He had just passed the Café Sol when it came to him that he had seen a familiar face in unfamiliar company. He walked another twenty yards and then retraced his steps.

Yes, it was Malcolm – talking to a strange woman, who was wearing a beige-coloured dress. She looked as if she was in her mid-forties, with long brown hair and an intense expression on her face. They seemed to be arguing.

Raynes kept on walking till he met up with Debbie.

"Malcolm's got himself another woman," he said.

"Has he? Jo will be pleased."

"That's just what I was thinking."

They passed the Café Sol once more.

"Did you recognize her?"

"No. I haven't seen her round the hotel."

"It looks more like business than pleasure."

It was business – and Malcolm was not pleased. Against

73

his advice, Wendy had decided to come out to Majorca to keep an eye on her lawyer's activities. He had tried hard to discourage her on the phone on Sunday night but she had flown out on Monday evening and left an urgent message for him at reception. Since the Café Sol was some distance from the *Hotel Aphrodite*, it seemed the ideal place to meet.

"It's not for my sake – it's for the children."

"I appreciate that," said Malcolm.

"Not that they are children any more. Timothy's nineteen and Victoria's twenty-one."

"You feel that they should benefit in some way from all their father's hard work?"

"Well, don't you? There's no reason why she should hog it all."

Malcolm felt that they had covered the same points many times before, back in England. But Wendy was naturally obsessive about her children's perceived rights, even though she had accepted a generous cash settlement in 1977, renouncing all future claims.

"Have you spoken to her about it?"

"Yes," lied Malcolm. "We discussed it briefly on Sunday afternoon. She is not unaware of your children's position but she cannot help feeling that the settlement you and Charles made eleven years ago was a fair one. Neither of you realized at the time that the value of the company would increase so dramatically. I think one could safely say that she is embarrassed about it."

"Yes, but is she going to do anything about it?"

"I have to appeal to her conscience – and that's not easy. I have to win her confidence and trust – and you can't expect that to happen in a couple of days. She's a very astute business-woman – changing her mind will take time."

Malcolm knew that time was not on Wendy's side. The money from the settlement had long since gone – and the house was currently up for sale. Time was running out.

"How long d'you think it'll take?"

"I think that by the end of the fortnight, I shall be in the best position to get her to change her mind." Malcolm knew that he was being vastly optimistic – so he deliberately raised the spectre of Neville. "Unfortunately, there's an unforeseen factor in all this. For the past seven months, she's been seeing a lot of this publisher. He's been sending her roses and muttering sweet nothings in her ear. His firm's in a very bad way and I think he's hoping she'll bail him out. If that were to happen, she might not be in a position to make a decision in your children's favour. If she were to marry this man, that would, of course, make the situation even worse."

"Is there any chance of it?"

"I've been doing my best to smash it up. He's a bit of a wimp – but she seems very fond of him. I'm still hoping to throw a spanner in the works. Give me time."

Wendy looked despairingly at her lawyer.

"You did say that you thought her sister might be more of a push-over?"

"Oh, yes. Jo's a completely different cup of tea. A much softer, nicer girl. She's got a conscience. She would see the injustice of the whole thing. I don't think we'd have any trouble with her."

"D'you think she would speak to her sister?"

"No. She's got no influence in that direction. But, as I said to you before, if anything happened to Sarah, the estate – including your late husband's company – would pass to her."

"But if she were to marry this publisher?"

"It would pass to him."

There was a very long silence as Wendy mulled over the possibilities. Malcolm looked covertly at his watch. He would have to be getting along. He had only slipped out for a few minutes. Jo would be wondering where he was.

Eventually, Wendy looked up.

Her face looked very hard.

"I've got a pistol."

"A pistol?"

She nodded.

"How on earth did you get that through the airport?"

"I didn't. Someone gave me the address of this shop in

Palma. I bought it yesterday – and the ammunition. I tried it out this morning. It works."

"Good heavens!" said Malcolm. "You mustn't do anything like that!"

Wendy did not look as if she cared what Malcolm thought.

"Why not? You said that the sister would be a softer touch. If there's any likelihood of Sarah marrying this man, I've had it. You've just told me. I don't believe in leaving things to chance. I did that last time – and look where it got me. No one knows I'm here in Majorca. No one except you. I don't think that Sarah would recognize me after all these years."

"But you can't murder her!" said Malcolm as quietly as he could. "That's going too far. You'd be taking the law into your own hands. No good would come of it."

Wendy looked at Malcolm – and smiled.

"Which is why you're going to succeed. You're going to win her over. Get her to make fresh provisions for Timothy and Victoria. Generous provisions year by year. And if you don't succeed, I will."

There was no mistaking the threat.

Wendy was serious.

Shortly before they reached the hotel, Debbie and Richard met Sarah's mother.

"Good afternoon, Mrs Hickson!" said the Inspector.

She seemed slightly taken aback.

"That's very clever. How did you know my name?"

Raynes smiled.

"Your suitcase..."

"Of course, how stupid of me.''

Debbie asked: "Have you been in to see your daughters?"

"Yes. I intend to drop in every day or two. Just for a few minutes to see if everything's all right."

"We've been keeping an eye on them too," said Raynes. "Sarah and Jo seem to be coping quite well but there's friction between the men."

"I'm not surprised."

"Malcolm's been laying into Neville about his publishing

76

company and Neville's hinting that Malcolm rips off his clients whenever he gets the chance."

"I've heard that."

"And he seems to have quite an eye for the ladies!" said Debbie, thinking of her encounter with Malcolm during the dance.

"I've heard that too," said Mrs Hickson. "Jo'd better be careful."

"In fact," said Raynes, "he's actually seeing another woman at this very moment!"

"Really?"

"In the Café Sol," said Debbie. "Just along the prom. She's got brown hair, a thin face and a beige-coloured dress."

Mrs Hickson looked sad.

"I'd better do a bit of detective work and see what's happening."

She hurried away along the street and arrived just opposite the café as Malcolm and Wendy were leaving. Mrs Hickson paused behind one of the palm trees and took off her shoe as if to empty out some sand.

Then, as Malcolm set off back to the hotel, she followed Wendy back to her apartments – the Vistamar. Wendy was not hurrying so she was quite easy to follow. When they got to their destination, Mrs Hickson allowed Wendy sixty seconds grace before she followed her into the building. In front of her was the lift. It was in motion. She looked at the light indicator. It stopped on the second floor.

A little more detective work revealed that there were eight doors on each floor. Mrs Hickson walked up the steps cautiously to the second floor and listened at each door. Only three seemed to be occupied. In 202 and 206, there was a sound of children's voices. In No 208, a lavatory flushed.

By bedtime, Mrs Hickson had discovered that the woman Malcolm had been seeing was Charles' first wife – Wendy Bridges. Now there was food for thought! Why was Malcolm Clark seeing her? Mrs Hickson felt worried.

12: *Ut turpiter atrum*

Detective-Inspector Raynes was very fortunate to have avoided the Spanish night at La Calobra. It was every bit as awful as he had expected.

The farmhouse was in the middle of nowhere, surrounded by old farm carts, derelict ploughs and large round stones, once used for grinding wheat. The barn, in which most of the evening's entertainment was to take place, was crudely decorated with streamers, masks and posters. The only authentic features were the old orange carriage lamps which flickered along the bare stone walls. Trestle tables and benches had been laid out, together with litre bottles of country wine. A rather battered disco was mounted on a stage and 'happy' music was being played whilst the victims trouped in. In the background – but immediately recognizable – was the delicate aroma of fried onions.

Judging by the number of places set, about ninety people were expected – tourists from Alcudia as well as Pollensa had signed up for the night. The quartet from the *Aphrodite* had decided that it was a night for 'slumming' and had dressed accordingly in old jeans and bright cotton shirts – not a gold chain or ring in sight.

Neville instinctively headed for the table furthest away from the disco and sat down. There were as yet no glasses on the table; were they expected to drink from the bottle?

Sarah sat down gingerly on her bench.

"It's like being back at school again!"

"Worse!"

Around them, various people were screaming – trying to make themselves heard over the noise of the music.

"Over here, George!"

"Gladys, we've got a seat for you! Gladys!"

Within about five minutes, everyone was at long last settled and ready for the fun to begin.

Angie was the first to appear. She was dressed in pink

harem pyjamas with a turban, a rhinestone belt and Turkish slippers.

"Hello, everyone! Guess who I am tonight!"

Various obscene suggestions were made.

"No, I'm not! I'm Marie Antoinette. And you'll remember; she lost her head – no, I mean it! Well, I want to warn you that the country wine you'll be drinking tonight is pretty strong stuff – and we don't want you to lose your heads! Go easy, if you can!"

Malcolm looked at the nearest bottle.

It was clearly marked. 9%.

Angie made way for Mandy, who was in black fish-net tights, a black basque, a red hunting jacket and a top hat. She carried a leather whip and clearly intended to be recognized as Mistress of Ceremonies.

Marc was duly introduced. A smaller, less virile figure than one had been led to expect. Quite a little chap, in fact – about five feet four, with short-cut blond hair, black sweatshirt and tartan trews. He pulled up his shirt to reveal a massive tattoo front and back. He was given a cheer for his pains.

Various other couriers were introduced – and cheered – and then the transparent plastic cups were handed out. Bottles were opened and the wine sniffed at and sipped.

Jo thought it was not bad.

It was certainly not plonk. It had a rugged, country taste. Fruity and fairly sweet. People smiled and nodded happily. It was a taste they could live with.

Various party games now took place – all designed to get everyone shouting and yelling – and drinking as much as they could. Each table was organized as a team. Things had to be collected and rushed up to Marc. Malcolm very soon lost his shirt and Sarah, a 2000 peseta note. Fortunately, they were returned later along with another couple of bottles for each successful team.

Running through all the games was a ruling that when you drank, you must use your left hand. Anyone who used their right hand was obliged to stand up on their bench and drink down a cupful of wine. Naturally, all one's neighbours were extremely vigilant and within half an hour, there were very few people who had not been caught out at least once.

All this effectively broke the ice. People on each table got talking to each other. Inhibitions were broken down. One or two people had already drunk more than they could cope with and were laughing hysterically. Now was the time for supper to be served.

Neville had no idea what a medieval banquet would really have been like, but Megatravel had certainly done their best. Trayfuls of garlic bread circulated rapidly – and it was thick and juicy. They were followed by pink plastic goblets containing generous helpings of prawn cocktail. After a short break for more wine to be poured, the long-expected onions made their appearance, accompanied by chunks of steak, chicken drumsticks and large greasy sausages – and, of course, huge helpings of chips. The meal was served piping hot and was surprisingly tasty. Finally, there came the *grand finale* – Black Forest gateau and ice cream. It was probably as good as anything one could reasonably expect in the circumstances.

After the meal was over, everyone was herded out into the rear courtyard, where a short firework display was being given – whilst the tables and benches were re-arranged indoors.

Malcolm was making his way out to the yard when he saw a familiar brown face and a pair of mischievous dark eyes. He looked round to make sure none of his own party was anywhere near him.

"What are you doing here?"

"Same as you. Enjoying myself."

Malcolm felt that that was a bit of an exaggeration.

"Any chance of seeing you later?" he asked.

"Sure."

"When?"

The Brown Baby, now wearing a dark blue T-shirt but still in the same grubby, white shorts, looked at her watch.

"See you during the disco. About ten?"

"O.K."

Malcolm took a deep breath.

He had been hoping that if Sarah became sufficiently drunk, he and she might go for a little walk round the farm. But Sarah could always be saved for another day. The grubby little stranger was a treat to be seized *en passant*.

They watched the fireworks, then went inside where Marc was ready to demonstrate the full power of his 50 watt speakers.

Malcolm looked at his watch. 9.30pm. Half an hour.

"Two and a half hours to go," said Neville.

"No time off for good behaviour," said Jo.

"Have another glass," said Malcolm.

"I'm very tipsy as it is."

"Well, we're all going to end up tipsy. As long as they get us back on the bus, nothing else matters!"

"Cheers!"

The drunker they all were, the less likely they were to notice his departure. Malcolm made sure that his table had plenty of wine. He took Sarah up for a dance but Jo refused. She said it was too noisy – and anyway, she didn't feel too secure on her legs. Neville looked as if he was about to fall asleep.

Marc's disco was soon into its stride, blasting out old familiar numbers from the sixties. Tom Jones, the Beatles, the Stones, Elvis – everyone had heard them a thousand times before – but they still loved them. Couples jived, waltzed, twisted, rocked, did a conga, rubbed bottoms, crawled on their hands and knees. It was a splendid, boisterous night. Bottles were knocked over; people screamed; more bottles were brought in. Everyone was resigned to the fact that they were going home smashed – so why bother? If you collapsed, someone would pick you up.

Malcolm did not drink.

He was keeping his head clear.

As his watch reached 10.00pm, he stood up.

"I'm just going for a breath of fresh air," he said.

No one seemed to take any notice.

No one volunteered to join him.

The Brown Baby was standing just outside the door of the barn, telling one of the male couriers to leave her alone. When Malcolm appeared, the courier got the message and departed quickly.

The Brown Baby took Malcolm's hand and led him round the back of the farm, through a metal gate, up a flight of steps, under an archway and into a long block of stables. It smelt strongly of horses but there were no animals in sight. She led him over the cobbles to a distant corner where it was quite dark.

"You seem to know this place rather well."

"I've been exploring."

"Finding the ideal place?"

"Sort of."

"You're an enterprising young lady!"

The Brown Baby held both of Malcolm's hands and pulled them up to her face. She had a broad and heavy jaw and he knew she had thick lips.

"Kiss me!" she commanded.

Malcolm stroked her long brown hair and kissed her. The Brown Baby opened her mouth and sucked him in. Her strong tongue explored Malcolm's mouth. She smelt of wine and chips and cheap scent. Like an animal, she was definitely on heat. After two or three minutes, Malcolm broke away slightly breathless.

"What's your name, stranger?" he asked.

"Fran," she said. "What's yours?"

"Malcolm."

"You a doctor?"

"No, I'm a lawyer."

She sniffed at that.

"I don't have much to do with lawyers."

"You're a wise girl. Keep well away from them!"

The Brown Baby obviously felt there had been sufficient preliminaries and pulled Malcolm back for another powerful bout of kissing. He put his hands round her waist and down her grubby shorts. Her bottom was bare – deliciously bare. He felt deeply aroused.

He lifted her T-shirt and pulled it up over her head.

Even in the darkness, he could see her round, heavy breasts. The Brown Baby was wearing no bra. He cupped them with his hands and felt her hard, button-like nipples. Eventually he unbuttoned her shorts and they dropped to the floor. Now she was completely naked and defenceless. He ran his hands over her, enjoying her passivity, relishing the thought of penetration in just a few minutes time.

Whilst he was caressing her, she was undoing the buttons of his shirt and rubbing her lips against his chest. Then she undid the buttons and zip of his trousers and grunted with deep satisfaction.

"My! We are ready!" she said. "Such a big thing for such a small girl!"

"It's never failed yet!" said Malcolm proudly.

He stepped out of his trousers and briefs and rubbed his naked body lustfully against hers. She put her hands between his legs and caressed him. He felt almost ready to burst.

"Do you want it from the front or from behind?" he asked conspiratorially.

"The front'd be fine. I'll bend back against the wall. You open your legs."

She held Malcolm firmly by the wrists as she leant back against the wall. Then, suddenly, without the slightest warning, he received a violent blow between the legs, smashing hard against his testicles. She had used the full force of her right knee with crushing power against the most delicate and vulnerable part of his body. A red-hot, searing light flashed through his brain and he was instantly doubled up in pain and crumpled in a heap on the cobbled floor. For a long time he could say nothing – not even cry – and in retrospect he reckoned that he had probably been unconscious for a couple of minutes. Eventually his mind began to come to terms with the agonizing pain but he could do no more than hold himself, whimpering pathetically as he rolled over the dirty floor.

After delivering her savage blow, the Brown Baby put all her clothes back on and piled up Malcolm's shirt, trousers and briefs on a wooden bench near the door. She stood there looking down at him – without the slightest shred of compassion – a dark and menacing figure.

When she felt he was capable of taking in a few words, she spoke: "You don't know who I am. But even if you did, you wouldn't care. I know who you are. You're that crooked lawyer from Dartford who got my mum and dad thrown out of their house. It won't mean anything to you, but my dad had a heart attack because of that. He'll not be able to work again. I promised them I'd get you for it. This is just the first instalment. Next time, I'll make sure you suffer even more!"

It didn't seem to Malcolm that there was any way he could suffer more than what he was feeling at that moment. This was sheer agony.

"You bitch!" he said. "You filthy bitch – you've really hurt me!" He continued to hold himself tightly. Would he ever be able to have sex again? Were his testicles crushed beyond hope? How could he get essential medical help in this distant farmhouse? Wasn't it said that such a savage blow could kill people?

The Brown Baby took one final look at the pathetic figure on the floor, then she scooped up Malcolm's clothes and ran back the way she had come. It would be several minutes before Malcolm would be able to walk anywhere – let alone follow her. But just to make pursuit more difficult, she locked the metal gate which led to the stable-yard and threw away the key. There was no way Malcolm could climb over a wall in his present condition – he would have to go the long way round the building and she relished his embarrassment re-appearing at the disco wearing only his socks and shoes.

Who was it that said: 'Revenge is sweet'?

She parcelled up Malcolm's clothes more neatly and delivered them to his friends at Table 9. They were looking very much the worse for wear. Over the noise of the disco, she shouted:

"Malcolm's compliments! He's screwing some bird in the cowshed, but he left his clothes behind. I think he might need some help."

With that, she was gone. It was quite unthinkable that she should wait for the bus and meet Malcolm again. The best she could do was run away and hide. She headed down the road back to Pollensa and ten minutes later, she got a lift which took her most of the way. A quick cuddle in the back seat with an elderly Spaniard seemed a small price to pay for her escape. As she walked up the steps to her apartment, she wondered if Malcolm had yet made his grand appearance.

The sight of Malcolm's clothes roused Neville.

"Hey!" he shouted.

But the girl had gone.

Jo looked at the garments.

"Where is Malcolm?" she shouted.

"I don't know. He said he was going out to get some fresh air."

"Looks as if he got more than that!" said a near neighbour. "Caught with his pants down right and proper! Eh! What a laugh! He won't dare show his face!"

It was no more than the truth.

"What are we going to do?" Neville asked.

Although she was still suffering from the noise and the wine, Sarah was immediately her practical self. "We've got to go and find Malcolm – and take his clothes with us."

"What did the girl say?" asked Jo.

Neville looked at her coldly.

"She said he was screwing some bird in the cowshed. It's probably a practical joke but it could be very embarrassing."

Jo looked ready to cry.

"What the hell did he need to do that for? He's got me!"

"Uncontrollable urges," said Sarah. "All men are the same."

They made their way out of the disco.

"Which way should we go?" asked Neville.

"I think we should stick together," said Sarah.

They went round the back of the barn and came to the locked metal gate. They called out several times: "Malcolm!"

In due course, a voice replied: "I'm here."

"At least he's alive," said Sarah thankfully.

"We're behind this gate," shouted Neville, "but it's locked. We'll come round the other way. Just hang on!"

It took a full five minutes to find their way round the other side of the farm and all its outhouses. Eventually, they discovered Malcolm leaning over a wall, looking at a number of pigs. He looked as if it was the most natural thing in the world to be standing in a farmyard at 11.00 at night virtually stark naked.

Neville handed over the clothes.

"Thank you," said Malcolm.

He put on his briefs awkwardly and obviously with some pain.

"Have you been hurt?" asked Sarah.

"Yes," said Malcolm. "Badly."

"Whereabouts?"

Malcolm gritted his teeth and pulled on his trousers.

"I'll tell you later," he said.

"I think you deserve everything you got," said Jo angrily. "Fornicating in a cowshed with some cheap tart!"

Malcolm buttoned up his shirt with dignity.

"I haven't fornicated with anyone."

"The girl said you did."

"Did she? Well, she was wrong." He sighed deeply. "She may have wanted to fornicate – but she didn't."

"What did she do?" asked Neville curiously.

Malcolm could see no way of avoiding explanation.

"If you must know," he said reluctantly, "she kneed me in my private parts. It's bloody painful. I can hardly walk."

Neville laughed.

He couldn't help it. There was Malcolm thinking he was having a little on the side without anyone noticing – and the bloody girl had got in first. Not only kneed him in the groin – but also pinched all his clothes. Now perhaps Joanne would see what sort of man Malcolm was.

Jo saw only too well. She felt deeply humiliated. As Neville had said, Malcolm was not a man to be trusted. She had imagined that her body and her passion would be quite sufficient for him. After this, their relationship was well and truly shattered.

She walked away crying.

Sarah put her arm around Malcolm.

"Just walk slowly," she said. "It's bound to be painful. But the pain will lessen."

"It's a lot better than it was," said Malcolm, glad to have some sympathy. "I don't know how much damage she's done. I'll have to see a doctor. She may have crippled me for life. I believe you can kill people doing that." He stopped dead in his tracks. "Take it easy," he said.

They were now alone in the farmyard.

Neville had gone ahead to comfort Jo.

"Do you know who the girl was?" asked Sarah cautiously.

"Somebody called Fran," said Malcolm. "I saw her on Monday on the bus trip. She spoke to me in the Cathedral. She was being very suggestive. Tonight I met her again just as we were coming out to the fireworks display. I didn't expect anything like this. I thought she was just a little scrubber eager for a poke."

He decided not to mention the Dartford connection.

"Are you going to report her to the police?"

"I'll break her bloody neck if I see her again! Oh!"

Malcolm came to a sudden halt.

"Well, that won't do much good. You'll end up going to jail – in Spain. I can't imagine that'd make things any better."

"No," said Malcolm. "It's my own fault. She led me up the garden path. Right up the garden path."

They were now on the south side of the farm. The sounds of the disco could be heard in the distance. They were still alone.

Malcolm stopped again.

"You've been very understanding," he said.

As he said it, his emotions got the better of him. Tears poured down his cheeks. He tried to choke them back. It was ridiculous. He had never cried for years.

Sarah understood his distress. She pulled him closer to her.

Malcolm was shaking all over. It was a delayed reaction. He hugged her close to him. From there, it just developed.

Within minutes, they were kissing as hard and as passionately as he had ever dreamt. Sarah was pressing herself close against him. It was strange that adversity and humiliation should have brought them together when other more straightforward approaches should have failed.

No words passed between them.

The feelings on both sides were too deep for words.

Joanne and Neville had been standing near the door of the barn waiting for Sarah and Malcolm to re-appear. After several minutes had gone by, Neville began to be anxious. Something might have happened. Malcolm might have collapsed. He looked at Jo.

"We'd better go and look for them."

They walked back across the dusty farmyard and round the southern corner of the building. The noise of the disco music muffled the noise of their steps.

Neville and Jo stopped dead.

There were Sarah and Malcolm engaged in a deep, lingering embrace, their hands slowly caressing each other's bodies. They were quite unaware of anyone else.

Neville looked at Jo despairingly.

He coughed.

Sarah and Malcolm slowly and unwillingly broke apart.

Although he was seething with anger, all Neville could say was: "Don't you think you've had enough for one night?"

He took Sarah roughly by the hand and pulled her away.

13: *Alma Mater*

"Good morning, Mrs Hickson. Back again?"

Raynes had been out to post a few cards. He had been told that it sometimes took almost a fortnight for them to reach the United Kingdom. As he returned, he met Sarah's mother coming down the hotel steps.

"You haven't heard?"

"Heard what?"

"Malcolm's been attacked. They've had to call in a doctor."

"Who attacked him?"

"Some girl at the disco."

Raynes was surprised.

"I'm glad we didn't go."

"Well, Sarah said it was frightful. Now she's wishing they'd never gone. But it's a bit late for that!"

"Why did the girl attack him?"

"I think it's what your wife was saying yesterday afternoon. Malcolm has an eye for the ladies..."

Raynes nodded.

"... Apparently he pursued this young hellcat out to the stables but then she rounded on him. Kicked him... you know where..."

"Really?"

Raynes could not help smiling.

"Hurt him terribly. Sarah said Malcolm could hardly walk. She had to help him. Naturally Jo's frightfully upset. She's been up crying half the night. And she's asked the hotel to move her to a single room. They're all in a frightful stew. Neville's trying to talk her out of it."

"Perhaps she didn't know what Malcolm was really like. She's only just found out."

"I'm afraid she's had stars in her eyes ever since she met him. Last week, she was hoping that he might propose whilst they were out here on holiday. But I'm afraid there's no chance of that now!"

"What a chapter of accidents!" said Raynes.

"Not half! And Neville's not speaking to Sarah! He's annoyed because he thinks she was being too friendly with Malcolm. She says that she was only trying to comfort him – giving him a cuddle – but Neville says there was more to it than that! And Jo's angry with Sarah. She thinks she was trying to pinch her man! Really! It's like a wasps' nest in there."

Raynes said he was not surprised. Judging by one or two of the conversations he'd heard, Malcolm was asking for trouble; but he was sorry to hear the girls had got involved.

Mrs Hickson prattled on.

"When Sarah phoned me this morning, I could tell she was upset; so I came right over. There wasn't much I could do, but I did my best to calm things down."

Raynes commiserated.

Then he moved the conversation on to a question which had been circulating in his mind since the previous afternoon.

"Did you go to the Café Sol?"

"Oh yes, I did."

"And did you see them?"

"They were just leaving."

"A woman in a beige-coloured dress?"

Mrs Hickson nodded.

"I followed her back to her apartments – the Vistamar. She's in room 208."

Raynes was impressed.

"We shall have to get you into the force."

Mrs Hickson smiled happily at the compliment.

"Too old for that, I'm afraid. But I've found out who the woman is. You won't believe it! She's Charles' first wife – Wendy. Wendy Bridges. The journalist he was married to before Sarah enticed him away. She's here in Pollensa. I don't know what she's here for; but if that lawyer's involved, you can be sure it's something nasty. I told you on the plane, there's mischief in store – and that woman's part of it!"

"It certainly looks like it," said Raynes, making a mental note to contact Detective-Constable Carlisle and ask him to find out all he could about Wendy Bridges. He put on a puzzled expression. "Where did you say she lived?"

"Bexley. South London. There's no love lost between her and Sarah. If those two ever meet, then feathers will really fly!"

"You didn't tell Sarah about her being here? And that you'd seen her speaking to Malcolm?"

"I had to. I wasn't going to – but when I found out how unpopular Malcolm was this morning, I thought I might as well throw in my tuppenceworth. Might persuade him to go! The trouble is, Sarah does so love this place. She thinks of it as a sort of Garden of Eden – but today, it's rather like the gateway to hell."

Raynes tried to look at the situation positively. "Well," he said, "at least she'll be on her guard. Now she knows the worst. If Wendy tries to attack her, at least she'll be prepared."

"That's the way I see it." Mrs Hickson's eyes twinkled behind her spectacles. "But there's worse to come."

"No?"

"I'm afraid so. Neville was so upset by the way Malcolm treated him that he's decided to get even with him. Long before last night. He knows some people called Latimer..."

"From Dartford?"

"You know about them?"

"No. But I gather it's an incident that causes Malcolm some embarrassment. Neville mentioned it the other night at dinner. It proved a most effective show-stopper!"

Mrs Hickson repeated the lurid tale that Neville had told Sarah and Joanne. Raynes added yet another inquiry to his list.

"They've been hoping to see Malcolm. Talk to him man to man about the way he's treated them. But since the court case, Malcolm won't have anything to do with them."

"That's understandable."

"Well, the trouble is, Neville has phoned the Latimers and told them that Malcolm was staying in this hotel – and they're flying out today!" She shook her head. "I think our lawyer friend is going to have a very unpleasant time."

"He'll talk his way out of it. Lawyers always do!"

"But don't you think it has all the makings of a thoroughly unpleasant holiday?"

Raynes smiled broadly.

"I can't wait for Act 2!"

A little later, when he had reached Room 301, he said to Debbie: "Guess what? Malcolm got kicked in the goolies last night!"

"Where?"

"In the goolies."

"No. Where?"

"At the disco."

"We should have gone!"

"No, we shouldn't. Apparently, it was frightful. But Sarah's taking pity on Malcolm. That's upset Neville and Jo. They're both writhing with jealousy. And that woman we saw in that café, yesterday afternoon, that was Sarah's husband's first wife! The question is: 'What's she doing here?'"

"She was talking to Malcolm."

"Yes. The plot thickens." He smiled grimly. "It has all the makings of a first class fight."

"Gosh! How awful!" said Debbie, thinking of the elusive £200. "Is he badly hurt?"

"The doctor's been in to see him, so it must have been pretty bad."

"And who did it?"

"Some little charmer he met at the disco. She didn't take kindly to his advances!"

Not for the first time, Debbie thought how hopeless these amateurs were. If people just stuck to the professionals, they would fare so much better. If he'd come to her, Malcolm would have been £200 poorer; but he would still be physically intact.

To Richard, she said: "I suppose that means curtains for Jo?"

Raynes nodded.

"I should think so."

14: *Nihil Carborundum Illegitimae*

Sarah sat out on the terrace alone. She was thinking what a mess it all was. She should never have suggested that Jo and Malcolm come out to Majorca. She should have treated them to a dinner in some London hotel. One night would have been quite enough.

But, instead, she had invited them to her favourite resort, quite convinced that the four of them would get on well together. Unfortunately, Neville had taken an immediate dislike to Malcolm. He had felt threatened – and ever since that moment, he had done everything he could to discredit Jo's boyfriend. He had told both her and her sister everything he knew about the lawyer's past life and the way he had treated his clients. Now he had invited the Latimers out to Pollensa with the deliberate intention of causing trouble.

Sarah had been looking forward to meeting Malcolm. She had wanted to see what sort of man Joanne had picked up this time. Although, physically, he cut a less impressive figure than Neville, he was without doubt a much cleverer and more able man – and Sarah liked clever men. There was no doubt either that Malcolm was attracted to her. He had said so on Sunday afternoon. Quite rightly, she had resisted him. But last night, in his despair, he had turned to her. At a time of acute misery and humiliation, he had found comfort in her arms. He had fondled her with a depth of passion which seemed – even in retrospect – completely genuine. And then Neville and Jo had come upon them and misunderstood the whole situation.

It had been a disastrous night for Jo. She had lost control of her man. She had let him slip away to that little bitch. That was bad enough! But when they found Malcolm naked and in pain, Joanne couldn't find it in her heart to show the slightest bit of sympathy. She had walked away and left him. Now Jo was convinced that her sister had pulled a fast one over her and was actually accusing her of pinching her lover!

As if Joanne was even wanting him now!

She had not spoken to Malcolm since they left the farm. She had spent the night on the bathroom floor and this morning had asked the hotel for a single room. Malcolm was not the sort of person to tolerate such behaviour. Why should he? What was the point of staying on in a hotel where everyone was at daggers drawn? Sarah very much hoped that Jo would forgive Malcolm and apologize to him. Otherwise, she could see Malcolm packing his bags and heading home.

So, this morning, she had made a deliberate point of asking

him to stay – for her sake. She had felt she was being very disloyal to Neville because she might have given Malcolm false hopes about her feelings for him. She had given him another long cuddle and then sent him off to the local doctor to see what needed to be done. The local doctor had told him to spend the rest of the day in bed. He'd been given some strong pain-killers and she had made sure he had been tucked up and made comfortable.

Then her mother had come to see her and told her about Wendy. If there was one person likely to act as a red rag to a bull, that person was Wendy! She was like a leech. It had taken Sarah three years to fight her off last time. Now she was back again. It had almost broken Charles' heart, losing his children. He had sacrificed his house; he handed over half a million pounds but neither sacrifice had hurt him half as much as being parted from the children.

Wendy had been rotten! They could so easily have had a friendly separation – a quick, clean, easy divorce – and made civilized arrangements for looking after the children. But no! Wendy had really put him through it. She had used the children as a weapon – a form of punishment. First of all, she had said that he was not fit to be considered their father. She had resisted access. Any presents sent had been returned unopened. The children had been encouraged to think that their father had deserted them, didn't care about them, would do nothing for them. When he was allowed to visit them, the children were put in a very awkward position. They didn't know who to believe.... who to be loyal to. Very soon, he had given up the visits. They were too painful.

So why was she here now?

Probably the money had run out! She would be wanting more. And Malcolm was acting as her lawyer... It was very easy to put two and two together. She would have asked him to screw a few more thousands out of the firm – even though the divorce settlement had been quite explicit. No further claim could or would be made.

But Malcolm was a clever lawyer. He might have discovered some legal loophole which could give Wendy what she wanted. He had deliberately bumped into Jo in the supermarket and she had sucked up all his guff about cooking! Getting her into bed was child's play. And then all he had to say was: 'I'd love to meet your sister' and Jo would promptly pass on the request – as she had. Then Sarah had been stupid enough to invite them both to Majorca. She had even paid their tickets and their hotel! It was madness! It was, she was sure, all part of the plan. Malcolm would ooze with charm. (That's what he had been doing on Sunday afternoon.) Softening her up. The next thing he would be suggesting was that she should think of Charles' children... Don't be mean! Don't be unkind!... Share a little of your success with them!... It won't cost you anything... If you do it this way, it'll probably be tax-deductible! She could see it all most clearly. He would remind her that it was Charles' firm; they were Charles' children. How could she refuse? And if she did agree, then of course he and Wendy would take their cut!

It was a nasty business.

But the important thing was that Malcolm did not know that she knew about Wendy. So long as he remained in ignorance of that fact, he would continue to play his dangerous game. And so long as he thought he was in with a chance, he would not leave Pollensa!

For Malcolm to withdraw – that would be defeat. For him and for Wendy. She would encourage her lawyer to keep trying. And with a bit of luck, Malcolm might be torn two ways! He might still be working on Wendy's behalf – but if she could pull him over to her side, he might ditch Wendy. That might be fun! After all, she, Sarah, had financially far more to offer Malcolm than Charles' ex could ever do. Malcolm must see that.

In view of what her mother had just told her, she could not afford to let her physical pleasure get mixed up with business. She must not get too close to Malcolm – she must quickly withdraw to the position she had occupied on Sunday afternoon.

In fact, they must all retreat to that same position. Neville must be persuaded that the scene he had witnessed at the back of the farmhouse was no more than an act of kindness to an injured man. If he could not accept that, they were finished as a couple. But she did not believe that Neville really wanted to fall out with her. He also needed her desperately. Probably he was being cold just to punish her. If she could show that she was really sorry about hurting him, he would probably be glad to be won round.

Joanne was more difficult. She had now lost all faith in Malcolm – and she was bitter towards her. The time had come to take a stronger line with Jo. To tell her it was her fault all this misery had come to pass. If she had not introduced this particular bull, the china shop would not have been wrecked. Sarah had done a lot to finance Joanne's independence; so why should she put up with all this moaning and whining? Jo must be told to get back to Malcolm and look after him. He was her responsibility. She would make it clear that she had no interest in Malcolm – none whatsoever. And perhaps the sight of her and Neville once more united would convince her?

Sarah was uncertain whether Jo would go back to Malcolm. Perhaps Malcolm himself would not want her back? But Sarah reckoned that if the holiday was to be saved, there would have to be reconciliation all round. First, between her and Neville; secondly, between her and Jo; and then some forcible diplomacy with Malcolm – working on the assumption that the lawyer, goaded by Wendy, would have every incentive to stay, pursuing his brief, and yet at the same time hoping for even more. For something he would not get. But of course, he wouldn't know that!

It took Sarah nearly an hour – and several black coffees – to work it all out, but by the end of Wednesday morning, she could see her way out of the dilemma. Everyone was feeling raw and distrustful – they would be walking on eggshells for the next day or two – but Sarah did not see any alternative.

She phoned her mother and told her what she had decided. She also asked her mother to keep a close eye on Wendy.

15: *Magnas inter opes inops*

Mrs Hickson sat on the balcony of her apartment, knitting. Her mind was not so much on the job in hand. Rather, she was wondering how she could get rid of Wendy Bridges.

Could she arrange for a bogus message – or a phone call – to say that one of Wendy's children was ill? The trouble was that she couldn't remember the name of either child. So the message would not exactly carry conviction.

She spent another fifteen minutes considering various outlandish plots and then decided that the best thing to do was to go and confront Wendy in person. It was something her own mother had always advised her to do. She had said that if you were at odds with someone, it was no use going around bearing a grudge – much better to have it out face to face.

But there was another problem. How could she speak to her as Sarah's mother? Would that not be completely self-defeating? Surely Wendy would just get up and walk away? She would need to be someone else. Someone whom Wendy might listen to – and not walk away. But who?

Mrs Hickson put down her knitting and looked at the purple bougainvillaea blossoming over the little cottage next door. It was so rich and glorious. What a pity one could not grow it in England!

She had stared at the flowers for about five minutes before inspiration came. Then she smiled to herself. It was a little deceitful, but only good could come from it. In fact, she was so pleased with her idea that she immediately put away her knitting, changed into a blue, flowery, cotton dress and went off to the Vistamar apartments.

But when she knocked on door 208, there was no reply.

Wendy Bridges was feeling depressed.

Despite all the beauties of Pollensa beach, the rich blue waters of the bay and the unremitting sunshine – with scarcely a wisp of cloud in the sky, her mood was grim.

Money was the root of all her troubles. There was never enough of it. She did not earn a sufficient amount to keep the house, the car or the children going. Every year, she had to pay out more – with less and less in the bank. Her voluptuous lifestyle of previous years had been drastically curtailed. Major repair bills to the house had knocked unexpected holes in the reserves. Very large holes. And the car was a constant nightmare. First of all, it had depreciated horrendously over the past three years. Probably she should not have bought a Jaguar, but it had seemed a good idea at the time. Now it was requiring a lot done to it; the insurance had soared with Victoria and Timothy – both young drivers – on her policy. If it was sold, she would still have to put up more money to buy another car. She couldn't win. Something would have to go – and it would have to be the house. Whether even that would stave off the evil day, she did not know.

She had met Malcolm through a mutual friend and he had held out hope. She had told him her story and he had seemed quite enthusiastic about the outcome. But it was now almost three months since he had made contact with the sister and it seemed to have taken him an age to get any further. After their conversation yesterday, she could not help thinking that he was spinning out the case as long as possible – doubtless to his advantage – not to hers. She had suspected this back in England and that was why she had come out to Majorca – to push things along.

But even here, nothing seemed to be happening. She had phoned the *Hotel Aphrodite* three times that morning, trying to contact Malcolm. But each time, the girl at reception had said he was unavailable 'Was he in or out?' she had asked. But still the same reply. Mr Clark was unavailable.

She had roamed around her apartment like a caged beast. But after the third call, she had conceded defeat and went along to the Café Sol for a glass of wine and a prawn sandwich.

She had nearly finished her snack lunch when a tall woman in a blue cotton dress bent over her and looked at her.

"Isn't it Wendy Bridges?"

Wendy quickly swallowed a final mouthful of sandwich

and acknowledged that it was. The woman in blue sat down at her table.

"You don't know me. I'm Marion Latimer. I'm a friend of Mr Malcolm Clark. I'm staying at the *Hotel Aphrodite*."

Wendy responded instinctively to her motherly approach.

"I've been trying to contact him all morning but the hotel switchboard says he's unavailable."

"Well, I'm afraid they're right. He had a nasty fall at the disco last night and he's been confined to bed for the rest of the day."

Wendy felt mildly relieved that his injuries were no more than temporary.

"He'll be all right tomorrow?"

"I expect so. He and his friends are going out on the pirate ship – going to explore Treasure Island, I believe."

Wendy felt her gloom return. Once again, Malcolm would be enjoying himself whilst she was kept waiting.

"Are you one of his friends?" asked Mrs Latimer kindly. "I believe he has an eye for the ladies!" She smiled. "Such a wicked man, I'm told."

"He's never made a pass at me," said Wendy honestly. "Not yet, anyway. No, he's doing a bit of business for me."

Because Mrs Latimer was a complete stranger, Wendy found herself explaining about her need for money. She told her story about the divorce from Charles, the financial settlement over ten years ago – and how money was now running out. She had twice been made redundant by the magazines she had worked for – and the present job was being maintained on a month-to-month basis.

Mrs Latimer listened with obvious sympathy, making the appropriate noises such as: "Oh, I see"... "How sad"... or "I do understand"... As indeed she did.

She had told Inspector Raynes in the plane that she had felt very sorry for Charles' first wife. She had always regarded her daughter as very much the villain of the piece and the more she heard of Wendy's troubles, the more sympathetic she became. In her heart of hearts, she resolved to speak to Sarah and see if something could be done.

But for the moment, her chief aim was to get Wendy Bridges out of the way. Once the pressure was off Malcolm, perhaps he would go – and then everybody would be happy. As long as the lawyer kept pursuing Sarah and her money, there would be trouble.

She smiled in an understanding manner.

"So you are hoping that Malcolm will persuade Charles' second wife to make a fresh allowance to help the children?"

Wendy nodded.

"It's my only hope."

"And how old are the children?"

"Victoria's twenty-one, Timothy's nineteen."

"Quite grown up? Are they going to University?"

Wendy told her quite a lot about the children before returning to Malcolm and his dilatory ways.

"I'm afraid that doesn't surprise me," said Mrs Latimer. "He took a frightfully long time recovering a bungalow we'd let out to some tenants. We couldn't get rid of them – and he took the case to court. He won, of course, but he wasn't cheap – and he wasn't quick. But these things always take time."

"That's what he says. He's trying to get to Charles' second wife through her sister. He set it up very carefully. He watched her movements and then he met her – as if by accident – in a supermarket. That was three months ago. He tells me that they're now very close – I suppose that means they're lovers – and through her, he got this invitation out to Majorca. Everything paid! I ask you! Some people have all the luck!" She scowled angrily. "But he doesn't seem to be making much progress. I'm frightened he might be so busy enjoying himself, he might forget about me."

Mrs Latimer looked serious.

"If I were you, young woman," she said, "I'd be far more worried about Malcolm falling for Sarah. He's quite unscrupulous, you know – and from what you've told me, she's a right bitch!" (It seemed rather a hard thing to say about one's own daughter but, at times, Sarah could be quite vicious.) Mrs Latimer continued: "I don't want to upset you but, from what I've seen in the hotel, Malcolm and Sarah seem to be getting on like a house on fire. Far more pleasure than business, if you ask me!"

She bent over the table and spoke in a quieter voice.

"In fact, from what I've heard, that was the reason why Malcolm had his fall at the disco. He was attacked by Neville... that's Sarah's real boyfriend... the one she brought over to Majorca with her. He caught them kissing and cuddling together. I believe Neville was quite incensed."

Interested though she was to hear the gossip, Wendy's spirits sank even further – as Mrs Latimer had intended they should.

She waited a few moments before delivering her final word of advice. She was remembering something Sarah had said to her on the phone just before lunch.

"You know, my dear, I would think twice before I went any further with Mr Clark. You may not get as much as you hope for – and you can be sure he will take a very big cut for himself. Malcolm Clark's not a man who helps the poor simply for the pleasure of it. I'm sure he already realizes that Sarah could put much more business his way than you ever could. In fact, if she put her mind to it, she could easily buy him off! Had you thought of that?"

"No, I hadn't."

Wendy bit her lip.

Things looked even worse.

Mrs Latimer watched her reactions with almost clinical interest. She had achieved her goal. Wendy's faith in Malcolm Clark was rapidly approaching zero.

"If you'll take my advice – but you probably won't – I should write to Sarah direct. Put it all down on paper. You're a journalist. I'm sure you're good with words. Don't grovel! Don't be spiteful or nasty! Tell her the facts. Give her a breakdown of your income and expenditure. Say exactly what you need – and I think she'll respond."

No thought was further from Wendy's mind. Pride alone would prevent it. Nothing would compel her to beg. It was out of the question. But this nice lady was trying to be helpful. She didn't really understand the background. She was a complete stranger. She had certainly done her best to be kind. It was no use being rude and rejecting her suggestion.

Wendy put on a bold smile.

"So you think I should approach her direct?"

"I would, my dear. It's much the best way."

Wendy nodded.

"You've been very kind. Thank you for taking pity on me. Perhaps we could meet again. I'm in the Vistamar apartments. Room 208."

Mrs Latimer didn't say that she was already quite aware of this. She produced a small notebook from her capacious handbag and wrote it down.

They shook hands.

"So nice to meet you!"

"Goodbye!"

Mrs Hickson walked down the road feeling a warm glow of satisfaction for a job well done. She'd spoken to the 'other woman' and not been rejected. Her disguise had been complete. She'd been told the whole story, given her the best possible advice and had left on good terms; there would be no problem if she wanted to see her again.

Wendy looked at her empty glass.

She caught the waiter's attention.

"Another glass of wine," she said.

But to herself, she muttered:

"Approach her direct? Yes, perhaps I will. But not in the way she thinks!"

16: *Ira furor brevis*

The Brown Baby sauntered along the promenade and entered the Megatravel office. She wanted to go on the pirate ship tomorrow, but only if her boyfriend was going as well.

Angie recognized her as someone who had been on their Monday trip to Palma and the Tuesday night barbecue at La Calobra, so she was more inclined to be helpful than she might otherwise have been.

"What's his name?"

"Malcolm. Malcolm Clark."

Angie looked down the list.

"Yes, he's going."

"He hasn't cancelled?"

"No. Why should he?"

"Just wondered."

The Brown Baby put down eight grubby 1000 peseta notes on the counter. Angie picked them up gingerly and put them in the till.

The Brown Baby went out on to the beach, took off her blue sweater and tried to become even browner.

Sarah and Neville went for a walk.

It was a very long walk – out past the *Hotel Illador*, climbing over the protruding roots of the large pine trees – out almost as far as the lighthouse on Cape Formentor.

During the walk, Sarah put her cards on the table. She didn't say anything about Wendy – but she made it clear that, although she might have taken pity on Malcolm and let him do things to her that she wouldn't otherwise have done, there was no way that she was really 'interested' in him. Malcolm was not to be trusted. Sad as it was for Jo, he was likely to go for any woman who took his fancy. If she, Sarah, were to take him as her lover, there would always be someone else tomorrow.

By contrast, Neville was a trusted friend. They had known each other a long time. They had developed a deep understanding over the past seven months and, basically, they were very happy together. It would be a shame to throw it all away. Sarah said that she hoped he would not hold one night's foolishness against her. She had drunk too much at the disco last night. In fact, she could hardly remember what she had said – or done. The whole thing seemed rather vague.

Anyway, the upshot was: 'Would he forgive her?'

Neville was surprised that she should eat so much humble pie. He was totally dependent on her. He was surprised that she didn't realize that. Even if she had gone the whole way with Malcolm, it wouldn't have made any difference to him. Sarah was an impetuous creature at the best of times and he was learning to live with all her whims and fancies. Like the French count who lived through the German siege of Paris in 1870-1, it was enough to say: 'J'ai survecu!' One did not quarrel with one's benefactor, however fickle that benefactor might be.

In fact, the depth of Sarah's apology made Neville even more suspicious. He found himself wondering why she should go to such lengths to appease him. There must be some reason for it, but for the life of him, he could not think what it was. However, if all she wanted was forgiveness, he was happy to oblige.

In a sandy clearing, they made up.

Neville was tempted to ask whether this meant they could now think of getting married. But he controlled himself. One step at a time. Perhaps it would be wiser to pop the question at the end of the holiday?

They walked back to the hotel hand-in-hand.

Joanne did not receive such gentle treatment.

Sarah tracked her down to the yachting marina where she found her sitting at the top of a flight of steps, looking out to sea. The coloured sails of the windsurfers dotted the surface of the bay, which was now a shimmering silver blue. It seemed hard to think that all these people were so carefree and happy whilst she was feeling so bitter and angry.

"You've got to pull yourself together, Jo! It's just not on! You brought Malcolm out here. You can't just abandon him."

Jo said nothing.

"He was badly hurt last night. I think you should have shown him some sympathy."

"You showed him quite enough!"

"And upset Neville..."

"... You upset both of us!"

"But if you'd given him a bit of tender loving care, he'd probably have ended up hugging you."

"It's you he's interested in – not me."

"Oh, don't be ridiculous! He may be interested in me, but I'm not interested in him. Neville and I are still perfectly happy."

"You weren't this morning!"

"Well, we are now. We've been for a long walk and he says he quite understands."

"Men will do anything for money!"

"So will women!" said Sarah brutally. "You invited yourself out here. And remember who paid for you both! I thought I was paying for you two to have a happy holiday. Instead, you've both been an absolute pain!"

"It's Malcolm's fault. He betrayed me."

Sarah was getting impatient.

"He hasn't actually done anything wrong – at least, not yet. He may have contemplated knocking off that little bitch – but he didn't do it. He suffered physical pain and a considerable loss of face. But Malcolm today is still the same man you brought out here on Saturday. He's probably always chased women. In fact, I'm sure he has – even during the three months you've known him! But what you didn't know didn't worry you! Why change now? He enjoyed your company then – why not let him enjoy it now?"

"I don't think he'd want to see me. I'd always be second best."

She sniffed.

"Oh, don't be so bloody petty! Malcolm will be as glad to have you as anyone!"

"Thank you."

"He was happy with you last week. Why shouldn't he be happy now?"

"Because I know what he's like."

"And he knows what you're like. You're no angel. You've slummed around – as I have! Sex is sex – and love is love. While you've got a man – use him!"

"Like Neville?"

Sarah was beginning to get angry.

"Look, Jo! Stop being such a stuck-up bitch! I've done a lot for you. Will you kindly do something for me? Look after

Malcolm for the rest of the holiday. What you do when you get back to England is your problem – but at least look after him here. I'm going to speak to him now, this afternoon. And I'm going to tell him that if the two of you don't make up – right away – then you can pack your bags and go. I want to enjoy this place, but if you two are going to make it a bloody hell-hole, you can get out now! And I mean that."

Sarah turned on her heel and returned to the hotel.

There was a knock at the door.

"Come in."

Sarah swept into Malcolm's bedroom, wearing a white cotton trouser suit with gold buttons. Her face was flushed after her walk along the marina and her hair was all over the place. She had deliberately not made any attempt to tidy herself up before going in to see the lawyer. Even so, she still looked extremely attractive.

"Ah," said Malcolm, "Beauty and the Beast!"

"Precisely," said Sarah.

"Come and sit down beside me so that I can feast my eyes on your charms."

"You're not feasting on anything, Malcolm!" said Sarah. "You're going to listen to me – very carefully."

She stood at the end of the bed – well out of reach.

She did not trust herself to go any nearer.

"Neville and I came out here to have a peaceful holiday together..."

"Sex on the rocks!" Malcolm laughed.

"Listen to me! We came here for *our* pleasure. You only came out here because my sister asked. I invited you out here in good faith as her boyfriend. I wasn't looking for another partner. I had no desire to be involved with you – and I still haven't."

"Didn't feel like that last night. You were practically throwing yourself at me."

"I was comforting you."

"Why not do some more of it?" He pushed away the sheets. "I think we're back in business."

106

Sarah shook her head.

"I don't think you understand. I'm giving you and Jo one last chance. Either you two pick up where you were yesterday afternoon or you go straight back to England tonight. Either you go – or we go!"

"The lady is being serious."

He was mocking her.

"Very serious. I know what you're up to – and I'm not tolerating it. You either do what I want – or you go."

"And what exactly do you want?"

Malcolm pulled back the sheets.

"I want you and Jo to make up. I've spoken to her. She's very hurt. About what you did with that girl..."

Malcolm laughed sarcastically.

"...And what about what she did to me?"

"I think you deserved it. Anyway, as you said, you're feeling better. But if you are better, I'd be very glad if you'd concentrate on Jo. She's very fond of you. Not just as a lover – but in you as a person. She knows you're not the faithful type – but she'd be faithful to you."

Malcolm was amused by Sarah's request.

"If I stay, do I get a chance for a second bite at the cherry?"

Sarah shook her head angrily.

"Do be serious," she said. "I mean it."

Malcolm pulled himself up on the pillows.

"So I've got to be good and kind to your big sister? We've got to pretend nothing has happened. We've got to kiss and make up. She's going to make me a good wife – and I'm to be a beast of a husband?"

"Third time lucky!" said Sarah viciously.

Malcolm ignored her taunt.

There were quite a few things he could say about her marriage; but Sarah was offering him a lifeline. Whether she was wise to offer it to him, he doubted. He still had every intention of having her before the holiday was over. He had felt the strength of her passion the night before. Even though she had dampened down the fires, they were still there. But, obviously, if he stayed, he would have to play his cards more carefully.

Now that she knew his real reasons for being in Pollensa, Sarah could understand exactly the thoughts that were going through his mind. He wasn't really interested in accepting her offer, he was simply buying time. He was, as the French might say: 'reculant pour mieux sauter.' (It sounded better in French.) For if he went, he got nothing.

"And how long do I have to make up my mind about this ultimatum?"

"Till dinner-time."

Malcolm weighed up his position.

"Jo'll find it harder than me."

"Much harder. That's why you'll have to help her."

There was nothing more to say.

Sarah left the room without a single backward glance.

Malcolm got up and went to the toilet. He brushed his hair and gently touched his private parts to see if they were any less bruised.

All seemed to be well.

He looked at his face in the bathroom mirror and said to himself: "He who fights and runs away, lives to fight another day." There was nothing else he could do.

That afternoon, Debbie and Richard hired a car and went to look at some of the small villages on the west coast of Majorca. Raynes had not thought to bring his driving licence with him, but Debbie had come prepared and in her name, they rented a small Fiesta from a firm recommended by Megatravel.

The Inspector had been through the Police Advanced Drivers' Instruction Course – and had had several refresher courses over the years. It was therefore a distinct shock to his system to be driven on the wrong side of the road by a young woman whose driving skills could best be described as 'modest'.

It was a long time since he had been in such a small car as a Fiesta – and sitting on the right in the passenger seat, without a wheel or pedals in front of him, he felt exceedingly vulnerable. As at other happy moments, Debbie chatted away, hunted for maps or opened the sun roof without slackening momentum or paying much attention to the white lines on the road.

Raynes was inclined to say something caustic about her driving, but he realized that a harsh rebuke would only spoil their holiday. Up to now, Debbie had been sweetness and light – a perfect holiday companion. As she swung into a little Spanish village, narrowly missing an elderly donkey, Raynes decided that if death were to come, he would try and meet it with a smile.

Just before closing time, the tall American student from Arkansas University called in at the Megatravel office. He seemed quite breathless – but then, he was still chewing a fairly large pink lump of gum.

Angie looked at him with some disgust.

What a vile habit!

"Ri-oja," he said in a low voice.

"Pardon?"

"The boat trip – tomorrow."

He seemed to be having some trouble speaking clearly.

"You mean the pirate ship?"

The student nodded.

Angie fancied there might be a twinkle of humour in the eyes behind the dark glasses.

He put four crisp 2000 peseta notes down on the counter.

Angie looked at his long brown fingers. She could see that at one point he had worn a ring. There was an indentation on the third finger of his left hand.

'Fancy anyone marrying him!' she thought.

(But money was money wherever it came from.)

"What name was it?"

"Russell. Jack Russell."

After he had left the office, Angie added his name to the list for tomorrow's excursion. Then she looked up. Was he having her on? Weren't Jack Russells some kind of dog?

She smiled. At least he had a sense of humour.

Mrs Hickson phoned Sarah to ask if things were any better. Sarah said that she had just spoken to Jo and Malcolm and she thought that it might work.

Mrs Hickson did not mention her conversation with Wendy Bridges. She felt that Sarah would be angry and accuse her of interfering. She would mention it at some later date when tensions were not running quite so high. Instead, she asked:

"Is Neville all right?"

"He's fine. We've been out for a long walk and he's forgiven me."

'Probably the only one who has!' thought Mrs Hickson.

But Mrs Hickson was being unduly cynical.

By dinner-time, Sarah reckoned that she had succeeded in bringing everyone together again. Certainly the atmosphere was subdued and people were being extremely polite. But, at least, to the outward eye, everything looked normal.

Even though he was once again seated at a neighbouring table, there was very little to interest Inspector Raynes.

Jo had been a long time coming back from the marina. Every step had been dogged with self-doubt. What could she say to Malcolm? What would he say to her? Would it all end in tears as she feared? Or could they rebuild their relationship?

She slipped into their bedroom almost as if she were a sneak-thief.

Malcolm was having a shower. She took off her clothes. It might be better to meet him naked.

She walked into the bathroom.

"It's me," she said.

"So it is," said Malcolm cheerfully. "I'd never have recognized you with your clothes on."

She smiled.

Malcolm switched off the shower and picked up a towel.

"Your sister's been in here reading the riot act. She tells me we've got to behave. I've got to stop chasing other women and you've got to satisfy my baser needs. Or at least, some of them!"

With Malcolm in such an easy-going mood, it was not hard to make up. As she soaped herself down in the shower, Malcolm called through: "Do you want champagne now – or after?"

"Now," she replied.

'Bloody cow!' said Malcolm to himself. 'Do anything for booze!'

But none of these ugly feelings were visible in the dining-room of the *Hotel Aphrodite*. Malcolm and Neville kept away from any explosive subject. Sarah was grateful to Neville for being so understanding.

"I think," she said, "we might venture to keep our appointment with Brendan tomorrow."

"Treasure-hunting!" said Malcolm. "Bet it'll only be an old boot or a cheap bottle of Spanish plonk!"

"I was looking forward to seeing the Blue Grotto," said Jo. "I believe it's beautiful."

"I wonder if there'll be any female pirates?" said Malcolm provocatively.

Neville managed a broad smile.

"Well, if there are, I suggest you keep your hands off them or Sarah'll make you walk the plank!"

It was all fairly innocent stuff.

In fact, it was only after dinner that the proverbial horse manure struck the legendary fan. It happened in this way.

Malcolm had gone into the bar to have a quiet, solitary drink. In reality, he was intending to phone Wendy to let her know how things were going. But since nothing was happening, he would have to be inventive.

Sarah and Jo had gone away for a quiet evening walk to 'discuss things', and Neville had excused himself and gone upstairs, because he had a strong idea of what was about to happen.

So Malcolm was just taking the first sip of his beer and preparing his forthcoming soliloquy, when a familiar voice spoke in his ear.

111

"Fancy meeting you here, Mr Clark!"

He swung round on his stool.

There, in front of him, stood an unsmiling Mr Latimer, his wife right behind him, looking daggers.

"Spending your ill-gotten gains, I see."

Malcolm kept calm.

"As I said before, I'm not prepared to discuss anything." He looked at them coldly. "Are you here on holiday?"

Mr Latimer looked at his wife.

"Well, I think we'd rather call it business. We've been trying to track you down ever since the trial. You're a very elusive man, Mr Clark. We've left numerous messages with your secretary – but had no reply."

"Did you expect one?"

"We expect justice," said Mr Latimer, his voice ice-cold. "You may think you can rip off your clients and get away with it. But you've chosen the wrong ones this time. The wife and I are not going to rest until we get our money back."

'How tiresome!' thought Malcolm.

He looked pointedly at his watch and drank a little more of his beer.

"You were so encouraging when you took up our case," said Mrs Latimer. "You told us it would be quite straightforward and simple."

"Well, it wasn't," said Malcolm.

"You should have warned us at an early stage. You let the whole thing mount up."

"You'd have saved quite a packet if you hadn't sued me," said Malcolm. "That added at least £20,000 to your costs."

"Yes," said Mr Latimer, "and you're going to pay it all back."

"Am I?"

Malcolm's voice could not have sounded more contemptuous.

"Sooner or later," said Mr Latimer. "Every bloody penny – if you value your skin."

"Are you threatening me?"

"This isn't England, Mr Clark. You're not on home ground

112

now. No little policemen to protect you. No secret tape-recorders hidden under the desk. This is very much neutral ground."

"You are threatening me."

"Yes," said Mr Latimer, "I am. This is the first time we've had a chance to meet man to man, face to face. It won't be the last. We shall make your life hell – like you've made ours."

"You're not only a crook – you're also a coward!" said Mrs Latimer.

Malcolm was holding his glass on his knee.

At Mrs Latimer's words, he flung the remaining contents in her face.

Mr Latimer grabbed the beer mug with one hand and hit Malcolm a savage blow on the mouth with the other. Malcolm fell off his stool. He got to his feet rather shakily.

"Another move like that," said Mr Latimer, "and I'll kill you now."

He produced a short, ugly-looking knife with a razor-sharp blade.

Malcolm looked at it apprehensively.

This was a man who meant business.

"I've castrated pigs with this knife, Mr Clark. And that's not the half of what I intend to do to you, if you don't pay up."

Malcolm silently pondered on the fact that twice in twenty-four hours, the Latimer case had brought him physical injury with threats of worse to come. Last night, Fran was vowing vengeance because her family had been evicted. Tonight, Mr Latimer, who had recovered his sodding bungalow, was threatening him with castration. He wished he had never touched the bloody case!

"We shall be expecting fifty thousand, Mr Clark. Fifty thousand cash. None of your fancy cheques. They might bounce. We want it in full – and we want it soon. You can keep ten thousand for your services!"

"Ten? You must be joking!"

Mrs Latimer looked at him with a steely eye.

"Mr Latimer does not joke."

113

Malcolm remembered that even at the best of times, Mr Latimer had not had much of a sense of humour.

"Justice," said Mr Latimer, pointing his knife at Malcolm's groin. "Justice – and £50,000. You'll not forget?"

Suddenly the barman appeared.

"Another glass for you, sir? A couple of glasses for your friends? All drinks half-price during our Happy Hour!"

Looking back on the incident a little later, Malcolm felt that it had all the essential ingredients of a bad dream – but he did not doubt that the incident in the bar had really happened.

How had that swine caught up with him? Who had told him that he was in Majorca? Even Fran had known where to find him. Had people been following him – or was there a conspiracy?

Fortunately, no one had witnessed his second humiliation in twenty-four hours. He rubbed the side of his jaw. It was beginning to swell. He bathed it in cold water and took another two pain-killers. Unfortunately, just at that moment, Wendy chose to call. All day, she had been brooding on what that woman had said to her at the café. She was not in the mood to be trifled with.

"Is that Malcolm Clark?"

"Speaking."

"It's Wendy."

"Ah, yes. I was going to phone you earlier."

"I've been trying to phone you all day."

Malcolm took a deep breath. Importunate women! "What can I do to help you?"

"You can give me a progress report."

"There's very little to report."

"All pleasure – and no work?"

"There's not much pleasure at this moment." He rubbed his jaw tenderly.

"Have you spoken about it to her today?"

"No. I haven't seen much of Sarah today."

(Which was true.)

"You're not ditching me?"

"Pardon?"

"You're not thinking of giving up my case?"

"Certainly not. I said I would do my best – and I'm doing it. The domestic circumstances between the two sisters have been a little bit difficult today – but they're easier now. I still expect a positive discussion on the matter before I leave Majorca."

"But you're here for a fortnight."

"That's right."

"I'm only here for a week."

"I told you there was no point in coming. I'll handle this in my own way."

"Apparently you have a reputation for being slow and for charging horrendous fees."

"Who told you that?"

"A lady I was speaking to this afternoon. She also told me that you had been attacked at the disco last night. Are you all right now?"

"I am." Malcolm was curious. "Who was this woman?"

He was suspicious of everybody.

"Mrs Latimer," said Wendy. "A very nice woman. She said she knew you quite well..."

Malcolm did not exactly scream. He squawked. All his emotions came together in a single moment. With dire fury, he slammed down the telephone – hit it again – and stormed out of the room.

Wendy looked at the telephone.

Had she been cut off?

It seemed very much like it.

She phoned back the *Hotel Aphrodite* and asked again for Mr Clark. The receptionist tried the number but said there was no reply. Did she want to leave a message?

No, she didn't.

She was in no mood to have any further dealings with lawyers. Mrs Latimer was right. They just cost you a lot of money and mucked you about. She would be better using her own direct methods. At least it would command instant attention.

She opened her bedroom wardrobe and took out the rolled-up blue towel. She sat on the edge of her bed and weighed the pistol in her hand. It was very heavy for its size – but it was quite easy to handle. She checked to make sure it was not loaded. Then she flipped off the safety catch and pressed the trigger several times. It felt good. She put on the safety catch and rolled it up again in her towel.

Malcolm had thought she was exaggerating when she said she had a pistol. Perhaps he would take her more seriously when he discovered it was true?

17: *Serenitas maris*

On Thursday morning, a large and noisy group of people met outside the Estacion Maritime, where Brendan was trying to drum up a few more last-minute passengers, making powerful use of a dark-blue plastic loudhailer.

"Roll up, my friends, roll up! Your final chance to join us for a fabulous trip to the Blue Grotto. A day of surprises for everyone. Free food. Free drink. Free sunshine – aboard Majorca's most notorious boat! Glamorous mermaids and sea-nymphs are waiting to greet you. There is treasure to be found on Long John Silver's island. Rally round, my hearties! The *Jolly Rioja* leaves in fifteen minutes. Don't delay – come today!"

The sound of his voice carried quite some distance; it could even be heard on the terrace of the *Hotel Aphrodite*. Raynes, who had heard the speech three mornings running, noted that Brendan's patter did not change much from day to day.

The Irishman turned to the couriers.

"How many have we got now?"

"Fifty-six."

"Better than yesterday. We only had thirty-two. Scarcely worth going."

He lifted up his loudhailer and repeated the message.

Almost on cue, a white taxi pulled up outside the Estacion and four more people emerged.

"That's enough!"

Brendan smiled happily.

It would be another highly profitable day.

Angie and Mandy quickly got the crowd into order, ticking off those who were already on their list and taking money from the extra passengers who had joined at the last minute. Raynes looked at both of them, trying to decide which one he liked best. Mandy was dark-haired; Angie was blonde. Otherwise, they were much the same. Small breasts, good legs, brown arms, big smiles. Today they were both wearing red blouses and short white pleated skirts with white ankle socks and white trainers. The Inspector wondered if they were hoping to meet a merman – or was Brendan enough for both of them?

Once everyone had been accounted for, the passengers were led about three hundred yards along the quay to where the *Jolly Rioja* was berthed.

She was quite a large boat – about ninety feet long, with a high prow and a high stern. In between, there was a well-polished gun-deck with a white canvas awning to protect those who didn't like the sun. There were about twenty seats on the prow and the same number on the stern. Being in the vanguard of the passengers, Debbie and Richard were able to choose where they sat. They chose the stern.

They sat on the starboard side, overlooking the gun-deck, and so had an excellent view of all that was happening. They watched the other passengers gingerly crossing the simple plank which linked the boat to the shore and recognized many of the faces who had been on the Monday trip to Palma.

Sarah and Neville were there – both dressed in white. Neville was carrying a pair of binoculars and a green canvas bag. Jo and Malcolm were mostly in blue but Jo had a pink chiffon scarf around her neck. Malcolm was wearing dark glasses and carrying a very expensive camera.

The Brown Baby was also making the trip – still wearing the same green and white grubby shirt and the creased shorts. As she came on board, the foursome from the *Hotel Aphrodite* turned to look at her. Raynes could imagine that

117

their eyes held a very frosty glare. Raynes reckoned that the Brown Baby could not be all that poor if she could afford a trip on the pirate ship.

The solitary student from Arkansas was also there, still in his hideous red and blue tracksuit – still chewing and spitting out his gum. But the cost had clearly deterred Mr and Mrs Average and the Tabloid family. In fact, looking round, Raynes was surprised to see there were no children on the boat.

Quite a few of the elderly couples who had been on the coach to Soller were also there – as were Mr and Mrs Latimer, who were among the last to board the boat. As they moved to the stern, to sit near Debbie and Richard, the party from the *Hotel Aphrodite* looked pointedly across the bay to the *Hotel Illador*. The only other person the Inspector recognized was a lady in a loose grey trouser-suit with a black bandana and very large sunglasses. At first, Raynes wrote her off as a complete stranger, but as the *Jolly Rioja* was being cast off and the mooring lines were slung on board, she took off her glasses and rubbed her left eye. At that moment, Raynes realized that she was the woman he had seen talking to Malcolm in the Café Sol. Wendy Bridges! What was she doing on this trip?

However, there was no time for further speculation. The *Jolly Rioja* was already edging away from the quay and gathering speed. Although there were a number of canvas sails flapping in the breeze, the boat was driven by an old diesel engine which at best could muster about six knots. It puttered slowly away as they passed the vast array of yachts gathered in the Marina. And then the ship turned right, on a southerly course, with the obvious intention of doing a tour of Pollensa bay before heading out to sea.

As the *Jolly Rioja* cut a happy swathe through the windsurfers, Brendan fired his one and only cannon at them. There was a puff of black smoke. A strong smell of gunpowder and the cannonball flew twenty feet and fell into the sea.

"Missed the buggers!" said Brendan sadly.

He picked up his loudhailer.

"Welcome aboard, shipmates! Remember this is a pirate ship. The only ship in the Mediterranean still flying the skull-and-crossbones. In the olden days, this was a great place for pirates, so we're upholding a fine old tradition.

"If we get sunk – or attacked by enemy submarines, remember the lifeboats only carry twenty passengers each! The rest of you will have to cling on to the wreckage. And don't expect the windsurfers to help you. They hate me!

"Later in the trip, we're going to have a little competition to find out who's going to be our Mr and Mrs Pirate. Nothing serious! Just a bit of innocent fun. The winners will collect a bottle of Spanish champagne..." Brendan chuckled to himself. "... There's a laugh! Spanish champagne! A bottle each. And then they'll walk the plank and get to the Blue Grotto first. But beware of the giant man-eating squid!

"For those of you who want to get sloshed, the bar's downstairs. Sixty feet long – so it's big enough for all of you. Don't forget to sample one of my ten Irish whiskies. Keep the peasants back home in business! And when you've drunk that – if you're still standing, try one of Brendan's 'corking specials' – one part vodka, three parts white wine, two parts peach schnapps and a touch of grenadine. Blow your guts to garters! And by the way, the toilets are also downstairs – at the back of the boat. But don't expect to find any toilet paper!" He laughed cruelly. "Just joking! Got you worried there!"

Brendan prattled on.

The pirate ship made a leisurely arc round the beautiful bay of Pollensa and then turned to starboard round the Cabo del Pinar and circled the beach at Alcudia – just to show the punters what they were missing.

As they approached the beach, Brendan picked up his loudhailer – and with a note of sudden panic in his voice he addressed those swimming in the sea and the children making sandcastles on the seashore.

"Beware!" he screamed. "There's a white shark just fifty feet from the beach."

Raynes and many other passengers crowded to the rails to see the dreaded monster.

Brendan repeated his warning twice more.

Everyone on the beach could hear.

Very rapidly, the sea emptied. Bathers rushed towards the shore. Mothers dashed into the waves to drag their children back to safety. Orange dragons and plastic play-rings floated out to sea. Windsurfers, caught unawares, changed direction. Many fell into the sea and scrambled frantically back on to their boards.

Brendan laughed hysterically.

"Always gets to them! Never fails!"

He hoisted his huge black and white pirate flag fore and aft and fired his cannon three times in the direction of the beach. This time he used blanks and a cloud of mulberry-coloured smoke covered the ship.

"Chap broke his leg last week!" said Brendan proudly. "Visited him in hospital. Took him a bottle of my special hooch! No hard feelings!"

Raynes could see why people hated Brendan.

As promised, their golden-haired captain moved on to give a running commentary on the sins of the rich and famous who had villas in the area. He was particularly hard on the Spanish film star, Daina Donja – the body of an angel, he said, and the lust of a beast. She was reported to have had over a hundred lovers in the past year.

"They don't get long," chortled Brendan, "but it's good while it lasts!" His voice took on a conspiratorial tone. "She's even had a member of the British Royal Family." He paused. "But I'm not going to tell you which one. You'll have to come on our night cruise to find out that! She doesn't care who she has! No taste whatsoever! I'm told that her last lover was some unemployed sheep-shagger from Australia! No Australians with us today, I hope?"

Two of the passengers put up their hands.

"Oh dear," said Brendan. "Done it again! Maybe I got it wrong. Perhaps he was Argentinian? No Argentinians on board? Fine! He was an Argentinian sheep-shagger..."

Debbie whispered to Richard:

"There's no such person as Daina Donja! I looked it up at home. He's making it all up."

Brendan carried on with his unrelenting cascade of character assassination. Black masses were performed in hidden chapels; women were chained up and whipped; homosexuals were hung by their nipples over candles and roasted till they screamed. To hear Brendan, you would imagine that the whole area round Cape Formentor was seething with vice. In fact, as their ship glided by over the calm blue sea, everything looked very beautiful – very normal; as indeed it was.

The object of relating all the scandal was to get everyone's hormones bubbling, to lower inhibitions and to put everyone in the mood for a bit of fun. To assist the feel-good factor, free glasses of Brendan's hooch were handed out. Seconds were freely available if you wanted more. Even if it was mostly cheap schnapps mixed with local wine with the odd slice of orange floating on top – it still had the desired effect. People loosened up; felt ready for a bit of slap and tickle. And as the boat drifted towards the grey cliffs beyond Cape Formentor, Brendan reckoned that they were now ready to play his favourite party game.

He picked up his loudhailer.

"Well, here we are folks! At the Blue Grotto. You can now see the fantastic cave built straight into the cliff face. The sand is like gold dust and the water – translucent blue. Pure magic! Never mind what anyone says! This is the real Blue Grotto. Blessed by His Holiness, the Pope."

"What about the one in Malta?" someone asked.

"A cheap imitation!" said Brendan knowledgeably. "Feast your eyes on this beauteous scene. We're going to cast our anchor here for about half an hour." He smiled. "And while we're here, we're going to select two star performers to be Mr and Mrs Pirate. They've got to be good climbers and good kissers. And if they could swim as well, that would help!" He laughed. "Because they'll be bloody drowned if they can't! We want to see them climb the ship's rigging – it's quite easy if you don't look down – touch our jolly old skull-and-crossbones and then scamper down and kiss five lovely people. Any five. The first two men and the first two ladies – will then be taken by myself and my Pirate Queen into the Captain's cabin where we shall select the winners. After that, we shall marry them and push 'em overboard in the time-honoured manner! All those wishing to walk the plank, step forrard!"

There was a buzz of excitement as people decided whether they were equal to the challenge. A pushy little woman from Warrington was the first to volunteer. She was wearing a mustard-coloured vest and blue denim shorts that were too tight for her.

Neville decided that he would take part but Malcolm shook his head. He was not going to make a fool of himself again – especially in front of *that* girl. He noticed that she was keeping well away from him and did not volunteer.

One or two of the elderly men fancied their chances and stripped off their shirts, revealing lean, mean, well-muscled torsos.

"I won this last time," said Debbie. "I think I shall have another go. At least we shall get a free bottle of champagne."

"He said it was crap."

"It's the principle that counts."

Before Richard could stop her, she had whipped off her blouse and skirt, run down the steps and positioned herself beside Brendan.

He looked at her thoughtfully.

"Hello, darling! Haven't I seen you before?"

Debbie nodded.

"Three months ago. In June."

Brendan laughed.

"You've come back for more. That's what I like!"

Jo looked up at the rigging.

"Do you really think it's safe?"

Sarah shrugged her shoulders.

"If Neville says he can do it, he will."

Malcolm smiled. "Well, if he breaks his neck, you two ladies will have to fight for my body."

"I thought it was already spoken for," said Sarah coldly.
Joanne gritted her teeth – and looked away.

Five men and four ladies were eventually assembled for the contest. They were lined up on either side of the gun-deck – gentlemen on the left, ladies on the right. Brendan appeared with a large cutlass and gave them their final instructions.

"When I raise this cutlass – you move!"

He looked round the assembled company.

"Are you ready?"

There was a flash of steel.

"Go!"

The contestants leapt up on to the ship's rails and scrambled on to the loose jute ropes which were knotted together in rough squares. The rigging sagged under the weight of the assault – which gave the impression of a large number of people wrestling in a hammock.

One of the old men seemed very adept. He raced up the rigging like a wizened monkey – but Neville was close behind him.

One of the girls climbed about ten feet and then froze. Another put her leg through the ropes and got stuck. Brendan poked her with his cutlass.

"Come on, sweetheart. Get it out or I'll chop it off!"

The little woman from Warrington was an aggressive bitch and twice pushed Debbie aside in her race to the top. Debbie bided her time but as the other woman reached for the flag, Debbie bit her arm above the elbow. The woman screamed – as Debbie reached past her and touched the flag. Whilst she was off balance, the woman kicked out at her and the rigging swayed alarmingly thirty feet above the deck.

Raynes' heart was in his mouth.

"Come on, girls! No cheating!" shouted Brendan. "Keep it clean!"

But as she had said, Debbie had done all this before. The other woman was no match for her. She came down the ropes, hand over hand, and breathlessly leapt down on to the deck.

She rushed over to Richard and kissed him. She kissed three older men and then finally flung herself into Malcolm's arms for a brief peck.

"Make the most of it," she breathed. "'Cos it's all you're going to get!"

The little woman from Warrington was busy complaining, showing Brendan the marks of Debbie's teeth on her arm. But Brendan was not impressed.

"I saw you kicking and pushing her," he said. "Count it evens."

The Pirate King and Pirate Queen took the winners into the Captain's cabin and poured each of them a glass of champagne.

"Now," said Mandy, "we've got to narrow it down to the last two. May the best man win!"

She put her soft arms round the older man who had come down first. He may have known a lot about ropes, but he didn't know much about women. He was nervous and grabbed her roughly. Mandy tried to look as if she had enjoyed it – but didn't. She turned to Neville with relief. He scooped her up in his arms and gave her a deep, deep, French kiss.

Debbie watched with interest as she waited for the little firebrand from Warrington to finish with Brendan. She was slobbering all over him. It was quite repulsive.

Free at last, Brendan turned to Debbie with lustful eyes. "Now, my little darling!"

After years of handling every different sort of man, Debbie had no problems with the Irishman. She yielded a little; pressed a little; sighed deeply with her eyes closed; pressed again – but harder; and moaned contentedly whilst Brendan poured his passion into her. When it was over, she opened her eyes and blinked unbelievingly. "That was great!"

The Pirate King had no doubt who was the winner – and neither did his Queen.

"It was a fix!" screamed the little woman.

"Bugger off!" said Brendan. "Or I'll throw you overboard!"

Neville and Debbie were led out into the sunshine and declared to be the happy couple. Red and gold satin mantles were wrapped around their shoulders and, exercising his traditional authority as captain of a sea-going vessel, Brendan waved his cutlass ceremonially over their heads.

"I declare you Mr and Mrs Pirate."

Everyone cheered.

Both Sarah and Richard looked on – both rather jealous, because Neville and Debbie looked the perfect couple.

But now it was time for the final act of the drama.

Each was blindfolded. The ship's rails were removed and a thick, wooden plank was run out six feet from the ship's side. Brendan put a couple of heavy metal weights on the end of the plank to hold it in position.

"Right!" he said. "We're ready for the big drop!"

Brendan saw Sarah's anxious face.

"Now," he said, "don't worry. The water's quite deep. About thirty feet."

He guided Neville on to the gangplank.

"Good luck, Mr Pirate!" he said.

Neville advanced only about four paces. Then he fell sideways. There was a gasp from the crowd. But Neville knew what he was doing. As he fell, he turned it into a perfect dive and entered the water with a graceful splash.

"Well done!" said Brendan admiringly. "Now, young lady, it's all yours."

Debbie approached her fate more slowly. Moving about six inches at a time, she felt for the edge of the gangplank before she moved forward. Everyone on board watched her slow progress with bated breath. Would she – or wouldn't she? She was five feet out – and paused.

"Get on with it!" shouted the woman from Warrington.

"Come on in," said Neville. "It's lovely and warm."

Debbie shuffled the last few inches and then leapt out into space. She went into the water feet first with her arms above her head. Everyone crowded to the side of the ship and looked down.

Debbie tore off her blindfold and received a kiss from Mr

Pirate. Then they swam to the foot of the ladder which would bring them back on deck.

Before she took hold of the ladder, Debbie turned to Neville. She smiled seductively.

"That was a terrific kiss you gave Mandy," she said. "Could you give me a bit of the same?"

Neville looked up at the deck.

"If you come in under the ladder, no one'll see us."

Neville swam up close to Debbie and pressed her against the side of the ship. On this occasion, there was no pretending. Debbie received a long, deep, satisfying, breast-tingling kiss.

If either Sarah or Richard could have seen the intensity of the embrace, it would have broken both their hearts.

"Thank you," said Debbie, as they broke apart and she pulled herself up on to the ladder. "We must get together again before the end of the holiday."

The kiss had made as deep an impact on Neville as it had on Debbie – but in a different place. He looked up at her bare, brown legs and the curve of her body under her wet swimsuit. He took a deep breath.

"It's a date!" he said.

18: *Fulmen Propria Horae*

At first sight, the island did not appear all that large, but the *Jolly Rioja* was approaching it endways on. As Brendan swept down its western coast, the passengers could see that it was about two miles long and half a mile wide at its broadest point.

The shore-line was rough and jagged, littered with huge limestone boulders which seemed to have been bitten out of the cliffs many centuries before and had since been washed and polished by the waves of countless storms. There were any number of narrow inlets and pebble beaches, protected by low-lying rocky pools.

"Good for crabs!" said Brendan. "Send your wives there!"

Above the shore-line, the main body of the island seemed to be a mixture of scrubby grass and rocks – with a central comb of small, dark pine trees which from the air looked like the letter S, giving the place its official name: *Caballito de Mar* – Seahorse Island. Brendan said that pilots letting down their planes for Palma airport often used it to check their position. If they were too close to the island, they edged northwards towards the lighthouse on Cape Formentor. Half-way between the two, they were spot-on for their approach.

Having given his passengers a chance to see the full extent of this island paradise on which they would effectively be marooned for the next four-and-a-half hours, Brendan swung his ship around the most southerly point and headed up the eastern shore, round a jutting headland and into a perfect little bay where the water shone a rich translucent blue over the deep, white sand.

The *Jolly Rioja* tied up at a small concrete pier and Brendan suggested that they should all go and find themselves a suitable place for a picnic – but not too far away from the ship. His crew would be laying out a buffet lunch on the main deck which would be served in about an hour's time.

Sarah and Neville were among the first to leave the ship. They had already decided that the headland overlooking the bay would make an ideal picnic spot. It was not far from the pier and it commanded a splendid view across the water to Cala San Vicente. They made their way rapidly to the top and unpacked their green canvas bag.

Jo and Malcolm followed – but more slowly. Every now and then, Malcolm would turn back and look anxiously at the other passengers as they came off the boat. He had just realized that the woman in the grey trouser suit was Wendy Bridges. What was she doing on the boat? Was she following him? Was she intending to make a nuisance of herself? It was bad enough having the two Latimers there, watching his every move. Now that he knew Wendy had been speaking to Mrs Latimer, things could get completely out of hand.

Joanne was aware that Malcolm was worried about

something, but since he hadn't bothered to tell her what it was, she didn't see why she should let it spoil her day. So, when Malcolm stopped for the fifth time, Joanne did not wait for him. She climbed steadily up the path to the grassy plateau and flung her bag down on the ground.

"Paranoia!" she said. "Advanced paranoia! He can't stop looking over his shoulder. I think he's frightened someone'll attack him."

"Can't say I blame him," said Neville, "after what that little bitch did to him the other night!"

"She's here too," said Sarah. "I recognized her. With the same dirty clothes she was wearing on Monday. We must make sure Malcolm doesn't do anything violent to her. We don't want another scene!"

The Brown Baby certainly had her eye on Malcolm. That was why she had come on the boat. She had threatened further acts of retaliation and she was already considering one or two juicy possibilities. Could she perhaps gatecrash his picnic party and claim that she was pregnant? Or would it be more infuriating if she just lay on the grass about twenty yards away and sunbathed topless? How could she embarrass Malcolm in front of his posh friends? She was surprised that he still had his lady-friend – but she didn't look very happy and they hadn't spoken much on the boat. One more blow would probably finish them off!

The Brown Baby sat at the landward end of the concrete pier, dangling her bare legs in the clear, blue water. There was no point in her going any further inland; she was desperately hungry and was determined to be first in the queue when lunch was served.

The Latimers chose a small stone bench on the other side of the bay and unpacked a travelling rug, two inflatable cushions, a bottle of good quality Spanish wine and a bright green bottle-opener. It was time for an aperitif. Mrs Latimer poured a generous libation into two plastic cups.

"A perfect day for a picnic!" she said.

"A perfect day for a spot of blackmail!" said her husband. "That bastard doesn't know what's coming to him. He's not going to leave this island till he's promised to pay us back every penny. I'm going to make sure I have it down in black and white." He patted his waistband to make sure he still had his knife. Then he lifted his plastic cup and pointed it mockingly towards the foursome on the cliff-top.

"Cheers!" he said. "Enjoy your lunch."

Raynes and Debbie headed up through the pine trees and over to the other side of the island. Debbie of course had been here before and she said she knew 'just the place'. It was down a narrow path, through a series of prickly bushes and under the lee of a very dangerous-looking cliff – but she was right. It was a simple crescent of white sand about thirty feet in length, beautifully sheltered from the wind but in full view of both sun and sea – an exceedingly private little beach.

"Told you!" she said, pulling off her pink top and baring two chubby, brown breasts. She unbuttoned her white shorts and slipped them off. "Come on!" she said. "What are you waiting for? Get your things off – and let's celebrate!"

Raynes looked at her with mixed feelings.

"What about lunch?" he asked.

"Oh, don't be so bloody unromantic!" she snapped. "Here we are on the most deliciously secluded beach on the whole island, enjoying the most glorious summer's day one could ever wish for... and you've got one of the world's most desirable women – just bursting for it! What could be more perfect than a squiggle in the sand?"

Raynes took off his green shirt.

He already looked much healthier and browner. By the end of the fortnight, he would be a new man.

"And it's no use dreaming about the food!" Debbie added harshly. "It's more than likely to give you gut rot! Brendan probably hasn't washed the lettuce properly – and the chicken'll be crawling with salmonella!" She smiled more appealingly. "At least I'm fresh! You can eat me!"

* * *

129

As Debbie had suspected, the lettuce was not all it might have been. Some of it was left over from the previous day. Old and new, Brendan mixed it all together and added a generous measure of French dressing to pep up the more wilted leaves and give them a better taste. He slashed up a dozen cucumbers and threw them on top of the lettuce and circumcised some colourful red peppers. Within a few minutes, the whole concoction looked quite appetizing.

Mandy was doing a similar resurrection job on the slices of ham and beef which, despite being wrapped in foil, were showing a distinct tendency to curl and shrivel up. With a sharp knife, she cut off the worst pieces and added a few face-saving tomatoes to cover up what was left.

Angie was carving up the bread – which was at least fresh that day. The potato salad was also quite wholesome and the onions were strong enough to demolish a nun at fifty yards. The chicken wings in the tikka sauce smelt encouraging but she had her doubts about the sausages on sticks. She had a feeling that she had seen them at least once before.

She shrugged her shoulders.

They'd probably be home before the squits hit them!

She moved over to the drinks table and poured litres of cheap red wine into large glass jugs. The oranges, lemons and other fruit were already cut up. She poured a measured amount into each jug along with a handful of ice cubes. Instant sangria!

Brendan put his arm around her beautifully shaped rump and stroked her right thigh hopefully.

"Darling!" he said. "That looks delicious!"

(He said the same thing – at the same time – on every trip.)

She giggled happily – more from the suggestive probing of his fingers than from the oft-repeated compliment. Brendan ran his fingers under her short, white, pleated skirt and whispered in her ear:

"What about taking a jugful down to the Captain's cabin for afters?"

Angie looked at Brendan sharply.

"I thought you were intending to pull that blonde who won the Mrs Pirate competition?"

Brendan sighed.

"Yes, I was," he admitted sadly, "but I've just remembered what happened last time I met her. She made me pay!" Brendan looked horrified. "Me! I ask you! She's nothing but a moneygrubbing little whore!"

Angie grinned.

"What does that make me? Just a cheap scrubber?"

Brendan shook his head and held her closer.

"You do it for love," he said. "Straight from the goodness of your heart." He looked out at the hungry punters roaming round the beach, waiting for the summons to eat. "Besides," he said, "what else is there to do on this bloody island?"

Wendy Bridges was not interested in food. She had much more serious things on her mind. Revenge... Murder... Call it what you will – that was at the top of her agenda. Before she had boarded the *Jolly Rioja*, she had spent nearly an hour examining a map of the island. She now had a fairly good idea of its layout and she reckoned that she could achieve her goal – and yet, cover her tracks quite easily.

Like Richard and Debbie, she had decided to establish her base on the western side of the island. She had watched the shore-line very carefully as the boat passed by, and had selected a very large boulder with a flat top as the ideal place to sunbathe. It took some time to locate the actual stretch of beach but when she found it, she laid out her towel and her bags. She took off her trouser suit and her black bandana and let her brown hair fall loosely round her shoulders. She felt much happier in just her navy-blue bikini. She rubbed some protective cream on to her arms, legs and shoulders and settled down to get a decent tan. There was no hurry. She had it all planned.

News that lunch was now being served was communicated to the world at large by a double round of the cannon and the

131

screech of a green distress rocket which streaked over the island and fell into the sea.

(Brendan had had some trouble with the authorities over this wheeze. The first time he had tried it, the lifeboat had been launched from Cala San Vicente and sent out to rescue the passengers on Seahorse Island. Once it had been discovered to be a hoax, there had been some very angry words followed by a visit from the police. But now it had become almost part of the local scene – two bursts of gunpowder would be succeeded by a green, red or purple rocket. It was now taken for granted that Brendan's customers were in no need of rescue – at least not from the sea!)

The Brown Baby was first at the trough. She grabbed a large red napkin and two plates and began to fill them to the brim. She armed herself with a large glass of sangria and escaped to the bows of the ship where she devoured her lunch. With her mouth smeared with tikka sauce and her hands slippery with French dressing, she felt on top of the world.

The Latimers also appeared promptly but were more conservative in their choice of food. Mrs Latimer looked closely at the cold meat and the salad – and then recommended the fried chicken wings, the potato salad and plenty of bread. Mr Latimer looked at the grilled sausages and was unable to resist the temptation. He chose beer rather than sangria.

Richard and Debbie completed their exquisite squiggle in the sand in record time. Then they plunged naked into the sea for a quick swim. The lunch-time rocket exploded over their heads and narrowly missed them as it plummeted into the sea. But it at least reassured Raynes that he would not have to sacrifice either of his two favourite leisure occupations. There was time for sex and sangria!

"And sardines!" said Debbie. "They're quite safe."

As she passed Brendan at the buffet, she gave his private parts a friendly squeeze.

"Lovely nosh!" she said sarcastically. "I see you're still using the same old lettuce!"

Brendan was about to grab her but he encountered Raynes' steely glare which said – quite unmistakably: "Keep your hands off her, you uncouth Irish brute!"

Brendan kept his hands off her.

The student from Arkansas also proved very selective in what he ate. He put his book down on the table whilst he reached over for the cheese and onion quiche.

Raynes looked at the title on the cover. Heidegger's *Of Divine Love*. 'Not much of that around here,' he said to himself. He was going to tease the student about his choice of reading matter but, as ever, the student seemed distant and aloof. At least he had given up chewing his gum. Looking at him closely, Raynes decided that he might be a lot older than he had at first thought.

In solitary isolation, he proceeded to the stern of the ship to enjoy his taste of culinary hell and his existential vision of heaven. Both seemed to bring equal satisfaction.

Whilst everyone else was eating their lunch, Wendy Bridges had put her rolled-up towel under her arm and set off back across the island. But instead of going towards the *Jolly Rioja*, she made her way round the back of the headland and fought her way through the mass of bracken and ferns. From here, she had a very clear view of the party on top of the cliff – especially when they sat up or stood.

She crouched down behind a tree and unrolled her blue towel. There was the heavy black revolver. She could tell it was an old one because it had lost all its shine and was in parts badly scored. She wondered how many people had used it; how many people it had killed. She tested its weight in her hand. It felt good. She knew it was a reliable weapon because she had already done a number of practice shots. It was just a question of taking careful aim and hitting her target. She hoped that one shot would be enough; but there were six bullets already in their chambers. She flicked off the safety catch.

She lifted the revolver with both hands and took a sighting on her target. She did this four times to make sure. At this distance, she could not miss. An airgun or a light hunting rifle might easily deflect – but not her weapon. The bullet would speed swiftly and accurately to its target.

She noticed that Sarah was laughing and lifting her glass. 'She won't be laughing in two minutes' time,' she said to herself. A good clean shot would put an end to ten years of hatred and humiliation. She held very steady for the shot and pulled the trigger.

Sarah had just eaten the last of her Camembert and was lifting her glass to wash it down with champagne when there was a sudden crack – and she found herself holding only the stem of her wine-glass. Both the champagne and the upper part of the glass had gone. She looked down in amazement.

"It's gone!" she said.

Jo had felt a sudden prickly sensation in her right shoulder. She looked down. There was a wet patch on her dress, a few shimmering shards of glass and emerging specks of blood. She too looked at it with amazement.

"Something's hit me!" she said.

Malcolm realized immediately what had happened.

"Down!" he screamed. "Get down!"

He lunged forward, grabbed Sarah by the hair and pulled her face-down into all the mess of the picnic lunch. And just in time – for there was a second crack – and Jo clearly heard the angry buzz of a bullet as it flashed past her.

Both she and Neville levelled themselves on the ground.

"What the hell is it?" asked Sarah angrily.

"Someone's just tried to kill you!" said Malcolm.

"Me?"

Sarah reached for a napkin and wiped duck pâté off her nose. She did not dare to sit up.

"Who could have done that?"

"Wendy Bridges... It's got to be her."

"I didn't see her on the boat."

"Grey trouser-suit. Sunglasses. I was watching her when we left the boat."

"Oh, is that who you were looking at?" said Joanne, understanding at last. "Charles' ex?"

"I knew she had a revolver..."

"You knew?"

"... She told me she had a pistol. I didn't think she'd ever dream of using it – but I think she just has."

Sarah was about to sit up.

"Don't sit up!" said Malcolm. "She's probably still there, waiting to get you with a third shot."

Sarah was getting very angry.

"What were you doing talking to her?"

"She wanted you to give her children some financial help. She's just about broke and she wanted me to approach you and ask you for money. That's why she came out to Majorca. She said that if I didn't succeed in persuading you, she'd shoot you."

"You never mentioned it."

"I didn't dare. I think I've caused enough trouble for the three of you already."

"You can say that again!" said Neville bitterly.

"And what are we going to do now?" asked Sarah. "We can't spend all afternoon lying on our faces. We've got to get up some time."

"I'll go and look for her," said Malcolm. "She won't shoot me."

"Famous last words!" said Neville. "But what do we do?"

"Wait till I've combed the immediate vicinity. Then I'll come back and tell you if it's all clear. If it is, then we can get Sarah back to the boat and she can spend the afternoon downstairs in Brendan's bar. It won't be much fun being cooped up – but it's better than being dead."

Malcolm rose to his feet.

There was no bullet.

He walked round the headland, looking down each side most carefully. There seemed to be no one in sight.

He said: "I'm going down. Stay where you are till I'm sure it's safe."

Malcolm came down from the high ground and made his way into the bracken and undergrowth where he was sure

Wendy had been. He could see that someone had trampled their way through the ferns – and where they had stopped behind a tree. He looked up at their picnic site. That was it. She had been here... but she was gone. He explored the whole area most thoroughly and then guarded Neville, Sarah and Jo as they packed up their kit and made their way back safely to the *Jolly Rioja*.

He waved them goodbye.

Now to find Wendy and get hold of that gun!

19: *Nemo me impune lacessit*

Malcolm did a thorough search of the island. He worked his way down the eastern coast, checking every bay and inlet. He reached the most southerly point where the pine trees stopped and there was just a series of gullies with heaps of rocks reaching out to sea. He continued his search along the western shore and eventually found her on a large flat-topped boulder drinking in the sun. He paused to make sure it was her. Then he climbed down the steep path and crossed the rough pebbled beach.

Wendy heard him coming and turned over on to her stomach. She looked down at him.

"That was a bloody silly thing to do!" he said.

She raised her eyebrows.

"Don't pretend you don't know what I'm talking about! You were within a couple of inches of killing her..."

"Pity I missed! I'll get her next time!"

Malcolm was extremely angry.

"There isn't going to be a 'next time'! Killing her won't do your children any good. It's only patient persuasion and negotiation that'll bring her round."

"It hasn't worked so far!"

"Bloody hell!" he said. "You can't change people's minds in five minutes. You've got to play it long... like a fisherman catching a salmon. It takes quite a long time to get the fish to rise to the bait and once you've got that far, it's still a slow business. You can't change the prejudices of ten years in the twinkling of an eye! For heaven's sake, be reasonable!"

Wendy gave Malcolm a grim smile.

"Well, at least she knows I'm serious! Deadly serious! And presumably you have now told her precisely what I want?" Wendy looked at him suspiciously. "You have told her?"

"I have."

"And what was her reaction?"

"She hasn't yet had time to consider the matter calmly. You can't think logically when there are bullets flying around you."

"You only told her after I'd fired my shots?"

"Yes."

"So you were stringing me along the other day in the Café Sol, saying you'd already mentioned it to her? In point of fact, you hadn't?"

"No. I was waiting for a suitable opportunity."

"You lied to me?"

"Yes." Malcolm was cornered. "But I had no option. You can't rush these things. There's a very tense situation between the two sisters – and Neville hates my guts..."

"We all do," said Wendy with some confidence. "You're a slimy rat! You always string people along. Charge them exorbitant fees. You rook even your own clients... and still leave them high and dry!"

Malcolm snorted.

"You shouldn't believe anything Mrs Latimer says. Theirs was a very exceptional case. We were dealing with some very difficult people..." He thought about Fran. "... some very violent people. There've been plenty of cases where I haven't charged my clients a penny. The Latimers' expectations were altogether too rosy – and then they sued me." His bitterness showed clearly on his face. "But that's got nothing to do with this business. I'd have got you the money for your children but you'd have had to be patient. Now that you've tried to kill her, it wouldn't surprise me if she switched off completely."

Wendy was quite unapologetic.

"Well, she knows what's coming to her. Her money – or else!" She drew an elegant line across her throat. "I give her two weeks."

Malcolm shook his head.

"That's not the way to do it. You're being very obtuse and stupid. I could easily report you to the police."

"You can't prove it was me!"

She smiled.

Malcolm did not smile back.

"We both know it was you... And you've still got the pistol."

"Have I?"

Another smile.

Malcolm was feeling increasingly frustrated, standing in the hot sun, arguing with an impossible woman about matters which – quite frankly – bored him stupid. There she was grinning down at him – being as awkward as possible.

"I want that pistol," said Malcolm firmly.

"Why? Are you going to shoot me?"

"No. But I'm going to stop you shooting anyone else."

"There isn't anyone else. It's only Sarah I'm after. Once she makes a suitable settlement, then I'll throw the thing away. No cash – no surrender!"

Malcolm decided that the only thing to do was to climb up on to the rock and force her to hand over the gun. Even if it wasn't there, he'd make her tell him where it was. He didn't see any need to be gentle with a would-be murderess.

Whilst he'd been talking, he had been sizing up the quickest way to reach the top of the boulder where she was lying. When she made her final declaration: "No cash – no surrender!" he said: "Is that your last word?"

"It is."

Without a moment's hesitation, he did a running jump on to an adjacent rock and then leapt across the gap to the boulder on which Wendy was lying.

She jumped to her feet.

Her bikini top fell to the ground.

"Are you going to attack me?"

138

"Yes."

She waited till he was three feet away from her and then rushed forward trying to push him over the edge. Malcolm grabbed her right arm and swung her round him so that she fell face down on the rock. He bent down, put his knee in the middle of her back and twisted her arm in a half-nelson.

"You're hurting!" she screamed.

"It'll be hurting a lot more in a minute," he said. He grabbed a handful of her long, brown hair, wrapped it round his fist, jerked her head up and then smashed it down on to the stone surface of the boulder.

She screamed again – several times.

"Tell me where the pistol is!"

"I'm not telling you anything!"

Malcolm was not inclined to argue. He banged her head against the stone a second time.

"You'll have to tell me – so you might as well do it now!"

He twisted her arm further until she whimpered with pain. He pulled her head up again...

"Third time lucky!" he said coldly.

"I'll tell you!" she said. "I'll tell you!"

Malcolm released the pressure.

"No fooling?"

"No fooling." She sniffed pathetically. Her nose was bleeding and her skull felt fractured. "It's under that rock on the right. You can see the blue towel it's wrapped in."

Malcolm looked in the direction she had indicated but could see nothing.

"Show me!" he said.

He lowered her off the flat-topped boulder, still keeping a tight grip on her hair. She led him over to the rock under which she claimed the pistol was hidden. He was expecting her to try and escape but she was sufficiently cowed. Her forehead had been cut and the blood from that and her nose dripped on to the rocks. She looked a mess.

"Pull it out – slowly!"

She tugged at the towel and the revolver clattered down on to the pebbled beach. It was a nasty-looking object – certainly not a toy. Malcolm was deeply shocked. That thing could really kill!

Malcolm escorted her back to the boulder.

"Up you go!" he said. "And stay there! I'm getting rid of that revolver so that you can never do anything so stupid again. I will speak to Sarah – as I promised – and ask her about a settlement for your children, but whether she'll do anything, I cannot say. But I promise to try. I know you're desperate – and she knows that now. Count yourself lucky you're not in jail! You deserve to be!"

Wendy climbed back on to the top of her large boulder. She felt dizzy and sick. She was crying and the blood was still running down her face and was getting smeared all over her breasts. Even her fingers were sticky with blood.

"I shall never forgive you for that," she said. "You had no right to do what you did. If I ever get a chance, I'll kill you too, you... you..." (No insult seemed equal to her feelings) "... you fucking shark!"

Malcolm shook his head, picked up the pistol, checked to see if the safety catch was on and then tucked it into the waistband of his trousers. He was conscious of its weight and its awkward shape. He pulled his blue and white striped shirt over it.

He threw the blue, rolled-up towel to Wendy.

"I shall ignore your last remarks," he said. "They were made in the heat of the moment. I shall still do my best for you – despite everything."

Wendy spat in his face.

Malcolm walked up the steep path from the beach and wiped the sweat and the spittle off his face.

'What a way to spend an afternoon!' he said to himself. 'Chasing a bloody woman with a gun!' He shook his head sadly. Such a beautiful island! Such a perfect place for a picnic! And that stupid bitch had to go and spoil it! Someone had once said that money was the root of all evil. He couldn't be more right! It was amazing to what depths people could sink when their backs were up against a wall.

He struggled up the hill towards the belt of pine trees – and then stopped. There was someone standing in the shade beneath the trees watching him.

Mr Latimer.

Another of them!

He walked on – as if to pass.

"I hope you're not going to ignore me, Mr Clark?" The voice was low and menacing. "You remember what I said to you last night?"

Malcolm stopped and looked at him.

"I remember precisely every word you said."

His voice could not have been colder.

"Well, you would perhaps be expecting to see me?"

Malcolm sighed. "Quite frankly, no! I've had quite enough for one afternoon..."

"Beating up a defenceless woman? I saw you ramming her head against the stone. Pity I wasn't nearer. I might have come to her aid." He licked his lips. "But I had other fish to fry."

He produced a neatly typed document from his shirt pocket and handed it over to Malcolm.

Malcolm unfolded it and read:

I promise to pay Mr Peter and Mrs Marion Latimer of 25 Baron's Lane, Dartford, the sum of £50,000 – that being the sum owed to them by me during recent legal transactions on their behalf. I promise to pay them in full – in cash – within a calendar month of the date of this document being signed, the money to be paid into their account at the Dartford branch of Barclay's Bank at a date and at a time to be mutually agreed. I have made this declaration of my own free will – and not under any compulsion – so that the above-named couple will receive in full and final settlement the £50,000 I owe them.

Witnessed by: ....

Signed: ....

Date:................................

141

Malcolm looked up.

"No deal!" he said contemptuously. "You won't get anywhere with that!"

"Is that your last word, Mr Clark?"

"It is."

Mr Latimer drew out his sharp, evil-looking knife.

"You will remember, Mr Clark, what I said about castrating pigs? I put you in the same category! This is a quiet and secluded place. I don't think anyone is going to disturb us. The alternatives are rather stark. Either you sign – or else!"

Malcolm was no coward – even when the going was tough. He tore up the piece of paper into small bits and dropped them on the ground. He looked Mr Latimer in the eye.

"I'm sorry it had to come to this," he said.

He pulled out Wendy's heavy pistol from the waistband of his trousers. He flicked off the safety catch and pointed it directly at Mr Latimer's groin.

"One more step and you're the one who'll have a nasty pain in the testes! Drop that knife on the ground and walk slowly backwards! Drop it!"

Mr Latimer had no option but to obey.

He dropped the knife on the grass and walked a few paces backwards. Malcolm bent down to pick up the knife but his eyes never left Mr Latimer's face and his pistol continued to point in one direction. Malcolm looked at his victim coldly.

"You'll never get a penny out of me," he said. "Never! I'm sick and fed up of people like you! Count yourself lucky I haven't shot you! Now bugger off!"

20: *Vitae Summa Brevis*

Sarah, Neville and Jo spent a very hot, unpleasant and frustrating hour on board the *Jolly Rioja*. Brendan had not been pleased to see them because he had only just got all the food cleared away and was looking forward to spending a couple of hours with Angie and Mandy in his private cabin.

When he was told that someone had tried to shoot Sarah – and was shown the remains of the wine-glass, he became a little more sympathetic. But he refused to let them occupy the downstairs bar. It might cramp his style. He insisted instead that they should sit on the gun-deck, with their backs to the panelling. That way, Sarah could not be seen or targetted by anyone ashore.

So they had sat on the gun-deck for almost an hour. Even though there were canvas awnings to protect them from the sun, the heat was quite oppressive. Neville had opened the second bottle of champagne and they had finished off the rest of their food. They waited patiently for Malcolm to re-appear and say that the coast was clear.

In the meantime, they could not avoid hearing the bumps and squeals from the cabin below where Brendan was enjoying himself with the two couriers. Really, it was quite disgusting! How could he keep it up for so long? And why did they both have to scream so wildly every time he touched them?

Eventually, Joanne could stand it no longer.

"I'm going to go and look for him," she said. "He might have been injured. Someone might have attacked him. He may be needing help. Remember what happened at the barbecue! I'll go and see if I can find him. Nobody'll shoot me. It's you they're after!"

"Thank you very much!" said Sarah.

Jo was glad to leave the ship and be free once more to move about. She wasn't entirely clear as to where she should look for Malcolm. There was no one on the headland and most of the passengers seemed to have settled themselves on the northern corner of the island with the view across the water towards Cala San Vicente – but she couldn't see Malcolm there.

She wandered slowly down the western coast, looking into each small inlet. In the course of her travels, she inevitably came upon the secluded beach where Debbie and Richard were disporting themselves in what Joanne considered to be a rather perverted fashion. She watched them secretly for

143

several minutes and found her own libido beginning to rise and her juices beginning to flow. She turned away rapidly and resumed her search.

After another ten minutes, she decided that her efforts were quite pointless. Malcolm would probably by now be back at the ship, wondering where she had got to. They might even send out a search-party looking for her. So Jo turned back sadly towards the *Jolly Rioja* – sad because she too would have liked to spend the afternoon making love to someone on the sand – and sad because, whichever way you looked at it, it had been a wasted afternoon for all of them.

When she got back to the ship, she discovered that Brendan had satisfactorily accomplished his 'droits de capitaine' and was now once more in command of his vessel. Mandy and Angie had gone off to sunbathe and there was no sign of Sarah or Neville.

"What's happened to my sister and her fiancé?"

"Well, she hasn't been shot. No blood or anything!"

Brendan was bare-chested with an enormous gold crucifix hanging on a chain round his neck. He was wearing only a small pair of white swimming briefs which showed his manhood to full advantage and left very little to the imagination. He looked surprised at her question.

"Where d'you think, darling? Just gone down the beach to find a quiet corner for a bit of nookie – like every sensible person."

Joanne reckoned there was no point in asking Brendan whether Malcolm had come back to the ship because he wouldn't know who Malcolm was. Everyone was away enjoying themselves and she was on her own. She began to cry.

Fortunately, Brendan understood the needs of women in distress. Indeed, in his entire professional life, he had never ceased to capitalize upon it. He looked at Jo and saw that she was still a very attractive woman with a well-rounded and comfortable figure, good legs and all the rest.

Without the slightest hesitation, he said: "Now look, darling, there's no point you going off and looking for them.

I'll be ordering them all back to the ship in about fifteen minutes time. Why don't you come downstairs to the bar and join me in a very special glass of Captain's hooch?"

Joanne did not refuse.

About twenty minutes after Joanne had crept away from the sordid goings-on in the sand, Richard and Debbie decided that it was probably about time to make their way back to the boat. Passion had been slaked and there was no need to rush. Debbie suggested that they should take a leisurely walk round the southern end of the island which would take about forty-five minutes.

"Brendan always gives people plenty of warning," she said. "He fires his cannon three times and that's the signal for everyone to return. He casts off about twenty minutes later when everyone's on board."

"I wouldn't like to be left behind," said Richard. "It's a long way to swim."

They wandered hand-in-hand along the western coast of the island, keeping close to the trees and looking down into each of the bays where couples were either sunbathing or hunting for crabs.

"Litter-louts!" said Raynes, noticing a scattering of little pieces of paper on the grass.

Out of a sense of public duty, he went over and picked them up. One torn piece caught his eye: '... Lane, Dartford, the sum of £50,000...' Raynes collected the scraps of paper more carefully and put them into his back pocket.

Debbie had wandered ahead.

"Look!" she said. "Isn't that the woman who was in the Café Sol? I recognize her hair."

Raynes looked down at the small beach where a woman was spread-eagled on a large, flat-topped boulder, wearing a navy-blue bikini bottom and a large pair of sunglasses. She had a blue towel rolled up at her side.

"It could be," said Raynes. "I'm not exactly familiar with the rest of her anatomy! But it could be."

The next person they saw left no room for doubt. The

Brown Baby was stark naked, standing knee-deep in shallow water, washing her green and white striped shirt.

"And about time too!" said Raynes. "She's been wearing the same clothes all week."

"Hasn't got much of a figure," said Debbie sadly. "Her hips are far too wide and her thighs are much too thick."

"Good pair of breasts though!" said Raynes crudely. "Plenty to hang on to!"

Debbie shook her head in despair.

"You men!" she said. "You have absolutely no taste! All you think about is breasts! And yet, without a shadow of a doubt, they are the most imperfect parts of a woman's body! They're either too big or too small; they droop; they sag; they flop about..."

"Present company excepted?"

"Present company most certainly excepted!"

But for how long?

Debbie went silent as she contemplated the ravages of middle age which even the most beautiful of women could not escape.

"Ah, she's seen us," said Raynes. "She's waving to us. Wave back."

They waved cheerfully to the Brown Baby and walked on.

At the very end of the island – the most southerly point, they could see the student from Arkansas, sitting on a small rock, staring out to sea, his book still in his hand.

"A psychiatric case!" said Debbie shortly. "Sent over to Europe to sort himself out!"

"Probably a theological student," said Raynes, "trying to come to terms with the hereafter." He paused. "Not that there is a hereafter to come to terms with – but if it makes them happy..."

Raynes had always been a confirmed atheist. When you had seen as many bodies as he had – bodies burnt, half-eaten, savagely mutilated, chopped into little pieces – you tended to lose all faith in a loving God. Raynes found it impossible to look beyond the inherent cruelty of human nature – let alone to believe in anything better.

"Don't be too sure!" said Debbie reprovingly. "Things are not always what they seem. I had a grandmother who had second sight..."

But what Debbie's grandmother had seen – or heard remained a mystery for at that moment, there were three clear bursts of gunfire from the *Jolly Rioja*.

Instinctively, everyone began to pack their things together and make their way back to the boat.

The student from Arkansas sighed deeply, closed his book and delicately picked his way across the stepping stones, back to *terra firma*.

The Brown Baby had finished her washing but only her shorts were dry. Her T-shirt was still horribly wet and she had no doubt that the wet material would cling hideously to her nipples. But it would have to be worn. She squeezed it out one final time and pulled it over her head. She reckoned that being close to her small, warm body, it would soon be dry.

Mr Latimer took a long time to get back to the stone bench where he had left his wife. He had gone for a long walk round the northern end of the island to cool his anger and come to terms with his abject humiliation. Shortly before the *Jolly Rioja* fired her guns, he returned to his wife.

"Did he sign the paper?" she asked.

Mr Latimer scowled angrily.

"No, he didn't. He tore it up into little bits and threw them down on the ground."

Mrs Latimer looked surprised.

"I hope you didn't take it lying down? Did you threaten him with your knife? You said you would."

Mr Latimer looked glum.

"He pulled a gun on me."

"A gun?"

"An old service revolver. Pretty lethal, it looked." He sighed. "I wasn't going to quarrel with a gun. He threatened to blast my private parts into kingdom come! You're lucky to get me back in one piece," he added sourly.

"So we're no nearer getting our money back?"

Mr Latimer picked up the travelling rug and folded it into four. He packed the cushions back in the bag. It was a long time before he replied.

"You approach him next time," he said. "He probably wouldn't shoot a woman!"

But even as he said it, he remembered what he had seen Malcolm doing to the young woman on the beach; smashing her head against the rock and twisting her arm till she screamed. Clearly Mr Clark was no respecter of persons – not even of women.

Wendy Bridges heard the three blasts of the cannon. She knew what it meant. Failure! She had set out that morning with such high hopes – intending to settle her long-standing grievance against that woman who had pinched her husband and been the architect of her ruin. She had fired two shots and missed both times. Now she had even lost her gun!

Her lawyer – yes, her own lawyer – had bashed her head against solid rock – twice! She was bruised, cut, but no longer bleeding. Her arms were sore; her bruise was swollen and throbbing; and she also had more than a touch of sunburn. It had turned out to be a sodding-awful day. She had achieved nothing.

Now she would have to face them once more on the boat. Sarah might attack her or Neville report her to the police. Even though Malcolm had promised to continue pleading her cause, she could hardly expect him to receive a fair hearing. Sarah wouldn't care a damn what happened to Timothy or Victoria. They were no concern of hers.

Wendy put on her trouser-suit and her black bandana. She brushed her hair so that it would cover the bruise – and she put on her large sunglasses. She rolled up her towels and tucked them under her arm. Perhaps no one would notice.

When Wendy got back to the boat, Sarah and Neville were nowhere to be seen. She cast her eyes over the milling crowd of passengers to double-check – but she could only see Joanne. She was looking extremely worried and was walking up and down the concrete pier anxiously waiting for the rest of her party to return.

Just as the last few people crossed the gangway, Sarah and Neville appeared from behind the headland. Neville's arm was around Sarah's shoulder and both of them looked blissfully happy and relaxed.

"Where have you been?" asked Joanne angrily.

"Making up for lost time," said Neville. "No harm in that. We haven't kept anyone waiting."

"But where's Malcolm?"

"I don't know," said Sarah. "I thought you'd gone off looking for him."

"Well, I didn't find him. I came back to the boat and then found that you had gone."

"Sorry about that," said Neville. "We decided that we couldn't bear being cooped up any longer. Guns or no guns, we decided to chance it. And we seem to have survived."

Sarah yawned.

"I'm terribly thirsty. D'you think Brendan'll give us a gin?"

"But where's Malcolm?" repeated Jo.

"I don't know. Isn't he on the boat?"

Joanne felt she was getting no help from her sister. So she walked back down the pier and spoke to Angie who was standing beside the gangway, ticking off people's names as they came on board.

"One of our party's missing," she said. "A Mr Malcolm Clark."

Angie looked at her list.

"57... 58... 59... Yes, there's one more to come."

"Well, we don't know where he is."

"Brendan'll give him another five minutes. If he isn't here by then, he'll have to swim."

Joanne went over and sat behind Neville and Sarah.

"If he doesn't come in five minutes, they're going to leave without him."

"Serves him right," said Neville. "He'll have to become another Robinson Crusoe. Perhaps he'll find the cave?"

149

"Our cave," said Sarah dreamily.

Joanne choked back her anger at their lack of concern.

"But he could have fallen and broken his leg. He may have fractured his skull. We can't just leave him. Anything could have happened."

She got up and went over to Brendan and explained her anxieties. Brendan was feeling quite tender towards Joanne. "Don't worry, darling, we'll do our best to find him." He lifted his loudhailer. "Has anyone seen Mr Malcolm Clark?"

No one replied.

Those who had seen him were saying nothing.

"What was he wearing?" Brendan asked Jo.

"A blue and white striped shirt and dark-blue trousers."

Brendan lifted his loudhailer again.

"A blue and white striped shirt and dark-blue pants. Anyone seen him?"

One or two of the passengers said they had seen someone dressed like him – but that was over two hours ago. Otherwise, there was nothing to report. People began to speculate where Malcolm might be.

Wendy smiled quietly to herself.

Mr Latimer turned to his wife:

"Probably drowned himself!"

"Don't be so pessimistic!" said Mrs Latimer. "If he goes – so does our money!"

"So it does," said Mr Latimer more soberly.

Raynes watched the problem developing.

"Perhaps we should all go and look for him?"

"You're not going anywhere," said Debbie. "You're staying here with me."

But sure enough, five minutes later, Brendan was asking for volunteers to go back over the island to look for Malcolm. He said he would give them fifteen minutes. Each volunteer was to go to a different part of the island, to call out his name – and then listen carefully for any reply or cry. Then they would scour the nearest rocks and beaches to see if he was lying injured on the ground. After fifteen minutes, he would fire two more rounds of his gun. They should all return to the boat immediately, whether or not they had found him. If they had discovered his body, a proper stretcher party would be organized to bring him back.

Nine young men and three girls volunteered.

Brendan sent the young men to the northern and southern extremities of the island; the girls were sent to comb through the pine trees. They all set off in great haste.

Joanne sat in her seat feeling very numb.

What on earth could have happened to him?

In a few minutes, she could be nursing an invalid. He might even be brain-damaged. She would have to go with him to hospital. Where was the nearest hospital to Pollensa? How much would it cost? Would Sarah lend her the extra money? All these thoughts – and many others – swirled through her mind as the minutes ticked by.

After nearly twenty minutes, Brendan fired his two guns. And slowly the searchers returned. No one had seen Malcolm. There was no sign of any injured body on any of the beaches they had visited. No one was lying under the trees. The volunteers had drawn a complete blank.

By now, the sun was beginning to set.

The island was looking darker and less welcoming.

The pine trees seemed sinister and vaguely menacing.

Joanne burst into tears.

Brendan put an arm around her shoulders.

"Darling, I'm afraid we'll have to go. We can't wait any longer. I'm afraid it's a job for the police."

He gave a nod to his helmsman who pulled a lever and started the engine. With a slow putter of its diesel engine, the *Jolly Rioja* – now much less jolly – pulled away from the pier, turned out to sea and headed home to Pollensa.

21: *Pallida Mors*

It took the police forty-eight hours to find the body.

Although the island had been searched twice, it was a team of dogs which eventually found Malcolm's body. It had been hidden under a small heap of stones in a narrow gully at the southern end of the island. It was most probably the smell of blood that led the dogs to the actual spot, for as the stones were cleared away, it became obvious that Malcolm's throat had been slashed open and blood had poured down his body and drenched his clothes. But, caked as they were with dried blood, they were still recognizable as those of the British tourist reported missing. The dark-blue trousers, the blue and white striped shirt and the blue ankle socks were exactly as described. And just to dispel any lingering doubt, his passport and his wallet were found intact in his back pocket.

Robbery did not seem to be the motive for the murder. Malcolm's wallet was still stuffed with notes and none of his personal jewellery had been removed. It was a straightforward case of murder by person or persons unknown.

It did not take the police long to discover that the actual assault had taken place beside a small clump of pine trees. There was quite a lot of dried blood on the ground at that point and a trail of blood led to the narrow gully where Malcolm's body was found.

Copious photographs were taken of the murder scene. Samples of blood and soil were removed for examination at the laboratory. All the blood-spattered stones which had covered the body were placed in polythene bags and taken away for analysis. The body itself was covered with a grey blanket, strapped to a stretcher and carried off the island for an immediate autopsy. It was then taken to a mortuary in Palma where a police surgeon examined the injuries in more detail.

No stone was left unturned on the murder site – which was perhaps as well, for a pistol was discovered with the safety catch off and three bullets still in the chamber. The pistol was an old one – dating back to the Spanish Civil War, but it had recently been cleaned and re-bored. There were a few traces of Malcolm's blood on the weapon when it was examined under a microscope, but any fingerprints had been wiped away before the pistol had been concealed – once again under a few loose stones.

Of the knife which had cut so deeply into Malcolm's throat, there was no sign. A sizeable area of ground around the murder site was minutely examined by a large number of policemen – but nothing else was found. In the local branch of the Guardia Civil in Pollensa, the slim brown file on Malcolm Clark was changed from a routine 'missing person' inquiry into a full-scale murder investigation.

But it was a further twenty-four hours before anyone was informed that the body had been found. Then, early on Sunday morning, two English-speaking Spanish detectives called at the *Hotel Aphrodite*, knocked at the door of Room 313 and asked Joanne to accompany them to the local police station.

The Inspector received a panic call from Mrs Hickson.

"They've found Malcolm's body!"

"Where?"

"On some island."

"What happened to him?"

"He's been murdered. Jo's been taken down to Palma to identify the body. Sarah and Neville have gone with her."

"When did they discover the body?"

"I don't know. They didn't say. They just asked Jo to go to the local police station. They asked her a lot of questions and made her sign a statement. She was there for well over two hours."

"Good heavens!"

"And it wasn't till she'd been there over an hour that they told her Malcolm was dead. Then, of course, she broke down."

"Did they say how he'd died?"

"No. I think they were expecting her to tell them. But she hadn't seen him since Thursday when he walked off and left them. She reported his disappearance the moment she got off the boat. But they didn't seem to think there was much to it. 'A lovers' tiff', one of them said."

Raynes shook his head.

"But now they're taking it a bit more seriously?"

"Yes. They've obviously been to the island and searched it from end to end. What worries me is that they seem to suspect Jo. I mean, they wouldn't have been asking her all these questions and getting her to make a statement – not unless they suspected her, would they?"

Raynes tried to sound reassuring.

"It's probably no more than routine inquiry. When someone goes missing in England, we always ask a lot of questions. Many of them are quite pointless – especially when the person turns up a few days later. But once you've got a body, then the immediate friends and relatives are naturally prime suspects. The local police know nothing about them, so they've got to ask a lot of questions – just to get the picture..."

"So you don't think...?"

Raynes shook his head again.

"No. It'll probably be very unpleasant for all of them. But there's no other way the police can begin their investigations. They have to start with the people most closely connected."

Mrs Hickson's voice quavered anxiously.

"I don't think Joanne will be able to cope. She's never seen a dead body before. At least, not that I know of. When her father died, she refused to see him. Sarah's made of sterner stuff, of course. But it worries me – them being on their own in a foreign country. They don't speak the language. They might be kept in custody. D'you think I should approach the British Consul, if there is such a person? Or do you think I should phone up Sarah's office and get them to send someone out?"

"I wouldn't panic just yet," said Raynes calmly. "Wait and see what happens. If it's just a question of identifying the body, they won't keep them all that long. They'll probably take a statement from each of them and then let them go. But if they're not back by six o'clock, it might pay to phone Palma and find out what's happening." He looked at his watch. "What time did they go?"

"About half-past eleven. Sarah phoned me before they left. I do hope they'll be all right." She laughed sadly. "I'm afraid I'm a natural worrier."

"Well," said Raynes, "at least nothing has happened to Sarah. That's what you were worried about. Both she and Joanne are still alive. And so is Neville. If it had to happen to anyone, I'd rather it was Malcolm!"

"He certainly wasn't very popular."

"He was a born troublemaker."

Mrs Hickson still sounded agitated.

"I'm afraid my money's running out. I haven't any more loose change."

A rare burst of humanity came over Raynes.

"Would you like to come over to the hotel and wait for them here? Then you could use our telephone. It'd be easier than using a pay-phone. You'd be most welcome."

"That's ever so kind..."

The voice was suddenly cut off.

Raynes looked across at Debbie, lying on the bed, her legs crossed, reading the latest copy of the *Hello!* magazine.

"She got cut off."

"So I gather."

"Would you mind her coming across? So that she can wait for her family? They've gone down to Palma to identify the body."

"So he was dead?"

"Yes. Someone bumped him off."

"I'm not surprised. I felt like doing it myself."

"Why's that?"

Debbie continued to read the cookery page, trying to discover what she could do with a kumquat. At last she said:

"He tried to proposition me outside the ladies' on Sunday night. Offered me 40,000 pesetas for a quickie!"

Debbie looked up to see how Richard would react to this unexpected revelation. He looked quite startled. He was clearly unaware of the deep currents swirling around him. She smiled reassuringly: "You don't have to worry. I turned him down."

"I should think so!" said Raynes. "You're here with me. Surely you have some loyalty?"

Debbie lowered her eyes defensively.

155

"You haven't bought me! If I'd chosen to accept his offer, I could have done. I'm a free agent – and always will be. Anyway, I chose not to – because I thought he was a nasty piece of work."

"Well," said Raynes bitterly, "you've had it now. Not unless you're into necrophilia!"

Debbie put down her magazine and looked at her holiday companion. "Speaking of necrophilia..." she said. "It's nearly three o'clock. If that old bat's coming over here, we'd better get on with it."

Raynes took off his shirt and looked at himself in the mirror. There was a rather nice tan in the making. He appeared very healthy and virile. Quite a fine figure of a man.

"I think you exaggerate," he said.

Debbie smiled.

"Prove me wrong."

About an hour later, reception phoned to say that Mrs Hickson had arrived. Raynes went down to meet her and brought her up to their room. Debbie, now clad soberly in a silky beige-coloured dress and sporting the minimum of jewellery, soon put her at her ease, settling her into the most comfortable chair by the window and getting her something invigorating to drink.

"A gin and tonic?"

"I'd prefer a brandy."

Raynes looked at Mrs Hickson.

She was pale and nervous.

"Well," he said, "they're not back yet. Have you heard any more?"

"Not a thing."

Raynes picked up the local telephone directory.

"I think we'll start with the British Consul."

He looked up the number and dialled.

There seemed to be a long delay before the call was answered. Raynes was politeness itself:

"Good afternoon," he said. "I'm Detective-Inspector Raynes of the Grasshallows force – on holiday in Majorca.

I'm staying at the *Hotel Aphrodite* in Puerto de Pollensa and phoning on behalf of a Mrs Hickson, whose two daughters are at present in Palma helping the police identify a body..." He paused. "Yes. Malcolm Clark..."

He turned to Mrs Hickson.

"They seem to know about it. They've been in touch."

He listened to the voice at the other end of the phone. The message seemed to be reassuring – but not entirely satisfactory. The tone of Raynes' voice became correspondingly harder.

"But they've been there for quite some time. One of the daughters has been in police custody since about 7.00am. She's made a statement... Yes, long ago... It's about five hours since they went down to Palma to identify the body... yes, five hours. We were expecting to hear something before now..." He frowned. "Yes, I know these things take time. But their mother's getting anxious... Naturally..."

Raynes sighed.

How he hated officialdom!

He waited till the consular spokesman had said his piece. Then he said: "Well, I think they should have been able to phone us before now. To let us know what's happening... They haven't been charged with anything, have they?... No, I thought not. They're probably sitting round doing nothing. They've not been detained?... Not that you know of. Could you possibly find out and let us know? Yes, as soon as possible. And phone us back immediately." He gave them the hotel's phone number. "Room 301... Thank you. That would be most helpful..."

He put down the phone.

He looked at Debbie and Mrs Hickson.

"There's no reason why they shouldn't be in touch. Just the usual bureaucracy. Probably language difficulties as well. He's going to find out what's happening and push them along."

He smiled grimly.

"But we have quicker ways than that!"

He picked up the phone again and dialled through to police

headquarters in Grasshallows. "I know it's Sunday," he said, "but they'll be able to do something." He waited for the phone to be picked up. "Hello, Raynes here. Is Detective-Constable Carlisle in sight?" He smiled more happily. "Well, could you get him to phone me back immediately? It's a Spanish number." He repeated it twice. "Thank you."

Within two minutes, Carlisle was on the phone. The Inspector told him immediately what he had to do. Get in touch with Interpol and find out precisely what was happening. The more information the better. Contact the Spanish Embassy in London and put in an immediate complaint about British nationals being detained. Ask Scotland Yard to find someone who spoke Spanish to phone Palma's police headquarters and request a full report about Malcolm Clark. The results to be faxed back to the *Hotel Aphrodite* within the hour.

Raynes grinned – and put the phone down.

"That'll put a bomb under them."

"I do hope so," said Mrs Hickson, who seemed much happier now that Raynes had taken charge.

Debbie poured a second round of drinks whilst the conversation turned to other things. Mrs Hickson told them more about Sarah and Joanne – their childhood, their marriages, their affairs. Raynes told them about some of his more difficult cases and how they had been solved. Debbie spoke of holidays she had enjoyed, places she had seen – whilst they waited for the replies to come in.

It took almost two hours before the first fax arrived. Later, there were several phone calls – including one from the British Consul himself. Detective-Constable Carlisle called to report progress; said he hoped the Inspector would pay for all the calls made on his behalf; and wished him a happy holiday.

"Sarcastic bastard!" said Raynes.

But he had to admit he was enjoying himself. This was far more fun than sunbathing.

Eventually, shortly after seven, they got a call from Sarah herself to say they were about to leave Palma. A police car would be bringing them back but they did not expect to arrive in Pollensa much before 9.00pm. Raynes promised to let the hotel know that they would be dining late.

However, since both he and Debbie were starving – and Mrs Hickson was clearly needing something to soak up the five large brandies she had drunk, they decided to have their meal right away – and not to wait for the others. Mrs Hickson accepted Raynes' invitation to join them and ate a surprisingly hearty meal.

By the time Sarah, Neville and Jo arrived in the dining room, they had reached the coffee stage. Mrs Hickson immediately rushed forward to hug Joanne who burst into floods of tears.

"Was it awful?" asked Raynes.

"Pretty bad," said Neville. "It would have helped if we could've spoken the language. When you don't know what they're saying, you feel quite lost. And the interpreter wasn't very sympathetic." He sighed. "Most of the time, we've just been sitting around. Just waiting. No telephones in sight. I thought we were going to be there all night."

Mrs Hickson disentangled herself from her daughter's arms.

"You probably would have been!" she said brusquely. "If it hadn't been for the Inspector phoning all his friends, trying to find out what was happening. He even phoned the Spanish Embassy in London and registered a formal complaint." She looked at the dining-room table with its empty coffee cups. "They've also treated me to a lovely meal."

"How very kind," said Sarah.

Her reply was coldly automatic.

Raynes looked at her – and then at Neville.

"Would it help if I went through things with each of you tomorrow morning – so that we might get a fuller picture of all that's been happening?"

"I think we've all had quite enough," said Sarah.

"I don't think I could've endured another hour," said Joanne.

Neville said nothing.

Mrs Hickson asserted her maternal authority.

159

"I think you should accept the Inspector's kind offer. He knows all about murder – and that sort of thing. He'd be able to advise you – in case the police came round again."

"God forbid!" said Joanne.

Neville decided to intervene.

"I think your mum's right," he said. "We need all the help we can get. Not tonight, when we're all fagged out. Tomorrow, things'll look a lot better." He looked at Raynes. "Thank you. We'll accept your kind offer." He looked at the Spanish waiter hovering expectantly in the background, holding three large menus. "Right now, we need something to eat..."

"... And drink!" said Joanne.

"Champagne!" said Sarah. "The best – and plenty of it!"

Richard and Debbie slipped quietly away, leaving Mrs Hickson with her family.

"You deliberately engineered that!" she said accusingly. "You were determined to get involved. Right from the beginning, you've been sniffing around for clues!"

"Busman's holiday!" said Raynes philosophically. "You can't break the habits of a lifetime."

Debbie looked at him sadly.

To herself she said: 'Two can play at that game. You'll see!'

22: *Quis fallere possit amantem?*

Raynes tried to sound relaxed and not at all like a policeman. But the questions he asked were no different to what he would have asked had he been conducting the interview in Grasshallows. The only difference was that he was in the cocktail bar of the *Hotel Aphrodite* where he had just bought Joanne a drink – a large Cinzano Bianco with plenty of ice.

"Tell me," he said. "What exactly happened on Thursday afternoon?"

"We were having our picnic lunch..." she began – then halted. "Actually, it began some time before that... Malcolm

160

was sure he recognized someone on the boat... Someone he thought might be following us... Wendy Bridges. Do you know her?"

Raynes shook his head.

If the truth be known, he knew quite a bit about Wendy Bridges but he wasn't going to admit that to Joanne. He knew that she was the woman he had seen talking to Malcolm in the Café Sol on Tuesday afternoon. According to Mrs Hickson, she was Sarah's husband's first wife. She lived in Bexley, South London, and she had been wearing a beige-coloured dress. According to a phone call from Detective-Constable Carlisle, she was a professional journalist, had two grown-up children, lived in a large, run-down house and drove a rather battered Jaguar which had seen better days. She had no police record for anything other than speeding for which she had been booked five times. Although he did not know Wendy personally, Raynes had quite a clear picture of the lady involved.

"Well, it seems that Malcolm had been working on her behalf. She was wanting Sarah to provide more money to help her children and she'd asked Malcolm to act as go-between. He never said anything to Sarah about it till Thursday afternoon. He must have realized what a delicate matter it was. After the divorce, Sarah vowed that Wendy would never get another penny out of her. She'd screwed Charles for every pound he had and then she did her best to prevent him seeing his children... so if Malcolm had said anything, Sarah's reaction would have been pretty chilly. In fact, she'd have sent him away with a flea in his ear!"

"Why did Wendy come out here?"

"Presumably to push Malcolm along. They've been seeing each other in some café along the prom."

Raynes tried to look as if this was all news to him.

"Well, what happened on Thursday was that he suddenly realized she was on our boat. She was wearing those large sunglasses so he didn't recognize her at first. But once he knew who it was, it worried him."

"Why?"

161

"Because she had a revolver."

"Really! And how did he know that?"

"She must have told him. But he never thought she'd use it."

"Did she?"

"Well, that's what really started it. We were having our picnic lunch on the cliff top. Sarah didn't like the food on the pirate ship. She thought it was bound to be crawling with bacteria. So we'd brought our own food from the hotel. Well, we were just on to the cheese course when a bullet hit Sarah's wine-glass. Just blew it to pieces! Some of the champagne and bits of the glass hit me. I've got one or two little scratches." She pulled back the collar of her blouse to show the Inspector.

He looked at them closely.

She was wearing a particularly seductive perfume.

"Sarah didn't know what was happening and neither did I. But Malcolm put two and two together. He realized that Wendy had fired her gun at Sarah, trying to kill her. He pulled Sarah down – she got pâté all over her nose..." Jo laughed. "But it's as well he did, because there was a second shot that went just over our heads."

This was all news to Raynes.

"Malcolm told us what he thought had happened. Then he said he'd go and find Wendy and get the gun off her. He didn't think she'd shoot him. I thought it was awfully brave of him. He got to his feet and searched all round the cliff. He found where she'd been but there was no sign of her, so he escorted us to the pirate ship where he thought we'd be safe."

"And what did he do then?"

"He set off to find Wendy. That was the last time I saw him."

There were tears in her eyes.

She obviously cared a lot about Malcolm.

Raynes took a couple of sips of his San Miguel.

"Did you tell the Spanish police all this?"

She nodded.

"But I don't know if they believed me. They wrote it all

down but they kept making me repeat it – as if they thought I was making it up."

Raynes nodded.

That seemed reasonable.

"So did you stay on the boat for the rest of the afternoon?"

"No, I couldn't stand the heat. It was terrible. We sat there for about an hour but then I began to get worried about Malcolm... you see, he'd been in trouble earlier in the week. He got attacked at the barbecue... some girl... and I was worried he might have been attacked again." Jo looked worried. She was clearly re-living the emotions she had experienced on the Thursday afternoon. "So I left the others on the boat and I went to look for him. I saw lots of people..."

She hesitated.

"Go on."

"I saw you and your wife..."

Joanne blushed – but Raynes was not embarrassed.

"Trying for our first baby!" he smiled.

Joanne knew there was no way the Inspector and his wife were going to conceive a child with what she had seen them doing – but she let that pass.

"I saw lots of people – but not Malcolm. I thought that perhaps he had gone back to the boat. He might now be looking for me. Going back to the boat seemed the most sensible thing to do. But when I got back, even Sarah and Neville had gone! So I didn't know what to do."

"What did you do?"

Joanne was not going to say anything about her private encounter with Brendan. There was no need to. It had nothing to do with Malcolm.

She shrugged her shoulders.

"I just waited. Brendan was about to fire his gun to tell everyone to make their way back to the boat. So I went out on to the pier, hoping that everyone would come back safely. I hoped that Sarah and Neville would come back with Malcolm. But they didn't. He was dead!"

She burst into tears.

Raynes let her cry.

He drank some more of his San Miguel and thought about what she had told him. The story of Wendy shooting at Sarah added a completely new dimension to the story. But he had noticed that Joanne had hesitated towards the end of her account. There was something missing. But was it important?

When she had recovered a little, he asked: "D'you think Malcolm got the gun off Wendy?"

She shrugged her shoulders again.

"I don't know. The police said they'd found a gun near his body, but it wasn't the murder weapon. It might not have been the same gun. They said three bullets had been fired – but she only fired two at us. Anyway, it wasn't a gun that killed him. It was a knife. Slashed ear to ear. It was awful!"

She cried some more.

Raynes moved round the table and put his arm around her shoulders. After all, he was supposed to be a friend – not a servant of the Law.

She cried for a while, then pulled herself together.

"It was horrible seeing him like that. All grey. So dead. And that gash. All his clothes covered in blood."

"Do you have a knife?"

"No."

"Did Malcolm have a knife?"

"Not that I saw."

"So, if the gun was Wendy's, Malcolm must have taken it off her before he was killed." Raynes speculated aloud. "Or if she was there, she must have buried it."

"But why should she kill him?" asked Joanne, her eyes still full of tears. "She had far more to gain from him being alive and fighting her cause. He'd got into Sarah's circle. He obviously meant to approach her about the children. But he just hadn't found an opportunity to bring the matter up." She sighed. "It's been a very difficult week. Neville was angry with Malcolm. I was angry with him too."

"Why was that?"

Raynes had a vague idea of what had been happening from Sarah's mother, but he wanted to hear it from Joanne herself.

"Well, it's all a bit sordid. Malcolm had an eye for the girls. I knew that. But, on Tuesday night, at the barbecue, he went off with some young woman and tried to have it off with her. She led him up the garden path and kicked him where it hurts most. She hurt him quite badly. He was in pain for several hours. She also went off with all his clothes. But, strangely enough, instead of hiding them, she brought them back to us. So we went off to find him."

She paused.

"Could I have another Cinzano?"

"Certainly."

Raynes ordered a fresh round for both of them.

"We went off to find him and there he was – in the farmyard – stark naked except for his socks and shoes. He couldn't really stand up straight. He really thought she'd done him some long-term damage – but she hadn't. I felt extremely hurt. We're not married or anything, so there's no reason why he should be faithful. But since I'd brought him out here, I felt he should stick to me. I didn't like the idea of him going off with someone else. In the event, of course, he didn't have her – but the intention was there."

Joanne drank deeply of her second Cinzano.

"I walked off and left him. I know it was the wrong thing to do, but I was so angry. Neville also turned his back on him. He was disgusted. But Sarah took pity on him. She helped him get his clothes back on – and then, she says, he broke down and cried. And she kissed him!"

"Oh, dear."

"Yes. That didn't help. Because at that moment, Neville and I came back to look for them – and there they were smooching all over each other. It was bad enough him going after that little bitch, but we didn't expect him to be kissing and cuddling my sister as well. That really broke things up."

She laughed sadly.

"How petty it all seems now! Neville wouldn't speak to Sarah. I wasn't speaking to Malcolm. I wanted to go home. And then Sarah got angry with me. She said I'd brought the bloody man out to Majorca. It was my fault. She was quite nasty. Eventually, she issued an ultimatum to all of us. Either we all made up – or we went home."

"So you made up?"

"With difficulty."

"And the next day he was killed?"

"But it wasn't anything to do with us. We were all quite friendly on Thursday."

From what Raynes had seen of the family on the boat, he was inclined to regard Joanne's opinion as somewhat over-optimistic. From what he had seen, they had still been remarkably subdued.

"And you say that you didn't kill him?"

"Of course not!" Joanne was quite indignant. "Why should you even think that?"

Raynes put a gentle hand on her arm.

"I'm just thinking what the Spanish police must be thinking. Here you are in Majorca. You must be close to Malcolm but you're not his wife. Not even his fiancée. You are just his..." Raynes was going to say: 'his mistress' but he thought twice before he said it. "... You're just his holiday companion. You had quarrelled. You had all quarrelled the day before. Tempers had run high. A lot of jealousy. There was this other woman – Wendy Bridges. He'd admitted seeing her. And then he'd gone off with the young hell-cat! And you were hurt about that..."

"But not enough to kill him!"

"The Spanish police wouldn't know that."

"I think it's far more likely that that young bitch attacked him again."

"How could she?"

"She was on the boat."

Raynes suddenly realized that it must be the Brown Baby who had attacked Malcolm at the barbecue.

"You mean the girl in the green and white striped T-shirt?"

"The *dirty* green and white T-shirt!"

"She was the one who attacked Malcolm?"

"You didn't know that?"

"I wasn't at the barbecue."

166

"You were lucky."

Raynes thought the matter through carefully. Eventually he said: "It doesn't make any difference whether it was Wendy Bridges or this young woman. If the Spanish police think you were jealous or angry, there's still the likelihood that you might have gone off and killed him. They might easily think this was *un crime passionel* and that you were his murderer."

"But that's ridiculous! I wasn't anywhere near him. I wasn't anywhere near the part of the island where his body was found!"

"But you did go wandering round the island. Have you got any witnesses to prove where you were? The police might easily think that you came upon one or other of them canoodling with Malcolm – and in revenge, bumped him off."

"But I didn't!"

Raynes was at his most unctuous.

"You and I know that," he said, "but people in the police look at things very differently. They'll probably want to see both these women and hear what they have to say. Did you give them Wendy Bridges' address?"

"I don't know where she's staying."

"Did you mention the other one?"

"No."

Raynes continued to sound sympathetic.

"I think that's probably why they were hard on you. They must have felt you had a genuine motive, and that would make you a prime suspect."

Joanne continued to look very unhappy.

"Well, what else could I do? I told them the truth. If they don't believe me, there's nothing else I can do, is there?"

"No," said Raynes. "There's nothing else you can do. The only alternative is to find the murderer – and as quickly as possible."

"Do you think you can?"

It was Raynes' turn to shrug his shoulders.

"I don't know. I haven't got any authority out here. I don't know all the facts. The only thing I can do is ask people questions. I can't force people to say or do anything. All I can do," he smiled, "is to use my 'little grey cells'. But at my time of life, that may prove rather painful!"

23: *Veni, Vidi, Vici.*

The next person Raynes spoke to was Neville.

Sarah's boyfriend was looking cool, debonair and relaxed. His long, dark-brown hair was smoothly brushed back. He wore a gold bracelet on his left wrist and an elaborate Rolex on his right. All his clothes bore designer labels and he appeared in the lounge wearing a lemon-coloured shirt, immaculate white trousers and a dark-red silk cravat. Clearly Neville regarded himself as suitably dressed for an interview with the police – but he wore a similar outfit most mornings for breakfast. Although he appeared to be one of the idle rich, Raynes reckoned that there was more to Sarah's boyfriend than met the eye and, during the past week, his respect for the young man had grown.

"A bad business?" said Raynes.

"Not really," said Neville. "It may be cruel to say it, but the world's a cleaner place without him."

"He caused you a lot of embarrassment?"

"He was a bloody nuisance! From the word 'Go' he set out to be totally offensive. He'd been into all my affairs. Pried into my family background. Examined my company's financial accounts. Even before he came to Majorca, he was regaling Joanne with scare stories about me – and she was relaying them to her mother. In consequence, she got deeply worried – that's why she came out here – thinking I had evil designs on her daughter. But if anyone was a shark, it was Malcolm. You never knew what game he was playing. I didn't trust him an inch. Judas Iscariot was a saint compared to him!"

Raynes listened with a faint smile on his face.

"But surely you did have some designs on Mrs Hickson's daughter?"

"Nothing that a healthy, red-blooded male wouldn't have for an attractive young widow!"

"A rich young widow?"

Neville laughed heartily.

"Don't you start, Inspector! I had enough of that from Malcolm! Take it from me, Sarah's more than capable of looking after her business interests. When it comes to looking after her balance sheet, she's as hard as nails. But when she goes on holiday, she's a different girl."

"So how has Malcolm affected your relationship?"

Neville looked reflective.

"Strangely enough, it seems to have brought us closer together. On his first night here, Malcolm did his best to drive us apart. It was a very unpleasant evening. Then, for the next three days, he did his best to win her over. You probably heard what happened at the barbecue..."

Raynes nodded.

"... But Sarah put her foot down. She realized the damage he was doing to all of us – particularly to poor Joanne. It was breaking her heart. She actually loved him! So Sarah issued an ultimatum. Either he behaved or he went home. That did the trick! After that, he was much better."

"When did she issue her ultimatum?"

"On Wednesday. I gather he even tried to get her into his bed whilst she was reading the riot act to him! But then he must have realized he'd gone too far. By dinner-time on Wednesday night, he appeared to be a reformed character."

"What d'you think his game was?"

"Money... power... sex. All three. Wendy Bridges pointed him in our direction by asking him to get money out of Sarah. He then cast a fly over Joanne and she rose to the bait. He quite enjoyed screwing her and she provided him with a valuable entrée to Sarah and a free holiday into the bargain! As you know, Inspector, the *Aphrodite* isn't all that cheap! So there he was like a pig in clover. Two attractive women to play around with! Lots of lovely lolly – six million pounds – a rich widow waiting to be swept off her feet! There's no mystery as to what his game was!"

"But it didn't come off?"

"He was rumbled. He was sent packing."

"In rather a messy way!"

"In a rather effective way, I should say. Swift, dramatic and effective!" Neville smiled at the Inspector. "And it's no use asking me whether I'm sorry about his death. I'm not sorry. I'm delighted. Sarah's delighted. Poor Jo will probably take some time to get over it; but in the long run, she'll come to realize she had a very lucky escape."

"I'm not asking you whether you're sorry or not," said Raynes. "What I want to know is who did it? There are only a few people who knew Malcolm on this island, so the number of suspects is limited. No more than five or six at the most."

"I plead innocent!" said Neville.

"I'm sure you do," said Raynes. "Everyone does at this stage. You had the motive – a good motive – to eliminate a deadly rival. But did you have the means? That's what interests me. What did you do when you went back to the *Jolly Rioja*? You and Sarah and Jo?"

"Boiled... fried... baked. Take your pick, Inspector! It was excruciating – the heat! We were stuck on that top deck. Brendan wouldn't let us go downstairs. He was busy knocking off his birds – and you could hear it quite clearly where we were sitting. Every moan! Every *frisson* of desire! It was quite insufferable! Jo was the first to break. She was worried about Malcolm. Thought he'd fallen or something. Wanted to go and rescue him. I told her not to bother. Malcolm would be all right. And if he wasn't, who cared? Well, she did. She went off on her high horse and we never saw her again – not till we got back to the boat."

Raynes nodded thoughtfully.

"And when did you leave the boat?"

"About ten minutes after Jo. Sarah suggested we take a chance. She reckoned Malcolm would have got the pistol from Wendy by then. She said: 'Let's take a chance.' Well, I wasn't going to appear a coward, was I? It was her pretty head that would get the chop! So we scarpered off the ship, but we kept well away from the hoi-polloi. We went along the beach under the headland where we'd been picnicking..."

"The eastern shore?"

"Yes, the eastern shore, that's right! We walked along for about a quarter of a mile till we saw a cave. A cave in the rocks. It was cool, clean and quite fit for human habitation. I mean – no crabs, no seaweed, no Irishmen! So Sarah and I settled down there."

"How long were you there?"

"God knows! An hour? Perhaps a little longer?"

"Doing what?"

"Talking mostly. We were trying to decide what we should do when we got back to England. Whether we should move in together. Whether we should get engaged. Whether I should make Sarah a director of my company and let her sort out my problems."

"What did you decide?"

"Positive on all three counts. And we sealed the deal with a loving kiss."

"Is that why you were so late coming back to the boat?"

Nothing could embarrass Neville.

"Well, Inspector, you know what happens to women when you kiss them. I'm sure you've often had the same experience yourself. They want more than a kiss. They want the whole works! 'But don't rush me! Do it gently!' All the usual! Well, I'd no sooner got my pants off than Brendan gave a blast on his hooter. Sarah wasn't going to rush and neither was I! So that's why we were a bit late."

He grinned happily.

"So there you are, Inspector," he said. "Guilty of nothing but love!"

It sounded plausible – but Raynes was certainly not going to take his story at face-value. He and Sarah had had plenty of time to prepare their alibi. He decided to move to a quite different line of attack.

"These people," he said. "The Latimers. I heard you talking about them. They had some trouble recovering a bungalow in Dartford. Malcolm was acting for them, I believe?"

171

"Oh, yes! Dreadful business! He took an age to get the bungalow back and by the time he'd got it, the house was a total wreck. The tenants had vandalized it from top to bottom. A colleague told me about it. And then Malcolm had the brass neck to charge them a really exorbitant fee. Naturally, they refused to pay. He sued them – and won. I should think it cost them at least £60,000. It was a disgraceful business. Malcolm should have been ashamed of himself."

Raynes looked at Neville thoughtfully.

"Have you had any dealings with the Latimers?"

"I've never met them."

Raynes opened his eyes wider.

"I didn't ask you whether you'd met them. I asked you whether you'd had any dealings with them. That includes writing, phoning, sending a fax... something like that?"

Neville looked as if he would rather not answer that question. Raynes waited for a minute or so. Then he said:

"Would it surprise you to know that they are in Majorca at this moment?"

"Really?"

Neville looked acutely uncomfortable – and it showed. Raynes watched him squirm.

"Would it surprise you to learn that they were on Brendan's boat last Thursday... that they met Malcolm on Seahorse Island... and that, at this moment, they are staying at the *Hotel Illador*?"

"I didn't know where they were staying."

"But you knew they were here!" Raynes said accusingly. "And how did they come to be in Majorca at this time? In Puerto de Pollensa? How did they know their lawyer would be staying in this hotel? Travelling on the same boat? Did a little bird tell them? It couldn't just have been an accident, could it?"

Neville winced visibly.

"I would agree with you, Inspector. A little bird must have told them..."

"And that little bird was you!"

Neville reckoned there was no way he could avoid making a clean breast of it.

"Yes," he said, "it was me. Malcolm was really rotten to me that first Saturday night – making all sorts of insinuations about my motives for being with Sarah. It really riled me. Then he started making up to her on the Sunday. I could see what was going on. So I decided to get even with him. I guessed the Latimers must be feeling pretty raw. They'd tried to speak to Malcolm – but he put the phone down on them. They'd written to him but he wouldn't reply. They were anxious to meet him face to face and pin him down. I knew that. So, on the Sunday, I phoned a couple of friends back in England and got them to give me the Latimers' number. I phoned them and told them Malcolm was staying in the *Hotel Aphrodite*, here in Pollensa. I gave them the information. It was their decision whether to come or not."

"When did they arrive?"

"Wednesday afternoon. But I didn't know where they were staying. I imagined it would be somewhere nearby. I didn't think they'd stay here."

Neville paused.

Raynes noticed the pause.

"Why not?"

Neville noted that Raynes had pounced on even his slightest hesitation.

"Because I believe they met Malcolm here on the Wednesday night – a rather unpleasant and violent encounter."

"Were you there?"

"No. But I knew that he always had a couple of drinks in the cocktail bar after dinner."

"In fact, you told them precisely where to find him?"

Neville nodded solemnly.

"And they did find him?"

"I imagine so. Malcolm had a bruise on his cheek and lost a little bit of one of his teeth. He told Jo he'd had a fall but I think someone had hit him."

"That someone being Mr Latimer?"

"I would imagine so."

"So if it turns out that Mr Latimer killed Malcolm on the

173

island, it would be directly as a result of you telling him to come to Majorca – and to this hotel – where his victim could be found? You set it up."

Neville took a deep breath.

"If that turns out to be what happened, I still say that I don't regret it. Not one bit, Inspector! He deserved to die!"

24: *Si indicum requiris, circumspice!*

Raynes considered Sarah to be the main witness for the prosecution. He saw her in the hotel garden immediately after he had seen Neville. She too appeared cool and composed, sitting under a large sunshade, already half-way through her first gin and tonic of the day. She was wearing a pale pink, chiffon blouse and her long, white, pleated skirt.

She smiled as Raynes approached.

"Good morning, Inspector," she said. "It's very kind of you to help us. You were a great comfort to all of us last night and my mother said you were very helpful to her whilst we were away."

She looked down at the bubbles rising in her glass.

"Having slept on it," she continued, "things seem much better today. Would you like a drink, Inspector, or are you teetotal when you're working?"

Raynes smiled.

"Well, I've already had two beers with Jo – so perhaps I'd better stop there."

"As you wish," she said. "You can always have one later." She paused. "Now what was it you wanted to ask me? Fire ahead!"

Raynes looked out at the deep blue waters of the bay – the same view that he had looked out upon last Sunday afternoon when Malcolm and Neville had swum out to the breakwater. Then, there had been no thought of murder – or had there?

"Well," he said slowly, "it seems to me that you could easily be regarded as the architect of all this grisly business..."

Sarah raised her eyebrows.

"You invited Malcolm and Jo to come to Majorca. You paid for their flights and their accommodation. You decided to put them up in the same hotel. It was your relationship with Neville that provoked the first row and it was apparently you kissing Malcolm after the barbecue that broke up the happy party. It was you who issued an ultimatum and tried to put Humpty together again. Going further back – if I may rake up the past – according to your mother, it was you pinching Wendy's husband which has inspired all her hatred for you. It is your money which she has got her eyes on and it was you Malcolm came here to squeeze – on Wendy's behalf. And it was at you Wendy directed her shots on Thursday afternoon during your picnic lunch. So it would be true to say, would it not, that your own actions have played a central part in all this tragic business?"

Sarah took a large measure of her drink before she replied: "That would certainly be one way of looking at it," she said slowly. "But I don't really see that I've got anything to answer for. I've always done my best for my big sister – ever since she left Rex. I've given her money for clothes. I helped her to buy her flat. When she said she'd got this lawyer in tow, and she said that *she*'d like *us* to meet him, I invited them both out to Majorca – for the best of motives."

She smiled grimly.

"I had no idea Malcolm was going to lay into Neville. I still can't see why he did. But when he wasn't causing trouble, Malcolm could be a very charming person. He had a silvery tongue; he could coax the birds off the trees. He could make a woman feel very much a woman. I can see why Jo fell for him. But he seemed to go for every woman in sight. One was not enough! Last Sunday night, at the dance, he made quite a strong pass at me and I found him very difficult to resist. In fact, I didn't resist. But I certainly took pity on him after the barbecue when that little bitch attacked him. I was only intending to comfort him. Not to arouse him. If Jo had shown any sort of sympathy, he'd have been kissing her, not me."

Sarah was now in full flow and not to be stopped.

"Once I realized what was happening, I was the one who tried to pull everyone back together. But I did it mostly for Jo's sake. To spare her feelings. To get Malcolm and her even speaking to each other – let alone sharing the same bed! At one point, she was all for going home and leaving Malcolm with us!

"Of course, Neville was jealous! But that was quite understandable. I spoke to all of them. In fact, I thought I'd done rather well. By the time we went on that boat trip, at least everyone was speaking to each other. The sun was shining. The food was good. And the champagne was lovely.

"As for the past..." Sarah's face darkened considerably (as it always did when she thought about Wendy) "... *Charles* fell in love with me. I made him a good wife. He left his business to me and I've carried on his work. Done it rather well, I would say. Wendy fought a very dirty divorce case. She took Charles' house, most of his money and effectively deprived him of ever seeing his kids. She didn't go for his business because at that time, it wasn't worth much. But she took everything else. Charles was left with very little."

Sarah had her arguments well-rehearsed.

"Because he did very well with the business, we were not as poor as she would have liked. We built things up again. Got a nice house. Bought a couple of cars. Stashed away a few thousands in the bank. Now that she sees me doing well, she wants a second bite at the cherry! Not for herself – oh, no! But for the children – bless them!"

Sarah's voice had an increasingly bitter ring.

"It's because she's been so incompetent – such a poor manager – because she's run through all the money she got from Charles, that she's in trouble today. I didn't shoot her. *She* shot at *me*. I think she's already done pretty well out of both of us. But apparently, that isn't enough. Now she wants to kill me! She's crazy – deranged – mad! I didn't tell Malcolm to go and find her. He volunteered. I was shepherded like a bloody sacrificial lamb along to that boat – where I baked. The only good thing about Thursday was that Neville and I were able to talk things through..."

176

"And he was able to propose?"

Sarah smiled more cheerfully.

"It was a joint decision," she said.

Raynes smiled.

Sarah was not the sort of person to give way – even to the man she loved. She was determined to be mistress of her own destiny. And it was that thought which shaped his next question.

"So Malcolm wouldn't have succeeded in getting money out of you, even if he'd tried?"

Sarah looked thoughtful.

"The answer would have been 'No'," she said, "unless it was a clear case of 'your money or your life'. In that case, I would obviously have given way."

She drank the rest of her gin.

"I honestly think Malcolm realized that he was on to a loser," she added, "even before Wendy appeared on the scene. I think that by then he had... other priorities."

"You mean sex?"

Sarah gave the Inspector a sarcastic look.

"What else interests a man like that? He had eyes for everyone. Even your wife! You probably didn't notice – but at the dance last Sunday night, he couldn't keep his eyes off her. I was watching him. And when she went out to the toilet, he followed her."

Raynes managed a look of supreme surprise as if this was news to him.

Sarah laughed.

"I thought that would shock you! But you'll be glad to know she gave him the brush-off, because when he came back, he looked extremely annoyed. That's when he began to turn all his charm on me. Her loss was my gain!"

'Or vice versa,' murmured Raynes to himself.

Sarah looked at her empty glass.

"Shall we order another round?"

"I think I could manage a gin," said Raynes, looking round for the waiter.

"So," said Sarah gaily, "if we're going to be suspects –

then so are you! Where were you and your wife on Thursday afternoon? Did you see Malcolm Clark? Did you cut his throat? Were you consumed with jealousy – or motivated by a spirit of revenge? I think we ought to know!"

Raynes smiled.

"You've managed to turn the tables on me quite beautifully," he said. "Put me under the microscope instead of you."

"Well, Neville and I've got nothing to hide. We spent an hour in that wretched boat with Jo. And then another blissful hour alone in a cave. We've got no alibi for our movements – which is perhaps just as well – because most of them were pelvic!"

She laughed.

Two glasses of fresh, bubbling gin and tonic were delivered to their table.

"Did you tell that to the Spanish police?"

"Good heavens, no! I just told them we were on the boat."

"You lied?"

"Well, it's no use making yourself a hostage to fortune, is it? Once they've got an angle on you, they can twist it any way they want. It was bad enough having to admit that Joanne was on the loose, wandering round the island. At least we were able to vouch for the fact that she wasn't carrying any offensive weapon."

"Were you?"

She shook her head.

"Just a half-empty bottle of champagne. That was enough for the two of us."

"So," said Raynes, "if you rule out the three of you – and you rule out my wife and myself – who else is there who would want to attack Malcolm?"

Sarah had no hesitation in naming the murderer.

"Quite obviously, it has to be Wendy. She had the gun. She had an extremely strong motive; she must have been very frustrated with Malcolm's slowness in getting any money out of me. It was that frustration which brought her out to Majorca. It was a sort of helpless anger which made her want

178

to shoot me. She's not a nice person – and I should know. I think she's quite capable of anything."

"You'd rule out Mr and Mrs Latimer?"

Sarah looked vague.

"The bungalow people – from Dartford."

"I'd forgotten about them."

"They were on the pirate boat on Thursday. They're staying at the *Hotel Illador* – just across the bay. You didn't know that?"

"It's news to me."

"Neville phoned up some friends in England and dropped a large hint as to where Malcolm could be found. He was so angry by the way Malcolm had laid into him that he decided to get his revenge. They came out here last Wednesday."

Sarah shook her head again.

Raynes drew out of his pocket the unsigned declaration which he had found torn in pieces on Seahorse Island, which he had carefully Sellotaped together.

"Read that," he said. "I found it on Thursday afternoon."

Sarah sipped her gin slowly as she read the note.

Raynes continued: "Mr Latimer must have tried to get Malcolm to sign it – but he didn't. One of them tore it up – Malcolm, I should think. I would imagine that Mr Latimer then got extremely angry. He'd already sued Malcolm and lost a lot of money. I should have thought that this might have pushed him right over the edge. Wouldn't you agree?"

Sarah continued to sip her gin.

"Well," she said eventually, "if you're looking for potential killers, don't forget that little bitch who attacked Malcolm on Tuesday night. She was a very nasty piece of work. She led Malcolm completely up the garden path – and then kneed him in the groin. Malcolm told me – but I haven't told anyone else – that she informed him that this was just the first instalment. There was more to come."

"More to come?"

"Mm. She wasn't just resisting Malcolm's sexual advances, the little bitch. She had engineered the meeting in order to attack him."

179

"And why did she do that? Did Malcolm say?"

"It may surprise you again, Inspector; but it's all connected with those Latimers and their bloody bungalow. She is the *daughter* of the people Malcolm threw out!"

"Really?"

Scales fell from Raynes' eyes.

It explained everything.

"You see, she was getting her revenge as well. She found out Malcolm was going to be in Majorca. She followed him to Pollensa; don't ask me how. She was stalking him on Monday when we went on the bus trip to Palma. She was making sure he noticed her. Gave him a nod and a wink. 'I'm a sexy little animal. You only have to ask.' So that when she appeared at the barbecue, Malcolm already knew what was on offer. He didn't need any preliminaries. He went for it – and fell straight into her trap."

Sarah looked at the Inspector.

"Does that make sense?"

"So far."

"Well, she was on the boat on Thursday, wasn't she? Why was she there? Was she just out for a breath of sea air? Perhaps she was. One musn't be too cynical. But isn't it likely... much more likely...." (She emphasized her point by waving her glass vaguely in Raynes' direction) "... that she was still stalking Malcolm, just waiting for another occasion to put the boot in?"

Raynes nodded.

Her logic was faultless.

"I've been thinking about this," she smiled. "You may think I do nothing but drink – but I do think... a lot. And what I think is that she crept up on him stealthily. Malcolm wasn't shot. It was done with a knife. That suggests to me that the person who did it came up from behind. Like a mugger approaching his victim – except that she didn't take any of his money... I think that's significant! She came up from behind with a knife – the sort of razor my father used to use when he was shaving. What d'you call it?"

"A cut-throat?"

"Yes, that's right. Very sharp it was. All she had to do was slash him across the neck. One good cut. Malcolm didn't have a chance. She covered his body with stones. Threw the knife into the sea. And there you are. Bingo! The perfect crime."

Sarah turned to the Inspector.

"Do you think my theory holds water?"

"Perfectly."

"So now, you've got eight suspects – three of us, two of you and three others..."

"It's actually nine. Mrs Latimer's here with her husband."

"Well, nine then. But if you ask me, I think Wendy and that little bitch are the most likely. It seems to me the whole thing had a woman's touch. If Mr or Mrs Latimer killed Malcolm, they wouldn't get their money back, would they?"

Raynes thought there was more to Sarah's theory than she knew. For when she spoke about the assassin creeping up on Malcolm, the picture that had immediately flashed through his mind was that of the Brown Baby washing her shirt in the sea. Why was she naked? Why was she washing her clothes? Obviously, to get rid of the blood-stains! She couldn't have killed Malcolm without getting a lot of the stuff on her hands and clothes. It was a vital addition to the picture.

But he wasn't going to say anything about that to Sarah. What he did ask her was whether she knew the young woman's address.

Sarah shook her head.

She didn't even know her name.

Raynes wasn't worried.

Mr Latimer would certainly know her name. Then he would make the rounds of the travel offices till he found where she was staying. For all he knew, she might already have flown home. If he had been the murderer, he certainly wouldn't have stayed.

Raynes was amused to think that Sarah had included himself and Debbie among her list of suspects. She had skilfully enlarged the field of potential murderers in order to minimize her own family's involvement. For the more the Inspector could be persuaded to look at Wendy, the Latimers and the Brown Baby, the less he would be looking at them. It was clever – but perhaps she was right.

At least she had given him plenty to go on.

Raynes thanked her for her help and asked her if she would like another gin.

"Tell them to bring the whole bloody bottle!" she said with a laugh.

Raynes did just that.

He reckoned she was worth it.

25: *Auri Sacra Fames!*

Immediately after lunch, Raynes set off for the *Vistamar* apartments. Mrs Hickson's excellent detective work had located Wendy Bridges in No. 208. The Inspector hoped that she might be enjoying a late lunch or a quiet siesta so that he might catch her in an unguarded moment.

In fact, Wendy Bridges was packing. Her short holiday in Majorca was due to end early on Tuesday morning when she flew back to Gatwick. So the blue suitcase was out on the bed and the bottom layer was already neatly packed. She was just wrapping up a small bottle of expensive perfume which she had bought for Victoria, when there was a knock at the door.

She was surprised that anyone should be visiting her. No one knew where she lived. She opened the door and saw a tall, pleasant-looking man with cheerful brown eyes. After a few seconds, she remembered that he and his wife had been fellow-passengers on the *Jolly Rioja*.

"Hello," he said. "My name's Richard Raynes. I wonder if I could have a few words with you?"

"Come in," she said.

He immediately noticed the suitcase on the bed.

"Are you leaving?" he asked.

"Tomorrow morning at 1.00am the coach comes for me. It's a dreadful time but I came out to Majorca on the spur of the moment and it was the only flight I could get."

"We're going back on Saturday," said Raynes. "Time

seems to fly when you're enjoying yourself."

Wendy looked at the clutter of clothes and shoes all over the bed and chairs.

"Would you mind sitting out on the balcony? It seems to be the only civilized place. Something to drink?"

"No, I'm all right," said Raynes, settling himself into a white plastic chair. "I'm sorry to disturb you, but I'm following up the disappearance of Mr Malcolm Clark."

"Are you a policeman?"

"A detective-inspector." Raynes smiled a disarming smile. "I'm on holiday at the moment but I've been doing some background enquiries and I believe you're a friend of his?"

Wendy smiled wryly at the thought.

"I don't think he'd call me a friend. I'm just a client seeking his professional help. And a dissatisfied client at that."

"Been dragging his feet a bit?"

"Very much so. I came out here to ginger him up; but my visit seems to have had quite the opposite effect. First of all, he got angry and now he's vanished into thin air."

"How long has he been working for you?"

"About three months. He seemed very enthusiastic at first. Told me there was no problem; he could easily get what I wanted. And then the whole thing seemed to go into cold storage."

Raynes was at his most seductive.

"Would you mind telling me about it?"

"Not at all. There's no secret about it. I'm a divorced woman who's fallen on hard times..." Without the slightest hesitation, she told the Inspector about Charles and Sarah, the divorce, the house, the children and all her current anxieties about her job and paying her way. She seemed to be a very open, frank person and, being a professional journalist, she explained everything in a very straightforward manner.

"I really didn't think of approaching Sarah – she doesn't like me; and I don't like her – but someone told me that her firm was doing very well. It's a printing firm which Charles set up. He built it up from nothing and what it is today is basically his work. I just felt that *his* children – our children – should benefit in some way from what their father had done – even though he's been dead these past five years. I'm sure, if he'd been alive, he wouldn't have hesitated to do something for them. I wasn't after anything for myself. Just for them. They're branching out into adult life and it's an expensive time."

Raynes nodded thoughtfully.

"Well, Malcolm said there'd be no problem getting Sarah to cough up. He found out who she was, where she lived and everything about her. He met her sister and got involved with her. He said he was combining business with pleasure; but if you ask me, I'd say there was more pleasure than business!"

She laughed coldly.

"His plan was to meet Sarah through her sister. Socially – rather than formally. To talk to her about her husband's family. To suggest that she might set up a trust fund for each of them. She'd never miss a few thousand a year! I don't want anything from her – nothing at all – but I think it would be a nice gesture towards the children. Help them get started properly in life."

Put that way, it all sounded eminently reasonable. But Raynes knew that Wendy had been far from reasonable. In fact, she had even contemplated murder because Malcolm had not been quick enough in getting results. Had he been questioning her at home, in England, he would have given her a much rougher ride. But here in Pollensa, he was geniality itself.

"So you came out to Majorca to give Malcolm a shove in the right direction. Did it work?"

She shook her head.

"He hardly wanted to know me. Too busy getting off with his new friends. We had one conversation last Tuesday, the day I arrived, but after that he proved very elusive. I left messages with the receptionist at his hotel but he never phoned me back. On Wednesday night, he actually slammed the phone down on me. Why, I don't know..."

"Is that why you went on the pirate ship last Thursday – to keep an eye on him?"

She nodded.

"And did you?"

"Very much so. I put the screws on him right away."

Raynes was as gentle as a cooing dove.

"I believe you brought a pistol with you?"

"Oh, you know about that?"

"I was told that you took a pot-shot at Sarah."

"Two, actually. She was very lucky to escape!"

"Forgive me for saying so," said Raynes, "but I can hardly see how you could make Malcolm move more quickly by shooting Sarah. Surely, if you had killed her, he would have dropped your case like a hot potato and you would've been facing a murder charge – in which case you and your children would have lost everything? Surely such an action was completely unproductive?"

"Of course it was," said Wendy. "But by that time, I'd given up all hope of Malcolm doing anything. I thought the time had come to take the law into my own hands. If I'd killed her, I wouldn't have minded. It would have brought to an end ten years of bitterness and hatred – I really hate that woman; I can't tell you how much. But if I had a near miss – which I did – then I thought that everyone would take my claim more seriously – especially Malcolm."

"Did it?"

Wendy sighed.

"I think it did – to start with. Malcolm was furious. He came after me and took away my pistol. He really hammered me..." She pointed to the still-visible remains of a large bruise on her forehead. "He smashed my head against a rock till I told him where I'd hidden it. He was extremely violent – but I was angry too because he said he'd only told Sarah about my claim *after* I'd fired the shots. It took that much to get him going! Once he'd taken my pistol away, he promised that he'd still pursue my claim. But after that, he just vanished. I guess he just couldn't face going back to them. He took the coward's way out..."

"You mean he committed suicide?"

"Suicide? Not him!" Wendy was scornful. "He was too

185

fond of the good life to do anything like that. No. I expect he hid somewhere on the island till we'd all gone; then he got picked up by some passing fishing boat. He's probably back in England by now – laughing at us."

Raynes listened to her carefully. It all seemed quite plausible. She seemed to think that her theory of what had happened to Malcolm was perfectly sound and reasonable. As it would have been but for the discovery of his body. The time had perhaps come to puncture the balloon.

"So you gave him your pistol?"

"He forced me to hand it over."

"Where did you get the pistol? Did you bring it out from England?"

"No. I bought it in Palma last Tuesday morning."

Raynes raised his eyebrows.

"Would it interest you to know that your pistol has been recovered?"

"Where?"

"At the southern end of the island."

"Really?"

"It'd been buried under some rocks, I believe."

She seemed quite pleased at the news.

"Can I have it back?"

Raynes shook his head.

"'Fraid not. The Spanish police have got it. It was found near the dead body of Malcolm Clark. He'd been murdered."

Raynes watched her reaction closely.

She seemed genuinely surprised.

She said nothing for several minutes.

Then: "Murdered? Well, well, well! I wouldn't have expected that. Of course, he probably had lots of enemies. Mrs Latimer told me that he had a reputation for feathering his own nest at other people's expense. Somebody must have decided to polish him off."

She paused thoughtfully.

"It could even have been one of his new-found friends."

"Why d'you say that?"

"Well, Mrs Latimer told me that since he came to Majorca,

Malcolm had been making up to Sarah. She said they were getting on like a house on fire. I wouldn't imagine that'd go down very well with Joanne! She said that Sarah's boyfriend had caught them kissing and cuddling and he'd attacked Malcolm. That was on Tuesday night. So they may have had it in for him. How interesting!"

Raynes looked at her in a kindly fashion.

"But," he said, "the pistol belongs to Wendy Bridges! The immediate family have told the police about the shooting incident. They have told them that Malcolm went off to find the person who did the shooting – i.e. you – and that was the last they saw of him. They went back to the *Jolly Rioja*, taking refuge against the possibility of a second attack. So what could be more logical than to suppose that the person with the pistol shot Malcolm?"

Wendy dismissed the suggestion out of hand.

"But he took the pistol from me. He did it extremely violently. How d'you think I got this bruise?"

"The pistol could have gone off during the fight and hit him in the head."

"Well, it didn't! He took it with him. I watched him leave the beach with it. He had it tucked in his trousers. I saw him speaking to some man up beside the trees. He was alive then! I didn't move from the beach till I came back to the boat."

Raynes nodded.

That seemed fair enough.

"Also," she said, "you are quite wrong to suppose that the 'immediate family' as you call them, were sitting on the boat all afternoon. I don't know about Joanne, but Sarah and her boyfriend were the last to get back to the boat. You saw them arrive. We all did. They'd been somewhere together. Knowing Sarah, I should think that she was quite capable of bumping him off. She has a vicious streak. All her family has it – even Joanne. They're quite capable of stabbing anyone in the back to get what they want. And I should know!" she said bitterly. "I imagine that if they wanted to get rid of Malcolm, they wouldn't have had any hesitation in shooting him. He wouldn't have been expecting it – not from them."

Raynes opened his mouth to speak.

"And thirdly," said Wendy, more aggressively. "What on earth do I stand to gain by killing my own lawyer, who had just promised me to continue pursuing my claim – even though I had told him I hated him and would kill him for what he had done to me? Now he's dead, I shall have to start all over again!"

Raynes managed to get a word in.

"Did I hear you correctly? Did you say you had threatened to kill Malcolm Clark?"

Wendy was quite unrepentant.

"I'm not hiding anything from you, Mr... Mr Raynes. I had just been physically attacked by Mr Clark. He had twisted my arm right up my back; he had grabbed my hair and bashed my head twice against solid rock. He had made me show him where the pistol was hidden. I can't say that I had any affectionate feelings for him at that moment. If I'd had the gun in my hands then, I'd certainly have killed him – without the slightest hesitation! At the time, it was just words; but I certainly meant it."

Raynes again opened his mouth to speak.

"But I didn't do it. He had my pistol. And I never saw him again that afternoon. So it wasn't me who shot him."

Raynes thought it better not to enlighten her as to the real cause of Malcolm's death. There was no point. She was so adamant that she was not involved. But he felt he had to caution her.

"Well," he said, "that may very well be true. But Neville, Sarah and Joanne have told the police that it was Wendy Bridges who had the pistol. They've probably told them that Wendy Bridges attempted to kill Sarah on Thursday afternoon. And that it was whilst pursuing Wendy Bridges that Malcolm disappeared. They don't know your side of the story. But if they act on the information they've been given, they'll be waiting for Wendy Bridges."

"You think I'll be arrested at the airport?"

"I don't know – but it's possible."

Wendy looked at him with wide, clear eyes.

"Are you going to tell the Spanish police what I've just told you?"

Raynes looked at her with equal frankness.

"No," he said. "I'm not. I'm not here in any official capacity. I don't speak Spanish and I have no intention of writing any official reports. I'm here on holiday – and I would like it to stay that way. But I am naturally curious as to how Mr Clark came to be killed. I thought I would meet everyone – in an unofficial capacity – to see if I could get to the truth in my own way."

"And beat the Spaniards to it?"

Raynes smiled.

"Why not? I am by nature a rampant xenophobe! Since you are a professional journalist, you will know what that means."

"A Little Englander?"

"Precisely. But it is a very interesting case. And I'm very glad I caught you before you left. If I had not met you – and you had vanished – it would have seemed a little suspicious."

"But you still think I might be arrested at the airport?"

Raynes shrugged his shoulders.

"It's just possible. But I shall do nothing to alert them."

Wendy looked relieved.

"Thank you," she said. "That's at least one burden lifted."

"Tell me," said Raynes. "One final question. How did you come to meet Mrs Latimer?"

Wendy seemed surprised by his question.

"She sat down and spoke to me in the café on Wednesday afternoon. She seemed a very well-meaning person – quite motherly, in fact. She tried to give me a lot of good advice but, of course, I didn't take it!" She smiled at the Inspector. "Why are you asking about her?"

Raynes pursed his lips together.

"Well, it just seems a little strange – that's all. You see, earlier today, I was told that Mr and Mrs Latimer didn't arrive in Puerto de Pollensa till about tea-time on Wednesday night. They flew into Palma at about 2.00pm. So, either somebody is lying – or somebody else was pretending to be Mrs Latimer."

"But why?"

"I haven't the vaguest idea," said Raynes. "But it makes one think. Doesn't it?"

26: *Arma Virumque Cano*

It was late afternoon when Inspector Raynes picked his way along the sandy shore which lines Pollensa bay. He walked past the splendid fish restaurant, *Los Pescadores*, past the roots of the large, dark pine trees which towered over his head – and on to the more civilized approaches to the *Hotel Illador*.

He approached reception.

"I believe you have my cousin staying here?" he said, lying happily. "Mr Peter Latimer of 25 Baron's Lane, Dartford, England."

The receptionist looked down the list of names.

"Room 117. Shall I call him for you?"

"No thanks. He's expecting me."

Raynes hoped that since it had been another very hot afternoon, the Latimers, having been out for a walk or a drink, would by now be back at the hotel, enjoying a quiet siesta before dinner.

He knocked at the door of Room 117.

Mrs Latimer opened the door.

"Yes?" she said. "What is it?"

Raynes put on his most formal voice:

"I'm Detective-Inspector Raynes of the Grasshallows police. I'd like to speak to you and your husband."

Mrs Latimer turned away.

"It's the police!" she said.

But Mr Latimer was already half-way across the room. He was wearing only a pair of white shorts. He had a slightly balding head but a very hairy chest. He seemed to be a slim, athletic type of man, very fit for his age.

"Come in, Inspector," he said. "What can we do for you?" He stopped. "Surely we've met before. You were on the boat last Thursday?"

190

"That's right," said Raynes, more amicably. "My wife and I were on the *Jolly Rioja*. But today I'm here in my official capacity."

"Do sit down."

Raynes sat down on one of the two tapestry chairs. Mrs Latimer perched on the end of one of the twin beds.

"What's all this about?"

"I believe you are clients of Mr Malcolm Clark?"

At the mention of his name, Mrs Latimer snorted.

"He turned up, then?"

"Eventually."

Raynes was careful not to let on that Malcolm was dead. Unless Neville had told them, there was no way they could have known about the murder.

"He's a slippery customer, Inspector. Marion and I have had no end of trouble with him."

Raynes nodded sympathetically.

"Something to do with a bungalow, I believe? Down in Dartford?"

"We came back from Hong Kong two and a half years ago. We felt we'd been abroad long enough. Time to return to our roots, so to speak. We'd rented out this bungalow some years before to a nice family... at least, they seemed a nice family. They assured us they'd have no problem paying the rent or moving out whenever we came back."

"We trusted them," said Mrs Latimer coldly.

"All went well for a few years – about six years actually. They paid their rent into our building society account. No problem. But I think the husband must have had some trouble at work. Lost his job or something. Well, after that, we never got another penny. The payments stopped dead."

"Without any warning," added Mrs Latimer.

"So I put Malcolm Clark on to the job. I was told he had quite a good reputation locally. Far away in Hong Kong, it's difficult to tell. Well, he said he would get our money for us – *and* he would get them evicted." Mr Latimer took a deep breath. "Well, he did get them out..."

"Eventually," said his wife.

"But we never got back a penny of rent – and the house... you should have seen it. It was wrecked. Not just natural wear and tear, but sheer calculated vandalism. The bathroom, the kitchen, the central heating system – you name it – they'd smashed it."

"Even my lovely conservatory," wailed Mrs Latimer. "Every pane of glass broken!"

"It broke our hearts," said Mr Latimer. "We couldn't believe it. We both decided we could never live there again. But we had to do it all up before we could sell it."

"And we didn't get any money from them. Not a penny!"

Mrs Latimer was rather like a Greek chorus supplying an antiphon to each of her husband's comments.

"And then he had the brass neck to send us the legal bill for the eviction. I don't know how many letters he'd written on our behalf or how many applications he'd made to Court, but it was an amazing sum..."

"Of course, Peter refused to pay."

"Any normal person would have done. So we let the bill gather dust. We just put it on one side. Then he sued us for non-payment of legal fees. We had to go to another lawyer. Go to Court..."

"And we lost!"

"We couldn't believe it! Of course, one lawyer won't go against another. I see that now. But we believed in natural justice. I wouldn't have minded if he'd got us some of the rent back. But, damn it, he only did half the job!"

"So, thanks to Mr Clark, we're £70,000 down."

"Between him and the house..."

"And you're trying to get it back?" said Raynes.

"Legally," said Peter Latimer. "Perfectly above board."

Raynes produced his Sellotaped letter pieced together from all the bits he had found on Seahorse Island.

"Is this yours?"

He did not give the letter to Mr Latimer but held it in front of him long enough for its authenticity to be verified.

"Where did you get that?"

"I found the pieces lying beneath a tree on the western side of the island. Someone had torn them up."

192

"He did that!" said Mrs Latimer.

Raynes pricked up his ears.

"Were you there?" he asked.

"Peter told me what happened."

"I asked him to sign the document – of his own free will. He knew he hadn't got a leg to stand on. I just wanted him to accept the justice of our case and help us to get our money back."

"Did you threaten him?"

"Me threaten him?" Mr Latimer looked highly indignant. "He pulled a pistol on me!"

"A heavy, service-type revolver?"

"Yes. A nasty-looking piece of work! He threatened to blow my private parts to kingdom come if I didn't leave him in peace."

"Did you leave him in peace?"

"Inspector, you don't argue with a revolver."

"So you parted peacefully?"

"He tore up my letter with complete contempt. Then he ordered me to go. I just went. There was nothing else I could do."

"He even took his knife!" said Mrs Latimer.

Her husband looked profoundly irritated at the mention of his knife.

"You had a knife?" asked Raynes.

"Only for self-defence," said Mr Latimer.

"So what did you do then?"

"I walked back across the island. I didn't go back to Marion. I was sizzling with anger. It really got to me. So I went for a long walk – on my own – to cool down."

Raynes looked at Mrs Latimer thoughtfully.

"And what were you doing, Mrs Latimer?"

"I was reading my book. Peter was a long time coming back. I thought I'd lost him."

Her reply did not ring true.

Raynes put it aside for the time being.

"I believe there was also an incident in the cocktail bar in the *Hotel Aphrodite* on the Wednesday night – just after you arrived?"

Mr Latimer looked suspicious.

"Inspector, why are you asking us all these questions? Has some charge been made against us by Mr Clark? We wouldn't want to be putting our heads into the lion's jaw..."

"Not again," said Mrs Latimer.

Raynes was blandness itself.

"I am making enquiries into an attack on Mr Clark on Tuesday night. The night before you arrived. Mr Clark was at a barbecue in a farmhouse near Pollensa when he was attacked by a young woman whom I believe you know. In fact, she was the daughter of the tenants you evicted from your bungalow..."

"The Roberts?"

"Did they have a daughter?"

"Yes. What was her name? Frances – or something like that... or was that the boy?"

"No. He was called Nicholas."

"So it must have been the girl."

The Latimers looked quite pleased to hear that Malcolm had been attacked from yet another quarter – even by their ex-tenants.

"Her grievance," said Raynes, "was the mirror image of yours. She was out for revenge because Mr Clark was the lawyer who evicted her family from your bungalow. So she came to Majorca to avenge her family's honour."

"Good for her!" said Mr Latimer.

"So what I'm trying to do," said Raynes, "is to get a fuller picture of all that's been happening. There was a further incident on Seahorse Island last Thursday and it may be that this girl was involved in that."

"Did she attack him again?"

"We're not sure. She may have done."

Raynes continued to look sympathetic and harmless.

"Well, now that you know what it's all about, perhaps you could tell me what happened in the cocktail bar at the *Hotel Aphrodite*. It may help to explain what exactly Mr Clark was feeling like on Thursday afternoon."

Mrs Latimer took up the story.

"We let him know we were here," she said grimly. "I reckon he got quite a shock seeing us behind him. The barman asked us if we'd all like a drink together as it was the happy hour! But I don't think he appreciated the joke. Anyway Peter put him in his place."

Raynes turned to Peter Latimer.

"Did you?"

Mr Latimer nodded.

"He threw his glass of beer in Marion's face. I saw red and punched him on the jaw. Knocked him off his stool. He was less cocky after that."

Raynes smiled.

"So there was no love lost on either side?"

"None whatsoever. But I tell you this! I'm not going to rest till I get back that £50,000. Even if he runs away to Australia, he'll never get us off his back."

"And that's for sure," said Mrs Latimer.

Raynes decided that the time had come to show his hand. "I'm afraid," he said, "you'll have some difficulty in pursuing him where he's gone. Let alone collecting your cash..."

Mr Latimer twigged immediately.

"Is he dead?"

Raynes nodded.

"On Thursday? On the island?"

Raynes nodded again.

"You didn't know anything about this?"

"First we've heard of it."

"Nobody tells us anything."

"He died from knife-wounds. Someone cut his throat."

Mrs Latimer looked quickly at her husband.

"Don't look at me!" he said anxiously. "I haven't got my knife. He took it away from me. Somebody else must have taken it from him."

Mrs Latimer advanced a theory of her own.

"Perhaps it was that young Frances that did it. Perhaps she made up to him. Got him into an uncompromising position – and then stole Peter's knife. If she hated him as much as we do, I'm not surprised she used it. It was a really good knife

195

Peter had. Really sharp. Peter used to use it to cut the testicles off the little porkers, didn't you, dear?"

Mr Latimer looked as if he wished his wife had never mentioned his blasted knife. Let alone speaking about it in such an endearing fashion. If Mr Clark had been murdered and his knife was the murder weapon – he foresaw trouble – big trouble. He tried to divert the Inspector's attention away from the knife.

"Did you say that the Roberts girl was on the island last Thursday?

"She was."

"I can't say I recognized her. We saw a few pictures of the family when this trouble first blew up..."

"She was an ugly little bitch," said Mrs Latimer.

"She was wearing a green and white striped T-shirt."

As he said it, Raynes noticed a glimmer of recognition in Mrs Latimer's eyes. She had seen her – but where? And when?

"Did you see her on the island?" he asked.

"I may have done."

Mr Latimer tried to be helpful.

"You probably saw her on the boat, when you were getting lunch..."

Mrs Latimer winced.

"Don't mention that food! I was in bed all Friday with acute diarrhoea. My stomach felt really dreadful. Someone should do something about that Brendan! He shouldn't be allowed to serve food in such unhygienic conditions. If he was in England, he'd be prosecuted."

She waxed indignant.

Her anger was a useful smokescreen for forgetting what Raynes had been saying. But the Inspector was not so easily deflected.

"Would you perhaps have seen her later in the afternoon?"

"I really wouldn't know."

"I thought you said you were reading your book, waiting for your husband to come back from his meeting with Mr Clark?"

196

"That's what I was doing."

The portcullis was firmly down.

Raynes decided to provoke her and see if there was any reaction.

"You wouldn't have followed your husband – when he went off to see Mr Clark? You wouldn't have been watching Malcolm pointing his gun at him – and taking away his knife?"

From the look on her face, Raynes could see that he was getting somewhere. Mrs Latimer's eyes looked exceedingly shifty and she was fiddling with her fingers – a sure sign of nerves. Even her husband, Peter, was looking at her anxiously.

"You weren't there, were you, dear?"

"I'm not saying anything."

"Did you follow me?"

Mrs Latimer was silent for a long time as she weighed the benefits and the disadvantages of disclosure. Eventually, she said: "You know I always like to keep an eye on you."

"So you were there!" said Raynes quietly. "And what did you do then?"

There was another long silence.

"I followed him."

"Mr Clark?"

She nodded.

"Why?"

"I wanted to have a word with him."

"You wanted to get back your husband's knife?"

"I never touched him!"

"But you spoke to him?"

"Oh, yes, I spoke to him. But that man hasn't got a civil tongue in his head."

Mrs Latimer was clearly distressed.

"You never told me any of this," her husband said.

"When you go wandering off on your own, it always gets you into trouble," said Mrs Latimer sadly. She was nothing if not maternal – but in a rather grim way. "When I'm with you, we can face these things together. You and your bit of paper! I knew he'd never sign anything."

"Did you have any more success?" asked Raynes.

"No," she shook her head. "He said: 'I've warned your husband and now I'm warning you. One more step and you get a bullet in your belly.' Well, I couldn't argue with that."

"So what did you do?"

"I left him. What else could I do?"

She looked surly and resentful.

Raynes decided to try his luck again.

"Is that perhaps when you saw the Roberts girl – the young woman in the green-striped T-shirt?"

Mrs Latimer paused – as if she was not quite sure what she had seen. At last, she conceded: "It might have been her. I wouldn't really know. I certainly saw a girl hiding amongst the trees – about one hundred yards away. She was watching us. I remember that because Mr Clark noticed me looking behind him and he turned to see who was there. But by that time, she was out of sight. There was no one to see."

Raynes was delighted with the fresh information he had received but Mr Latimer still looked distressed about the fact that his wife had followed him and witnessed his humiliation. He felt that Marion had been less than honest with him – and it hurt his feelings badly.

However, he still had one final piece of information for the Inspector.

"There was one more thing..."

"Go ahead!" said Raynes encouragingly.

"I saw our friend, Mr Clark, battering the brains out of a young woman who was sunbathing down on the beach. I was too far away to do anything about it – but he certainly knocked hell out of her. She was screaming quite pathetically. It was a nasty business – and no mistake. I don't know what wrong she'd done him, but he fairly dished it out to her."

Raynes didn't see why he shouldn't give Mr Latimer some information in return.

"That was the woman he got the revolver from," he explained. "She'd taken a couple of pot-shots at his friends, so he decided it'd be safer if he took the gun away from her."

"Oh, so it wasn't his?"

"No," said Raynes, "it was confiscated property. But if you'd caught Mr Clark ten minutes earlier, he would have been completely defenceless. I think you might even have had the upper hand." He smiled. "I think that faced with the prospect of instant castration, even Malcolm Clark might have been willing to sign your document."

'And that,' he said to himself, 'might have saved his life.'

To the Latimers, he said: "I'm most grateful for all the help you've given me. Even if it has been painful and hurtful to both of you. Most of what you've told me ties in with what I've been told already, but if there's anything you haven't told me, please don't hesitate to get in touch with me at the *Hotel Aphrodite*. Even the smallest detail could prove helpful."

He got up.

"When are you leaving?" he asked.

"On Wednesday," said Mr Latimer. "We only came for a week."

"It's been a pointless visit," wailed Mrs Latimer. "With him dead, we've lost everything we ever hoped for."

"Never mind," said Raynes soothingly. "You've still got each other. That's something."

His reassuring words did not seem to have much effect for as he said goodbye and made his way quickly out of Room 117, a violent row erupted.

"Why did you have to say all that to him, you stupid old cow? Now you've really landed us in it! Why couldn't you keep your mouth shut?"

Mr Latimer's voice was harsh and vicious. It was followed by several hefty blows and the sound of weeping. For Mrs Latimer, honesty did not seem to have been the best policy, but for the Inspector, it had been an enormous help.

27: *Gaudeamus Igitur*

Even when Raynes had discovered where the Brown Baby was staying, it took him some time to catch her in. She was very much an outdoor person and for most of the daylight hours, she was either sunbathing or roaming the countryside looking for food.

'Shoe-string' would have been the best description of her holiday in Majorca, as Raynes discovered when he managed to break into her studio apartment on the Tuesday afternoon. He found her passport, her return air-ticket, a scrubby suitcase, some dirty underwear, a half-empty bottle of vodka – and little else. Looking at her meagre belongings, he could not help feeling sorry for her. She was obviously one of life's waifs.

He checked her passport photograph to make sure he had got the right person and made a note of her home address and her passport number.

At 6.00pm that night, he returned and caught her in.

The Brown Baby was carving up a large water melon which she had 'appropriated' earlier that day. She had hidden it under a hedge to save herself carrying it about. Now she was slashing into the bright red flesh with a sharp steak knife and devouring it portion by portion – spitting the black pips into the sink.

When Raynes knocked at the door, the Brown Baby was wearing only her grubby white shorts. The sticky melon juice was dribbling down her breasts. She wiped them with the kitchen towel, pulled on her T-shirt and answered the door.

She recognized him immediately as the man with the tarty blonde from the posh hotel down the road.

"Come in," she said. "D'you want a slice of melon?"

"No," said Raynes. "I think I'll forgo the pleasure."

"Drink? It's only vodka, I'm afraid."

Raynes shook his head.

"If it's sex you're after, you're out of luck. I've got the curse."

Raynes assured her that he was not here to use her body or drink her booze. He was a police inspector and he wanted to ask her a few questions.

The Brown Baby looked disappointed. She liked a bit of drama in her life. Answering questions did not strike her as much fun.

"You are Frances Roberts, 23, from Dartford in Kent?"

"Most people call me Fran."

"Well," said Raynes, "what I want to know, Fran, is why you're here in Majorca?"

"Same as everyone else. Having a holiday."

She sounded defensive.

Raynes looked at her.

"I wonder if that is completely true?" he said thoughtfully. "You wouldn't have been pursuing a Mr Malcolm Clark, a lawyer from Dartford?"

The Brown Baby scraped a bit of melon out of her teeth.

"Never heard of him."

Raynes immediately registered her lie.

"Would it not be true to say that you are the daughter of a Mr and Mrs Roberts who occupied a bungalow in Dartford belonging to a Mr and Mrs Latimer? And wasn't it Mr Clark, their lawyer, who evicted your family from that bungalow – about a year or two ago? I believe you have a brother called Nicholas?"

The Brown Baby was interested to see that he had at least got his facts correct.

"Could be," she said obligingly.

"Well, if you are," said Raynes, "then Mr Malcolm Clark would be no friend of yours."

"No."

"So much so that members of your family – and you in particular – might hold rather a strong grudge against him."

"Very likely," said Fran. "But my dad's not able to do much about it. He's had a heart attack. He's in a bad way."

"I'm sorry to hear that," said Raynes – and realized that he meant it.

"He loved that house. Broke his heart to leave it."

Raynes avoided discussing the rights and wrongs of who owned the house because he thought it might antagonize her. Instead he asked her why her dad had loved it so much. He got her talking. Once she had unbent, he returned to her reasons for coming to Majorca.

"Mr Clark's friends tell me that at the barbecue at La

Calobra, last Tuesday night, you had an assignation with him..."

The Brown Baby laughed.

"A what?"

"A meeting with Mr Clark in a cowshed."

"He wanted to fuck me!"

Raynes smiled.

"But he didn't?"

"He tried."

"I hear that you kicked him in the goolies and ran away with all his clothes. Is that right?"

"Sort of."

Fran couldn't help smiling to herself. It had been one of the most amusing – and satisfying – parts of her holiday. She looked at the Inspector.

"Are you going to arrest me for that?"

"No. I'm not going to arrest you for anything."

The Brown Baby looked relieved and scratched her crotch.

"I was lying to you about the curse," she said. "You can have me if you want."

For all his experience of the seamy side of life, Raynes was taken aback by her open invitation. He covered his embarrassment with a joke.

"I should think," he said, "that after what happened to Mr Clark, most men on this island would think twice before they took you up on your offer."

"The peasants like me," said Fran simply. "I don't hurt them."

"Because they haven't done any harm to your family?"

"No. They're sweet."

She picked up the vodka bottle, which was now almost empty, and took a swig.

"Good stuff!" she said.

Raynes tried to continue his interview at her slow pace with continual distractions and side-tracking. Eventually he got her to the pirate ship and their visit to Seahorse Island on the Thursday.

"Brendan said he fancied me. He said I was 'a bonnie wee

lassie'. Not so wee though!" She giggled. "He's a naughty man! Did he do to your wife what he did to me?"

"I haven't the vaguest," said Raynes. "My wife never said..."

"Bet she enjoyed it!"

Raynes manfully got her back to Malcolm Clark.

"You were following him round the island?"

"Me?"

Raynes nodded.

"One or two people saw you hiding behind trees."

Fran waved her finger at the Inspector.

"Don't exaggerate!" she said. "*One* person saw me hiding behind a tree. A fat old bag with a sour face. I didn't think Malcolm was interested in her."

"I'm sure he wasn't."

"He goes for the older ones though..." said Fran reflectively. "There was this grandmother who worked at the off-licence down the road. He had her. Of course she was quite dishy – dyed red hair. 'Mutton dressed up as lamb', my dad says." She sniffed. "Still, there's no accounting for tastes!"

She looked at the Inspector.

"His present one's over forty," she said. "He picked her up in a supermarket. She's called Joanne. She's divorced."

Raynes was amazed.

"How d'you know that?"

"My friend told me. She works in the supermarket. I'm right, aren't I?"

"You are," said Raynes.

"But they're not very happy together. You only have to look at them. They're hardly speaking to each other. He only wants one thing off her..."

The Brown Baby was nothing if not a realist.

Raynes was gentle in his rebuke.

"I think they were probably quite happy till you appeared on the scene."

"Probably," said Fran.

"Now to get back to the tree," said Raynes, "and you behind it. What were you doing?"

"Having a pee!"

Raynes laughed.

"Do you expect me to believe that?"

"I have to go sometimes."

"You were behind that tree watching Mr Clark."

Fran tried to think of some other good reason why she might have been there – but couldn't. She therefore agreed with the Inspector that she had been keeping a wary eye on the lawyer ever since she came off the boat.

"I was frightened he might attack me."

"Don't you think he might have been justified in attacking you after what you did to him at the barbecue?"

"He deserved it. And more."

"Were you waiting... to give him... more?"

There was a long silence whilst the Brown Baby weighed the pros and cons of answering the question. Her natural, sly cunning inclined her to lie – but the Inspector had said that he was not here to arrest her – so perhaps it was safe to admit the truth.

"Sort of."

"Had you got any offensive weapon with you? A knife? A razor? Something like that?"

The Brown Baby laughed. "You've been reading too many detective stories," she said. "People don't go round with things like that!"

"Don't they?" said Raynes.

"No," she said, opening the kitchen drawer and producing a huge, stainless steel meat cleaver. "They go round with things like this!"

She slammed it down on the wooden bread board which promptly split in two.

"I didn't see you carrying anything like that," said Raynes suspiciously.

"No," said Fran. "I was just joking. But I always carry one of these." She picked up a small, serrated steak knife out of the drawer. "They're very handy."

She rubbed its sharp edge against her finger.

"It's really sharp!"

"I'm sure it is," said Raynes. "But the question is: 'Did you have that with you last Thursday on the island?'"

She nodded.

"Did you use that to attack Mr Malcolm Clark?"

The Brown Baby looked as if she would rather not answer the question. But having come so far, it was difficult to draw back.

"A girl's got to do what she's got to do," she said at last.

"That's not a proper answer," said Raynes.

Fran looked hurt.

"You don't understand," she said. "I promised the virgin I'd punish him for all the evil he'd done to our family – and she said it was all right."

"What virgin?" asked Raynes suspiciously.

"The Virgin Mary! I went down to our local church and spoke to her. 'Vengeance is mine,' I said to her, 'I shall repay.' And she said: 'It's O.K. by me. He's a shit!'"

"I can't imagine the Virgin Mary saying that!"

"Well, she didn't exactly say it in as many words. It was the feeling I got, talking to her. She seemed glad I was going to take him on and slay the wicked."

She picked up the meat cleaver and delivered another stinging blow to the bread board which splintered into two more sections. She laughed.

For a moment, the Inspector wondered if the Brown Baby was criminally insane.

"Sorry," she said. "I'm frightening you."

"No, it's all right," said Raynes, recovering his *sang froid*. "I'm just getting a little lost."

"Fear not!" she said. "Fran will find the way!"

"Will she?" said Raynes doubtfully.

"I was going to attack him. Sure! That was the plan. But when I saw him touting a pistol, I had second thoughts. I mean... There are places where you can call a person's bluff – like in Sainsbury's! They wouldn't shoot you there! Not beside the yoghurt counter! But out here, on a desert island, anything could happen. And I didn't want it to happen to me!"

"So what did you do?"

"I ran away. I may have small legs but they can move quite fast. 'Specially in an emergency."

"And this was an emergency?"

"What d'you think? *He* was chasing *me*."

"He saw you hiding behind that tree?"

"I think he must have done. He began to stalk me..." Her brown eyes opened wider. "...then he fired at me..."

Another detail clicked into place.

That explained the third bullet.

"... but it hit a tree."

"Perhaps he didn't mean to kill you? Perhaps he just meant to frighten you?"

"You don't think about things like that when you're being stalked by a maniac!"

"So he pursued you?"

"Well, he was trying to head me off so that I was cornered. You know – between the devil and the deep blue sea! I led him a pretty dance – but I didn't think of it like that. I was running for my life."

(There had been drama aplenty on Seahorse Island.)

"And you escaped?"

Fran calmed down.

"Yes, I escaped. I got into the sea and swam away from him. He couldn't follow me with his pistol. It'd have got wet. I swam away – and that's where you and your wife saw me. In the sea... I got very wet."

"I imagine you would – jumping into the sea," said Raynes. "But when we saw you, *you were washing your shirt!*"

"Got to do your washing some time," said the Brown Baby with a grin. "No time like the present!"

She laughed.

"Did you see my breasts? Did you like them?"

She pulled up her T-shirt and exposed her large, round orbs, deeply browned by the sun.

"Feel them!" she said. "They're real! No silicone there!"

Raynes shook his head and wondered what his colleagues in Grasshallows would make of this interview. They wouldn't believe him! In England, they would have said he was in acute moral danger – not to mention the very real possibility of blackmail! But out here he was able to handle it.

"Put 'em away!" he said. "I'm not interested in your breasts...I'm far more interested in what you were washing out of your clothes. Was it blood?"

"I told you..."

"Not your blood! Malcolm Clark's blood! Was that what you were washing out of your clothes?"

"Ah," she said, "that would be telling!"

Raynes was at his most gentle and coaxing.

"I would like you to tell me."

"Yes, I bet you would! Then you'd arrest me!" Fran was no fool. "You want me to confess that I murdered Malcolm Clark – but I won't."

"Did you?"

"Of course not! I'm not a violent person. Butter wouldn't melt in my...."

"But the clothes?" said Raynes impatiently. "They were spattered with the blood of Malcolm Clark. Is that true or not?"

"I didn't kill him!"

"You surprise me!" said Raynes sarcastically. "I thought you said the Virgin Mary had told you it was O.K.?"

"Well he certainly deserved to die. That's for sure...!"

"But you are saying that although he chased you into the sea – and although he shot at you with his pistol – and although your clothes were spattered with his blood – and although he died with his throat cut from ear to ear – cut with a knife very like that one there – you are telling me you didn't do it?"

"I didn't."

"Well, who did?"

"I don't know!"

Raynes had the feeling that she was on the verge of telling him the truth – but yet, each time, she drew back. She obviously knew who had killed the lawyer. Who was she shielding?

"Did you see the person who killed him?"

"No."

Raynes prodded her gently.

"Fran," he said, "you're lying! I can tell by the tone of your voice that you're lying. You know very well who cut his throat. Who are you protecting? Joanne – or her sister?"

Silence.

"Mr and Mrs Latimer?"

No response.

"Wendy Bridges?"

"Who's she?"

Raynes mentally ticked Wendy Bridges off his list of suspects. That left only five... or six, if you included the Brown Baby herself.

The Inspector waited for Fran to crack.

As he knew she would.

He let the silence go on – knowing that she would feel compelled to break it. She was churning up inside. Something would emerge. Minutes passed. The Brown Baby looked at the meat cleaver. Raynes followed her eyes. He hoped he had not guessed her thoughts too accurately. He watched her hands so that, at the first move, he could get to the meat cleaver before she did.

Eventually she spoke:

"I really can't tell you... He saved my life."

Her words electrified Raynes.

She had been a witness to the murder.

She held the key.

"Well," he said thoughtfully, "if you won't tell me who it was, can you tell me exactly how it happened? Don't tell me the person's name. Just describe what occurred."

There was another long silence.

"He didn't chase me into the sea... He chased me through the woods. I dodged back and forward so that he couldn't shoot me. I was trying to get close to other people so he wouldn't dare. But there was no one around. Then, just as I came out of the wood – where all the bushes are – I twisted my ankle..."

"Go on!"

"I fell. I must have caught my foot on some rock..."

Raynes nodded encouragingly.

"I couldn't escape..."

"No."

"He caught up with me."

"Yes."

"He was right over me – with his pistol pointing at my head. He said: 'It's no joke now, is it, you filthy little turd? I'm going to shoot you. No one'll notice. Not out here. Just a jolly little suicide. The gulls'll be eating your eyeballs for breakfast tomorrow morning!' I'm not sure that was exactly what he said – but it was something like that..." She paused – her eyes were filled with tears. "Not very nice, was it?"

Raynes was silent, waiting for the final dénouement.

"And then *he* came... grabbed Mr Clark by his hair... jerked his head right back... and slashed his throat. I didn't hear him coming... but one moment, Mr Clark was there; the next, he was dropping his pistol and reaching for his throat... and his blood was spurting out. It was revolting but I didn't mind too much. He saved my life. There's no doubt about it."

Fran did not have to exaggerate. The scene had been sufficiently dramatic to cater even to her degenerate taste.

"What did you do after that?" Raynes asked softly.

"We buried him. Slung him into a ditch and covered him with stones. Didn't give him no last rites or anything. Just bunged him in. We nearly forgot his revolver. We buried it separately. And that was that!"

The Brown Baby reached for the bottle of vodka and drank the final dregs.

"Gone – and good riddance! Thanks to my guardian angel. I expect the Virgin Mary sent him to protect me. I must light a candle for him when I get home."

Raynes admired the Brown Baby's simple faith.

"And what did your friend do then?"

"He left me. He didn't say much. Just told me to keep mum and say nothing about it. So I did – till now."

"And then you went and washed your clothes in the sea?"

Fran nodded.

"'Bout time too! They were stinking!"

"And then we appeared and waved to you?"

"That was quite a long time afterwards. It took ages to get the stains out of my shorts. I had to scrub them with stones."

She pointed to various marks on her shorts which seemed to have returned to their original condition over the weekend.

"And did your friend get blood on his clothes?"

"I expect so. I got most of it. Once he was sure he was dead, he flung him down on his face on the ground."

"Did you see what he killed him with?"

She shook her head.

"Not a meat cleaver?"

The Brown Baby laughed.

"No. Nothing like that."

Raynes was trying to respect her desire to keep her friend anonymous – and yet, at the same time, he could hardly control his curiosity – to see the final piece of the jigsaw and complete the picture.

It could only be one of two people. The violence suggested Mr Latimer, but the speed and the agility suggested Neville. If it was Mr Latimer, it was quite possible that his wife knew nothing about it. He had told Raynes that he had gone for a long walk before returning to his wife. During that time, he could have washed his clothes – and dried them out in the hot sun. That would explain why he took so long getting back.

But if it was Neville, Sarah must have known. Even if her fiancé had washed his shirt, she would have noticed that it was wet. If Neville was guilty, Sarah must know.

On balance, he was inclined to favour Mr Latimer. He was a morose creature – a man of few words – and he was no stranger to violence.

The Brown Baby watched the Inspector with some amusement.

"You're trying to work it out, aren't you? By a process of alimentation..."

"Elimination," said Raynes helpfully.

"... but you won't get it!" she said triumphantly.

"Why not?"

"Because it's not who you think!"

Raynes, who had been wondering whether he could bribe Fran to give him a clue, suddenly had a brilliant flash of inspiration. Not so brilliant really – the answer had been staring him in the face for the past five days. It was only when he was invited to think the unthinkable that the answer came to him.

"He was reading a book!"

The Brown Baby's face fell.

"You won't arrest him?"

"Of course not! I have no powers to arrest anyone in Spain."

"So he's quite safe?"

"Certainly from me."

"And you promise not to tell the Spanish police?"

She was easy to deceive.

"I don't know his name."

"And neither do I."

"So there we are," said Raynes. "All we know is that he is an American student from Arkansas University, wearing a bright red and blue tracksuit and a large baseball hat. He had large sunglasses and was reading a book."

Fran nodded.

"And that's all we know."

"Except that he's my guardian angel!"

Raynes was delighted to have solved the puzzle. He wondered how he could thank the Brown Baby for helping him in his investigations. Since he had been thinking of bribing her with 10,000 pesetas to give him a clue, it would seem churlish not to give her something to help her enjoy the rest of her holiday.

He took out his wallet and counted out 20,000 pesetas which he knew was about £100.

Fran's eyes widened.

"You don't have to pay for it," she said. "I've told you. . . "

Raynes shook his head.

"I'm not paying you for anything. I just want to give you a

small gift to help you buy a couple of decent meals, get yourself some new clothes and " – he looked at the empty bottle – "another litre of vodka. Now that you've been saved from death, you ought to celebrate! Buy your friend a drink when you next see him."

The Brown Baby stuffed the notes into a grubby pocket.

"Thanks!" she said.

Raynes went to the door.

"And remember," she added, "you're always welcome. Any time. If you and your wife would like me to come round for a twosome or a threesome, you only have to ask! I'm always willing to broaden my experience."

She gave the Inspector a cheerful grin.

Raynes had always thought that Debbie verged on the outrageous, but Fran was quite over the top. Perhaps they were like that down in Kent?

He smiled.

"Thank you for your kind offer," he said. "I shall keep it in mind."

But when he got out into the street, he drew a deep breath and, with a sigh of relief, he set off back to the *Hotel Aphrodite*.

28: *Festina Lente*

On the Wednesday morning, Raynes set out to find the student from Arkansas University. Once again, he directed his steps to the Megatravel office where Angie was on duty. Although she was suffering from a severe hangover after the latest Tuesday night barbecue at La Calobra, she gave the Inspector another of her gorgeous smiles.

"Good morning, sir. How can I help you?"

"I'm trying to contact all the people who were on the pirate ship last Thursday – you know – when that lawyer chap went missing."

"Oh, yes."

212

Angie sounded bored. Last week's problems were already consigned to history. She had paid for a coffin and arranged with the police to have Malcolm's body shipped back to England.

"I'm trying to get in touch with the American student who was on that trip. I believe he came from Arkansas University. You probably remember him. Kept chewing gum – wore a bright red and blue tracksuit."

A glimmer of remembrance came into Angie's eyes.

"You wouldn't happen to know where he's staying?"

Angie took down Brendan's file from the shelf and turned to the back page with last week's list of passengers. She ran her finger down the list of names. Then stopped.

"Yes, that's it," she said. "Russell. He came in here at the last minute on the Wednesday afternoon. He's not one of ours. He's probably with Thomson or Cosmos. You could go to their offices and find his address."

"Thank you," said Raynes. "Russell what?"

"Jack Russell," said Angie.

Raynes looked at her – and burst into laughter.

"That's the name of a dog!"

"That's what I thought."

Raynes shook his head.

"I bet that's not his real name. Is there anything else you remember about him?"

"Only that he always wore the same clothes. Like that wretched creature you were asking about yesterday. Always the same tracksuit. A most unsociable person. In fact, I thought he'd lost his voice..."

"Why's that?"

"When he came in here, he spoke in a sort of low whisper."

Angie continued to cast her mind back. When she got going, she had an excellent memory for faces but, this morning, her brain wasn't functioning properly.

Eventually she remembered one final detail.

"I think he's probably married. There was the mark of a ring on his third finger. Usual place for a wedding ring. He'd recently taken it off. I could see the indentation... I think that's all I can remember."

Raynes thanked her for her trouble.

He moved on to the other tourist offices and questioned their reps. But as he expected, none of them had seen the American student or had any record of anyone called Jack Russell.

Raynes walked along the promenade, deep in thought. This was a dead end. An intended dead end. The American student had never set foot in Arkansas University. (Not that Raynes had ever thought he had.) He was almost certainly British. Perhaps another of Malcolm Clark's ex-clients – as dissatisfied as the Latimers and the Brown Baby with his performance as a lawyer.

And he had been stalking Malcolm all week – just as they had. Raynes remembered him on the coach trip to Palma – always in the background. Always watching through those huge relective sunglasses – which meant you could never see his eyes. All you could see was the trace of a smirk on his sunburnt face.

Raynes decided to sit down and think carefully about Mr Jack Russell. The Café Sol was nearby so he turned in for a large cup of black coffee with plenty of sugar. He sat under a large sunshade and tried to picture the real man behind the glasses.

First of all, he must have a sense of humour. There were many other names he could have chosen – but he liked to joke. That was cheering. So many murderers were cold-blooded people, completely lacking any sense of humour. Perhaps that was half their trouble. The inability to laugh... Or, alternatively, perhaps the student had a Jack Russell terrier. Had loved it. Perhaps still loved it. Dogs! He must ask people about dogs.

Secondly, he was in disguise. Just as the Brown Baby went about in her green and white striped T-shirt, the red and blue tracksuit and the baseball hat were a perfect cover. Presumably the student would also have had to wash away the blood stains – just as Fran had done. But any discoloration would not have shown up quite so dramatically on his brightly coloured outfit. Had he deliberately chosen the clothes for just that purpose?

Thirdly, he had had a knife. Was it his knife? Or was it Mr Latimer's knife? But if it was, how had he taken it away from Malcolm? Only if he knew the lawyer personally... Raynes tried to remember whether he had ever seen Malcolm speaking to the student. He couldn't. If the knife were his own, then it suggested premeditated murder. The student had intended to kill Malcolm – not perhaps at that moment, but at some time during the course of the trip.

That was one possibility. The other, of course, was that the student had not intended to kill Malcolm at all, but had only done so when he saw him chasing the Brown Baby and threatening her with a pistol. He had not intervened when Malcolm was threatening Mr Latimer or his wife. But only when he attacked Fran. Was he not just her guardian angel – but also in some way a special friend? Was he watching over her? By God, she needed it!

Perhaps the student was one of Fran's secret admirers – suddenly moved to violence when he saw his loved one attacked? It seemed a bizarre theory – but then, the whole thing was bizarre. He remembered Debbie saying he was probably a psychiatric case. Debbie was very often spot-on in her judgement of people's personalities. And what had he said? He had suggested he might be a theological student! All because of that bloody book!

Raynes laughed out loud.

Several other customers looked at him curiously.

Who was this strange man who laughed at nothing?

The more he thought about it, the more ridiculous it became. A murderer wandering around with a book by Heidegger on divine love! He couldn't imagine anyone in their right mind reading such a book – but, of course, the student wasn't! He was using it to create a distance – a remoteness from lesser mortals, so that even someone like Raynes would think twice about approaching him or speaking to him.

And that was the purpose of the chewing gum. The vile pink bubbles billowing out of his mouth and the constant working of his jaws, put you off looking at him. You turned away in disgust. It was all very carefully thought out. But for what purpose?

Where would the tracksuit be now? And where was the book?

Raynes' quiet theorizing was suddenly interrupted by a high-pitched female voice.

"Inspector! Inspector!"

It was Sarah's mother, waving a newspaper in his direction.

The denizens of the cafe looked round to see who was being addressed in such deferential terms. To their amazement, it was the madman who had been laughing at nothing.

"Yes?" said Raynes, profoundly irritated that his deepest meditations should have been interrupted. "What is it?"

"Wendy Bridges has been arrested by the Spanish police!"

She thrust the local paper into his hands.

Although Raynes did not know any Spanish, the headline was easily translated: 'English Tourist Arrested for Murder'. Wendy's picture was recognizably her.

"What does it say about her?" Raynes asked.

"Well, I've only a smattering of Spanish," said Mrs Hickson, "but I got one of the locals to translate it for me. His English was almost as bad as my Spanish but at least I got the gist of it. It says that she bought a revolver from a well-known gun dealer in Palma. He has identified it. And she has admitted it was her property. Since the revolver was found beside Malcolm's body, she has been arrested on suspicion. She was arrested at the airport early on Tuesday morning."

"I did warn her," said Raynes.

"So did I. I told her there was no point in goading Malcolm into action. I told her that the best thing to do was to write a sensible letter to Sarah and put down all the facts and figures so that Sarah could see what her needs actually were. I was going to put in a word on her behalf."

"Well, she ignored both of us," said Raynes. "And it's done her no good."

"They haven't charged her yet."

"Just as well!" said Raynes, thinking of the elusive student. To Mrs Hickson, he said: "What are you doing now?"

"I'm going round to Sarah and Jo to show them the paper. I think they'll be most interested."

The news about Wendy Bridges completely distracted the Inspector for at least the next ten minutes. He reviewed Wendy's part in the events of the past week and how she could not possibly have murdered Malcolm – however unbalanced she was.

He returned – with great difficulty – to the student from Arkansas University. Was there any point in telling the police about him? Raynes couldn't give them a name, an address or a passport number. He had only the evidence of the Brown Baby as to the identity of the murderer and he certainly wasn't going to throw her into the hands of the police! They probably wouldn't believe her. She, too, would be arrested and get knocked about. It would not be fair either, because she regarded the murderer as her guardian angel – as perhaps he was.

When you thought what a beast Malcolm had been, even Raynes was inclined to think that his murder had been no bad thing. If he could not save Wendy by naming the murderer, he was certainly not going to involve Fran. The only way to save Wendy was to press on with his own investigations.

Where was he?

The tracksuit and the baseball hat? What would the student do with them when he came back from Seahorse Island on the Thursday night? He would get rid of them immediately. If he had any sense, he would have taken them out of town and burnt them in the open countryside. Of course, if he were not sensible, they might still be hanging in his wardrobe or hidden in some bottom drawer...

And the book...

What would he do with that?

Raynes found himself wondering how often the waste bins were cleared in Puerto de Pollensa. Where were the contents deposited? Who would know? He devoted himself to an orgy of lateral thinking. Everything he had thought about the American student had been completely wrong from A to Z. Could he take the investigation any further?

For another twenty minutes, Raynes sat under his sunshade – drinking two more cups of sweet black coffee – till the answer came. As usual, the truth was deliciously simple. *The book* was the key to unravelling the mystery. The student might have thrown away the blood-stained tracksuit and the baseball cap – but he wouldn't have thrown away the book!

Find the book and he would find the man!

Later on that day, Raynes bought himself one or two simple items to assist him in opening a locked door. On Thursday morning, after ensuring that the room would be empty, Raynes expertly picked a lock.

Even though he was a senior police officer, he had to admit that it gave him a pleasant thrill to be doing something illegal. He had always thought he had a criminal streak in him; now he was sure.

He went straight to the wardrobe and examined the clothes hanging there. No tracksuit. No baseball hat. Not even a pair of trainers. It was just as he had expected.

Undeterred, he opened all the drawers in the dressing table and the bedside cabinet – and smiled.

There was the book!

He opened it and read the dedication inside.

No doubt about it.

He wondered if he should take the book away with him – as material evidence. But the murderer obviously intended to keep it. It would remain in his possession, which was useful.

Although Raynes had now confirmed his deepest suspicions, he hunted through the rest of the belongings – including the suitcase on top of the wardrobe. His efforts produced three further items. A pair of large reflective sunglasses – several packets of chewing gum – and, in a zipped-up compartment of the suitcase, a wicked-looking cut-throat razor with a fine bone handle.

Raynes shook his head.

When would the criminal classes ever learn? It was essential – if you had been involved in any dirty dealing to get rid of *all* the evidence. Burn it... bury it... but get rid of it. That was the golden rule. But, every time, they left something to chance – a vital clue – which led to their arrest.

He had imagined that the student who had killed Malcolm Clark – who had even the quiet humour to carry around a book by Heidegger – would have had the sense to cover his tracks more effectively. But no! He was as flawed as the next.

Raynes put all the items back in their places – exactly as he had found them. He made quite sure the room was left precisely as he had found it. The whole operation had taken less than ten minutes.

That afternoon, whilst Debbie made her final assault on the local shops and bought the incredibly expensive blue leather handbag she had been drooling over for the past week, Raynes wrote a long letter to the Spanish police – in English. He posted it in the hotel lobby on the Saturday morning as he and Debbie waited for the coach which would take them to Palma airport for their flight home. He sincerely hoped that he would be back in the United Kingdom before they read his letter.

29: *Causa finita est*

Detective-Inspector Raynes settled back into his seat and fastened his safety belt – but not with any great enthusiasm. It was the same ancient Boeing 727 which had brought them out to Majorca. He had hoped for something better.

He looked at his watch.

At least it seemed likely to leave on time. And the runway at Palma was a long one. He shut his eyes and prepared himself for the ordeal which lay ahead.

A familiar voice roused him.

"Fancy them putting us together again!"

He opened his eyes and saw Mrs Hickson hovering uncertainly in the aisle with a carrier bag from the duty-free shop at the airport.

"You could have done worse," said Raynes, indicating two rough-looking men in the seats opposite.

He undid his safety belt.

"Here, let me put that in the overhead compartment."

"It's a couple of bottles of brandy – for my sister."

'For yourself, more like!' thought Raynes.

He stowed away Mrs Hickson's possessions and returned to his seat.

"Not her again!" muttered Debbie. "I'm bloody fed up with her and her family!"

"Be thankful it's not Malcolm!"

Debbie gave him a chilling look and drew out the in-flight magazine and turned to the page on perfumes.

Raynes settled back again.

Mrs Hickson immersed herself in the latest Catherine Cookson.

And there things rested until they had passed over Barcelona and the Pyrenees and were travelling up the French coast between Bordeaux and Nantes.

It was only after the lunch trays had been taken away that Mrs Hickson voiced her unspoken thoughts:

"It's been a very eventful fortnight."

"It has."

"You'll have to agree with me, Inspector, I was right. I knew something was going to happen."

"But not to the person you expected."

"No. I was misled. I thought it was Neville who was the problem; but it was Malcolm."

"At least Sarah and Jo are safe..."

She nodded.

"...That's what you were worried about."

"It's been a terrible ordeal for both of them."

"And Malcolm's dead?"

"Struck down by an unknown hand."

Raynes raised his eyebrows.

"I wouldn't say that."

It was Mrs Hickson's turn to look surprised.

"Did you find out who did it?"

"I most certainly did," said Raynes, "and what is more, I've just posted a letter to the Spanish police telling them whom they should arrest."

"And who was it?"

"The student from Arkansas University."

Sarah's mother looked puzzled.

"I don't think I remember seeing him."

"No, you wouldn't," said Raynes. "But he was always in the background. I first saw him when we were going on a coach trip to Palma. He seemed a very lonely chap. Always reading a book. Always chewing gum and then spitting it out on the pavement."

"He sounds vile."

"He was. But he was on the island trip as well. Kept himself very much to himself. We saw him sitting on a rock at the southern end of the island. He couldn't have been further away from the rest of us."

"And you think he did the murder?"

Raynes nodded.

"We have a witness."

Mrs Hickson looked excited.

"And who was that?"

"A young lady in a green and white striped T-shirt. If you weren't on the trips, you wouldn't have seen her either. But she was the young lady who attacked Malcolm at the barbecue."

"Oh, her? The young hell-cat?"

"Very much so. She'd been following Malcolm around just like the Latimers – waiting for an opportunity to get even with him. It was her parents Malcolm had evicted from the bungalow in Dartford. The eviction caused her father to have a major heart attack. I believe he's been an invalid ever since.

"Well, this young lady – she's called Frances Roberts –

she'd been shadowing Malcolm on the island last Thursday afternoon. Quite a dangerous thing to do. Because Malcolm was carrying Wendy's revolver and Mr Latimer's knife... but of course she didn't know that. She'd already led our lawyer friend up the garden path at the barbecue – and hurt him quite badly. And not only that. She had also completely humiliated him in front of Sarah, Jo and Neville."

Mrs Hickson nodded.

It was something Malcolm would be unlikely to forget.

"I saw him looking daggers at her on the boat. I think he would have liked to attack her then and there, but he couldn't do anything to her in front of all those people. But, given a quiet corner of the island, when no one was watching, I think he would have been less restrained."

"But surely he wouldn't have tried to shoot her?"

"Fran thought he would. She'd been watching him from a distance. She'd seen his angry confrontation with each of the Latimers. But when Malcolm was speaking to Mrs Latimer, he had noticed her eyes focus on something – or someone – behind his back. He turned round and saw Miss Roberts hiding behind a tree. He immediately ran after her – and fired a shot. That was the third bullet fired from the revolver. The first two were discharged when Wendy interrupted the lunch party.

"He wouldn't have fired that shot unless he'd been serious," said Raynes. "Fortunately, the bullet hit a tree." He smiled. "Unlike Wendy, he wasn't a very good marksman. But he intended to be a good deal more accurate with his next shot. I'm sure he intended to kill her..."

Mrs Hickson looked very upset.

Raynes continued:

"He chased her down to the southern end of the island where she fell and twisted her ankle..."

"So he caught up with her?"

"He did. And before he shot her, he gave her a little homily about why he was doing it. He told her she was a dirty little turd and the gulls would be eating her eyeballs for breakfast!"

"How horrible!"

Raynes nodded.

"I would guess that he would have arranged the scene to look like a suicide. He would have cleaned the pistol of all fingerprints – Wendy's and his own – and then put the gun into Fran's hand. No one would have worried about *her* disappearance. And if no one had put pressure on Brendan, he would have sailed without her. By the time her body was found, the gulls would indeed have done their grisly business."

Mrs Hickson shed several tears.

Raynes could understand her feelings.

"Fortunately," he said, "Frances was not alone in that part of the island. The student from Arkansas University was reading his book. They must have passed him. All he saw was a man chasing a girl, waving a gun. He didn't stop to think. He raced after them and just before Malcolm pulled the trigger, he jerked him back by his hair and slit his throat.

"His blood poured everywhere. Fran was covered with it. She had to wash all her clothes in the sea. We saw her topless but we didn't realize at the time what she was doing. We thought she was just exposing herself. She was a bit of an exhibitionist. Liked to shock people." (Raynes thought of the scene in the Brown Baby's apartment. She was really quite a girl! But he wasn't going to tell Mrs Hickson about that.) Instead, he said: "It took her quite some time to get rid of all the blood.

"But before she got down to washing her clothes, she and the student buried Malcolm's body in a gully and covered it with stones. Then they both went their separate ways. No one said much. But Fran is tremendously grateful to the student for saving her life."

"I'm sure she is."

"She intended to keep the whole episode a secret. But I guessed. He was the only other person around in that part of the island. It had to be him. Once I pointed this out, she told me the whole story."

"Did she know his name?"

Raynes shook his head.

"She regards him as her guardian angel. A *deus ex machina* sent by the Virgin Mary to rescue her in her hour of need."

"Perhaps he was?"

Raynes smiled.

"Yes. Perhaps he was. But if it hadn't been him, it might easily have been one of the others. Wendy... the Latimers... Joanne... Sarah or Neville. All of them were wandering round the island at one time or another. None of them with proper alibis. In fact, it could even have been Debbie or myself..."

He looked to his left – but Debbie was asleep.

At least, she seemed to be asleep.

Perhaps she was listening to his exposition.

"It was only when Mrs Latimer told me that Malcolm had seen a girl hiding amongst the trees and had run after her that I realized Miss Roberts was a key witness. So I tracked her down to her apartment in Pollensa. Miss Roberts had no intention of saying anything to anyone. It was very difficult to coax it out of her."

"I think the student did her a very good turn."

"Indeed he did – but murder is still murder. And, however much one dislikes Malcolm – and however justified his death might have been in the circumstances, people just cannot go round bumping other people off – even in a good cause."

"I suppose not," said Mrs Hickson. "But surely it would be better to let sleeping dogs lie?"

"Perhaps," said Raynes thoughtfully. "But remember! It was you who suggested I might help Sarah, Neville and Jo. It was they who provided me with all the background and helped me to understand what was going on. All the undercurrents of passion." He smiled grimly. "It was as a result of those conversations that I went to see Wendy Bridges, the Latimers and Miss Roberts. It's too late now to let sleeping dogs lie. Wendy has already been arrested for possessing the gun which killed Malcolm. She'll probably get charged with attempted murder. Sarah, Neville and Jo will have told the police about her shooting at them. Once they put those two facts together, Wendy'll be in for a very rough time."

"I think she deserves it!" said Mrs Hickson reprovingly. "She was extremely stupid."

"That's very true. But it may not let your family off the hook. The police may still come back to them. Especially Jo. How much longer are they going to be in Pollensa?"

"Another week."

"Well, it could still turn nasty for them. Much better to put the police on the trail of that student and let them start chasing after him."

"And that's what you've done?"

Raynes nodded.

"I've given the police the full story – from the barbecue right through to the end..."

"The end? Did you find out who he was?"

Raynes smiled more confidently.

"I found where he was staying. I found his book. I found his knife. I found his spectacles and his chewing gum."

"But not the young man himself?"

"No," said Raynes. "He'd vanished into thin air."

"So you don't think the police will catch him?"

"Oh, yes. I think the police will catch him. Very soon. Once they get my letter, they'll be straight on to him."

"It seems a bit of a shame. Especially after his good deed."

Sarah's mother naturally sympathized with the underdog.

But Raynes brought her back to reality.

"It's my duty," he said, "to track down criminals and bring them to justice. I'm sure that if Sarah or Jo had been murdered – as you once feared – you'd have been the first one to beg me to find their murderer."

"Of course."

Mrs Hickson looked admiringly at the Inspector.

He was a very clever man.

"And what was the young man's name?" she asked.

"Well," said Raynes, "we have a little problem there. The nearest he came to giving us his name was when he booked in for the trip to the island. On that occasion, he called himself Jack Russell."

Mrs Hickson laughed.

225

"That's the name of a dog!"

"Just so. Our student friend had a very pleasant sense of humour – which makes me warm to him. But it also seems to eliminate Mr Latimer, who had no sense of humour..."

"What has Mr Latimer got to do with it?"

Raynes' eyes twinkled.

"Because the student was actually someone else!"

"In disguise?"

"Most effectively. As I told you, he wore large reflective sunglasses. Chewed the most revolting pink gum. Spat it out on the pavement. He was very much a person who kept himself to himself. Not a person you would approach if you could help it." Raynes smiled. "It was an excellent disguise because it stopped you looking at the person too closely. If you had looked at the person closely, you might have seen who it was."

"And who was it?"

Raynes looked at Mrs Hickson's left hand with its thin band of gold.

"You!"

"Me?"

Raynes nodded.

"It was a brilliant piece of acting. Quite fooled me. But I haven't the slightest doubt that it was you who killed Malcolm Clark on Seahorse Island."

Mrs Hickson smiled apologetically.

"Inspector, I'm afraid you're very much mistaken."

"Not at all," said Raynes cheerfully. "It's amazing what a little lateral thinking can do. I found the spectacles, the chewing gum and the book in your bedroom. And I found the murder weapon – a cut-throat razor – in the zipped-up compartment of your suitcase..."

"You broke into my room!"

Raynes' eyes lighted with triumph.

"Thank you for admitting they were in your room. Yes, they were all there. Everything except the tracksuit which you at least had the sense to get rid of. It's a great pity you didn't dispose of the rest of the items. If you had, no one could have proved a thing. The fact that you hung on to the other items nailed you immediately as the murderer!"

Mrs Hickson felt faint.

Raynes continued: "I should have realized earlier. You came out to Majorca to keep an eye on your daughters. You told me that on the flight out. You didn't stay in their hotel. That might have been too close. But you settled yourself in a self-catering apartment on the other side of the resort. You called at the hotel almost every day. Like me, you enjoy doing a bit of detective work on holiday. You enjoyed tracking Wendy Bridges to the Vistamar – and then telling me about it.

"You found out that Sarah and Jo and their two escorts would be going on the coach trip to Palma so you decided to follow them. And you chose a very striking disguise. When people wear such a distinctive outfit, people tend to look at the outfit rather than the face. Even if they had looked at your face, all they would have seen would have been those large sunglasses and a mouth chewing away. You covered your face and hands with self-tanning lotion to make yourself look very brown. I suspect that you wore very thick-soled trainers to make yourself look taller and I would guess that you wore a wig underneath that baseball cap to cover your grey hair.

"I looked at you – and the other passengers. But I never recognized you. That must have given you confidence. The only danger point was if someone spoke to you; but you made sure no one did.

"The only time you did have to speak – when wearing your disguise – was when you went to the Megatravel office to book a seat on the island trip. Angie, one of the reps, told me that you spoke in a whisper as if you had lost your voice."

He looked critically at Sarah's mother.

"You had also taken the precaution of removing your ring. Angie noticed that too. Even if you do remove a ring, it is hard to get rid of the indentation it leaves. It was probably more noticeable off than on.

"So I knew I was looking for a person who normally wore a wedding ring. First of all, I thought of the men in the case. It could have been Neville. He has a very handsome signet ring; but Mr Latimer has nothing. And then I thought of the ladies; they have quite a number of rings between them – but none of them sports a wedding ring.

"Once I started thinking about wedding rings, I immediately thought of you. But you were an elderly woman – not a man – so I dismissed the thought from my mind. But when I moved on to think about knives, I remembered something that Sarah said to me last Monday morning. She said: 'Daddy used to have a cut-throat razor!' Which set me thinking. Widows are very sentimental people. They don't throw things away. I wondered whether, perhaps, you had kept your husband's razor and brought it with you to Majorca?

"I also realized – with a bit of a shock – that you had already impersonated Mrs Latimer when you were talking to Wendy Bridges at the Café Sol. Wendy told me that Mrs Latimer had sat down and talked to her – but Mrs Latimer told me that she didn't know who Wendy Bridges was. That surprised me. But then – again at the Café Sol, on Wednesday morning – you told me that you had warned Wendy not to push Malcolm too hard in approaching Sarah. You had told her to write a sensible letter to Sarah putting the facts on paper. Now if Wendy had known you were Sarah's mother, she would never have listened to you. Not for a moment. It was because she thought you were someone else, that she was prepared to talk to you. So, *ipso facto*, you must have claimed to have been Mrs Latimer.

"With these three thoughts in mind – the ring, the razor and the impersonation, I began to wonder whether I should look into your affairs more closely. I broke into your apartment on Thursday morning – and when I found the razor and the book, I knew it had to be you."

Mrs Hickson said nothing.

Inside, she was seething with anger. Anger with herself for failing to take such simple precautions which could have saved her. As the Inspector had said, it was sentiment which had persuaded her to hang on to things – a sentimental nature which had betrayed her.

The Inspector watched her.

"The book belonged to your husband?"

Mrs Hickson nodded.

"I read the dedication. He was interested in philosophy?"

"Yes. But I'm not."

Raynes smiled.

"You could have fooled me! The hours you spent reading that bloody book, you should have learnt something about divine love by now!"

Mrs Hickson was frightened to ask her next question – but it had to be asked.

"What do you think..." she asked nervously. "What do you think will happen to me now?"

Raynes looked at her with a long, steady gaze.

"When we get to Luton, you will be arrested. The police will be waiting for you on the tarmac. You will be taken to Luton police station where you will be asked to make a statement. If you have any sense, you will tell them the truth.

"Your baggage which, I imagine, still contains the razor and the book, will be collected separately. Your name is on the suitcase so they will know which one it is.

"I have already dictated a statement and sent it by fax to Grasshallows police station where I work. That will have been sent to Luton. If they need me, I will confirm that statement in person. In due course, the Spanish police will receive my letter. They may act upon it – or they may not. But either here or in Majorca, you will stand trial for the murder of Malcolm Clark and I shall testify against you. I should think – at your age – you will receive a light sentence."

Mrs Hickson looked like a cornered animal.

Raynes was frightened that she might panic or do something stupid. He decided to put her more firmly in the picture:

"When you got on the plane at Palma, you were rather surprised to find you were once again sitting next to us in the same seat. It wasn't an accident. It was all very carefully arranged. One of the stewardesses is a policewoman and she will escort you off the plane. If you should try to do anything violent to yourself, she and I are ready to restrain you. And those two rough-looking gentlemen in the seats opposite are also undercover policemen. So you are surrounded."

He smiled.

Game, set and match!

As Raynes concluded his exposition – with exquisite timing – the captain came on air, his calm, moderating voice filling the cabin:

"We're now coming in to land. Please fasten your safety belts."

Raynes turned away from Mrs Hickson. He had nothing more to say to her. He looked instead at Debbie who was busy counting up her Spanish money. She seemed to have a lot of it – mostly in ten thousand peseta notes.

Debbie turned to him and said sweetly:

"I think I've just about covered my costs."

"Costs?"

"The cost of the holiday – and the handbag."

For a moment his mind was blank. Then realization dawned. "You mean, you were...?"

Debbie put her finger to her mouth.

"Ssh! Don't say it! You were busy doing your thing – so I got on with mine. It's really been quite profitable. Saved me bringing back all that rubberware!"

Raynes felt deeply hurt.

Debbie put away the notes into the inner pocket of her new leather handbag. She looked at Richard.

"You've had your fun," she said firmly. "And I've had mine. And I'll tell you this! Neville was the best!"

"Neville?" Raynes was amazed. "You've had Neville? What would Sarah say?"

Debbie flashed her deep brown eyes, which no man could resist. "I'm sure she would agree. But his secret is safe with me!"

She looked at Richard who was still feeling shell-shocked. "Anyway," she said, "it was all your fault!"

"Mine?"

"You said it was a busman's holiday."
"More like a hooker's honeymoon!" said Raynes bitterly.
Debbie smiled sweetly and took his hand in hers.
"It's the same thing!" she said.

———————

If you have enjoyed this book, you may like to read other books which feature Detective-Inspector Raynes. They are part of our series – *Meadowside Crime*.

Next in line for publication is the sixth murder story featuring Detective-Inspector Raynes

MURDER ON THE MALLAIG EXPRESS

What could be more spine-tingling than a Murder Weekend? Molly Palmer, who is an experienced organizer of such events, has arranged her latest gathering at a sumptous hotel in Mallaig, in the north of Scotland. Detective-Inspector Raynes has been invited to supervise proceedings and enters fully into the spirit of the weekend. Unfortunately, it transpires that a woman's body has been thrown off the train which has brought the guests up to Mallaig and it becomes clear that one of Molly's guests may have been the murderer. The Inspector finds himself caught between frivolous play-acting and grim reality, in which even he has been allotted a sinister part. This is tabloid journalism at its most self-righteous and most brutal. Exposure is the name of the game. But who is exposing who?

Copies of books already printed and news about forthcoming titles can be obtained by writing to:

**MEADOWSIDE PUBLICATIONS
14 ALBANY TERRACE
DUNDEE DD3 6HR**

Or by telephone:
01382 223510